FURI'ON

C. P. CLARKE

The characters and events portrayed in this book are fictitious. Any similarity to real persons, living or dead is coincidental and not intended by the author.

Text copyright©2015 C.P. Clarke
All rights reserved.

Cover design by: The Smithy Creative
www.thesmithycreative.co.uk

ISBN-13: 978-1533285072
ISBN-10: 1533285071

Other titles by the author:

Life In Shadows
Stalking The Daylight
The Killing
Vicky Rivers
POV – A Personal Perspective of the Bible
A Question of Faith
Stories on a Wall

www.cpclarke-author.com

Dedicated to my dad, for believing in all the crazy stuff.

'There is a drowsy state, between sleeping and waking, when you dream more in five minutes with your eyes half open, and yourself half conscious of everything that is passing around you, than you would in five nights with your eyes fast closed, and your senses wrapt in perfect unconsciousness. At such time, a mortal knows just enough of what his mind is doing, to form some glimmering conception of its mighty powers, its bounding from earth and spurning time and space, when freed from the restraint of its corporeal associate.'

Oliver Twist
Charles Dickens

I reflected what a mortification it must prove to me, to appear as inconsiderable in this nation, as one single Lilliputian would be among us.

Gulliver's Travels
Jonathan Swift

C. P. CLARKE

Prologue

Thinking this could work - that was my first mistake. Committing my men - that was the second. I should have seen it all coming. It all happened way too quickly.

The landing pods were taking off. The excavation pad we had yet to assemble was being abandoned. I led a few circuit boards to the ridge of the crater on the far side of the river, more a stream, and climbed knowing that our only hope was to get high enough off the rock for a pod to hover over and dangle a Pa'as rope for our aid.

Looking back I could see some of my men fallen and being consumed by the very ground we had walked upon only moments before. It was alive, shape shifting and hungry, tearing and ripping apart flesh with ease to blend into the natural colour of the organic rocks that still didn't register on our scanners. Our weapons were hopeless. Even the circuit boards failed to make a dent in this strange new life-form we'd stumbled upon. The rocks would break well enough under a continued pounding of the androids but the broken pieces fell to a collective which simply merged to become a new beast as it fell to the ground.

I was glad to see some of my men reach safety and clear the ground. A few others were with me following my lead, mistakenly expecting the safest place to be with their leader, their undefeatable hero.

It was my duty to keep them safe. I didn't mind sacrificing the circuit boards, but my men were my family. I needn't have worried, the circuit boards were as loyal to my men as I was: they formed a perimeter as we ran uphill and took the fall in defence as they battled off the enemy.

The pods that had managed to take off saw our thinking and hovered near the ridge high enough from the surface not to be mounted by the living rocks. I wondered briefly what they would call those granite-like creatures and how they would categorise them on board the ship, but then dismissed the thought as nonsensical - I knew the odds of making it back, and anyone on board the ship monitoring my helmet display would be able to see my mind making the calculations.

"Apolly'on! Fire into the crater!" I bellowed.

Moments later the centre of the crater behind us erupted into chaos as it rained down a tumult of torpedos from the ship. It was a welcome distraction; not only did the rocks falter in hesitation but it boosted my men as their courage energised their legs believing they had a chance to reach the pods.

The readout of our survival still held in the negative on my visor, but I remained composed, unyielding.

"Continue the bombardment Apolly'on, we need more time!"

I didn't need to turn now to know that the base camp we had descended with was now obliterated and that debris was rising from the surface to fall to the gaseous giant that harboured the moon we rode upon

I felt rather than sensed the circuit boards fall from around us, our blanket of protection gone.

We were but steps away but the ground behind us was rising up steadily, drawing strength from the river we had crossed.

I read the readout on my visor, it was wrong. I knew the odds without relying on the calculations of a machine. This was what I did. I was the commander. I was the warrior. Battles were my domain!

I stopped dead in my tracks and turned to face my enemy, drawing both my swords from behind my back and screaming a deep roar of defiance that had terrified so many others in so many other battles. I swung wildly at any shape that dared to try to pass me, glimpsing momentarily as I span the climbing boots as they grappled for the ropes lowered to them. They called back to me but still I battled on, back stepping towards the lip of the ridge as I did so, but all was too late for me. As big a man as I was I couldn't hold the weight of barbaric rock determined to feed off the nutrient rich fluid they desperately craved. With sword in hand I fell. It was a good death.

Part One

The End, Back to the Beginning

e pluribus unum (out of many, one)

C. P. CLARKE

1

Unblinded by the bright lights of a mainland populace far up in the volcanic hills of Hawaii where the 4x4's are forced to park up on a levelled concrete field before their passengers can make the final ascent to the staging area of the main dish array pointing through the clouds to the heavens, sits the Mauna Kea observatories. The white eyeballs with their dark pupils staring on the forehead of the pacific at the stars above.

Marcus undid his seatbelt and stepped out after his wife Julie.

"Hey where you going?"

"I'm just heading up to the dish quickly," she called back at him climbing the metal frame steps that led above the facility to the newly installed satellite dish that sat filling the stomach of a deceased volcanic lake. Beneath the brilliant white dish lay puddles of crystalline greeny/blue water hidden from the fading light of day under the shadow of the white arc that balanced on its pedestal at a tilted angle skywards. "I just want to make sure it's calibrated properly before we bring it online."

Marcus nodded and headed for the doorway that burrowed into the side of the mountain below the facility that housed the telescopes.

"Don't be long, it will be dark soon and I want another go at charting that new cluster in Cygnus while we can still see it."

She raced off without acknowledging him but that was nothing unusual. To stop to reply would slow her down and she was excited about bringing the relay station online.

They had waited a long time to have the facility of both observing and listening in one place. Signals had been sent out from SETI for years with their own listening stations controlled by NASA, but private funding had finally allowed them to expand the Hawaii base, and they hoped their credentials would keep them in post here for the next five years at least.

They were both curious and determined astrophysicists eager to reach out to the stars in search of life and find that definitive evidence that intelligence wasn't limited to our own solar system.

As a couple they weren't deterred by the fact that they were just the latest in a long line of scientific theorists that had gone before them, but ever since they had graduated college together they had been convinced that now was their time, that the truth was out there and that the big wide expanse of night sky was about to be made smaller under their watch. They had proved their worth at the Harvard-Smithsonian Centre for Astrophysics, gaining respect and turning heads as a united and much adored young couple, often being asked to present work at IAU (International Astronomical Union) meetings around the world as well as domestically at state universities where many of their peers carried out their research. There were many who wanted to see them, the golden couple, fail, but in the field of searching for extraterrestrial life only the mad, the political, and the religious would begrudge a genuine find.

Marcus aligned the twins, the two primary telescopes that sat on the ridge platform closest to the newly installed dish relay. There were eight telescopes in total spread over a small area of the mountain summit which at times felt as though it touched the heavens themselves as cosmic lights danced a spectral aura as the gods showed off their beauty. The twins, officially named Keck I & II, were now, for the time being at least, under the control of Marcus and Julie Banstead and their British sponsors, Sentinel. Marcus flicked the switches on the new equipment. He could see Julie on the gangway of the dish. He pressed the intercom: "All good?"

She looked up to the camera and gave a thumbs up, and then reached over and pressed a button.

"Yep, looks good. Be back in five. Put the kettle on."

She blew him a kiss as he relaxed back in his chair ready for what was likely to be the first of many a long night.

2

The morning was cold and frosty, but no snow had fallen, something for which he was thankful; the bottles always got too slippery with a dusting of sleet. It wasn't so cold that the milk had frozen yet in the bottles but it was enough to burn the fingers for the first half hour, after that he got used to it and they warmed up beneath his fingerless gloves.

The whine of the electric motor of the cart echoed through the quiet street as all lay dormant waiting for the sun to rise, not that many would be getting up this morning as the holiday period slumbered on beyond the festive bank holiday into a luxurious weekend of family gatherings and slouching over excessive TV reruns, allowing that over indulgent lethargy to set in.

The crates on the open back cart rattled as he turned the corner into the familiar cul-de-sac. He hit the brake to allow for the black cat sat licking itself in the middle of the road to vacate his path and then pressed down gently on the other pedal to push himself forward again to his only drop at this end of the street.

The rounds were getting shorter these days. It wasn't like what it used to be back in the day when he'd started the job. Back then half the street got their milk delivered but now the big superstores were beginning to grow in popularity and convenience to accommodate the changing lifestyle of what was fast becoming a 24 hour society. It was the elderly that kept him in a job these days: those who couldn't get out regularly to the shops or those stuck in their ways, he wondered whether his fate was to join them when he retired - he hoped not.

He parked up in the middle of the street, the whining down and heavy clunk of the brake rattling his load once more. He stepped down onto the tarmac and back towards the crates. He didn't need to check the sheet, Mrs Dawldry had one bottle every other day, regular as clockwork. One day he knew he'd find it still sitting there and he'd have to make that call to the police; it happened now and again with the elderly, especially those on their own with no family around them. It was part of the job he wouldn't miss.

Being able to lay in in the morning was a luxury he was looking forward to, but he worried his body clock was too set in its ways to allow him a longer sleep. Still, to lay in a warm bed in the mornings and enjoy a late evening was something he could strive towards.

He reached into one of the crates and pulled out a bottle, mindlessly holding it between his two fingers as he ambled up the path. A cobweb caught his face as he walked through the unkempt bush bordering the gate. That was a new one; the spiders didn't normally spin across there. She hasn't been out for a few days, he thought to himself and quickly glanced down to the bottle holder on the floor. It was empty and he sighed relief. Christmas was a bad time to die.

He placed the bottle down and turned to walk back to the cart. As he did so something caught his eye beyond the hedge masking the next door neighbour's porch. He back stepped and peered through the hedge at the slumped figure lying still on the doorstep.

"Shit!" he muttered to himself and then quick stepped back down the garden path and back up the parallel pathway.

Half sat, slumped like an out all night drunkard on the doorstep was a white male in his late twenties. He was dressed in pyjamas and looked a deathly pale blue as though he'd been sat there most of the night. His eyes were fixed forward unblinking.

"You alright mate?" he asked already knowing the answer. He recognised him as being the usually cheerful father of two that often greeted him in the evenings when he came to collect his weekly money from Mrs Dawldry.

There was no response. He looked him up and down and could see no blood or bruising. No grey wisp of breath wafted out from his mouth.

He banged on the door as hard as he could for attention from the family then stopped and wondered whether that was such a good idea in case it was the kids that came to the door to find their father dead on the step.

"Bollocks!" he said to himself stepping back and looking up to the bedroom windows for signs of movement. The curtains twitched and he wondered whether the wife had any idea that her husband was outside. He saw her face appear from under the curtain, hair a mess and bleary eyed having woken from a deep sleep. She looked at him confused as if to say 'who are you, the milkman? You've got the wrong house!'

Her head disappeared back into the room and he bent to the letterbox to shout a warning before she walked down the stairs. As he did so he felt a hand grip his ankle causing him to jump out of his skin. His hand slapped the door in fright as he tried to balance himself. He looked down to the figure on the step who sat still, vacantly looking forward with breath held, the grip tightening on his leg the only sign that the figure slumped there wasn't dead.

3

In an echo of a dream I relived those last moments over and over again, expecting a different outcome, willing a different outcome. It was the dream of a thousand battles I'd had before. The flashback of thousands of scavenging trips and landing parties on virgin soil. It was the reluctant nightmares that recurred threatening to kill you and test you to keep you on edge, exercising the reflexes of the subconscious mind in those few dormant hours of travel between star systems.

Only somewhere in that sleeping mind I knew I was without a body and travelling far from where I'd left it.

Yet still I replayed the scene.

To get to the heart of a place you need to walk the ground, despite what the instruments tell you. It looked deserted. The gravitational pull was dense enough to hold us but not so much to crush us. The atmosphere was thin but toxic around the oceans but a terraforming helix dome could clean it up by the time a settlement could be established and a population of mine workers conveyed from another rock elsewhere in the quadrant. The rock itself was mineral rich, swimming in dusty heavy compounds ready for condensing and molding into fleet metals. The water was sparse, the oceans small and rivers almost non-existent, they ran thick and bloody, like the crust of hardened soil that layered the cold rock which lay in shadow, hidden from the sun by its parent gaseous giant that almost swallowed its tiny moons in its bubbling atmosphere.

As for life signs: the oceans were teaming with smooth faceless creatures which were typical of such a moon deprived of sunlight, they fed off the rock itself and emitted more of the same in excrement as they recycled, adding their own mineral rich deposits as they polluted the water and the air above it. The rivers strangely were less populated despite there being richer sediment for the fish-type creatures to feed on. The rivers should have been heavy with life, and the thickness of its composition denoted a greater defecation deposit than the amount of life present could produce. This was where I decided not to trust the instruments.

The readings on the machines weren't always right, weren't always trustworthy; they couldn't tell the variables and the instincts that you could read by stepping foot on the soil and reading the lay of the ground. So far as the instruments told all was safe for a scouting party: no other inherent life was present and there was a landmass suitable for us to drop down with a land-based excavator and leave it running with the preliminaries of a base foundation which we would leave behind whilst we searched out the rest of the quadrant. I requested the fleet move away from the giant which had the potential to disrupt our transmissions if the gasses spiked, and then assembled enough men to set the excavator running with a platoon of excess to help me explore the rocky surface near the river.

We dropped down on the open side of the moon, the fleet holding orbit on that side as we stared up to our home flying in the darkness above. We landed, secured our equipment, divided our workforce, and got to work. I hadn't even made it to the river with my men when the truth of our situation dawned and I realised that that last fleeting glimpse of my home reflecting red and yellow light from the planet's atmosphere was likely to be my last.

Of course I'd had thoughts of this sort before going into battle with a hostile alien brood, or falling injured and abandoned on an unfamiliar planet, not that my men would be privy to the inner concerns of my mind - a commander such as myself, renowned for his bravery and unflinching resolve never showed fear or emotion other than the willingness and enthusiastic desire to face a challenge head on.

All that being said, I knew immediately this was different. This time we were in trouble.

In what happened next I could understand the complexities of it through a combination of my own knowledge, experience, and that unnatural sense of premonition that I'd felt on one or two missions prior. Death was on us, I just couldn't see its form just yet.

But time has a way of freezing as we reach the event horizon of our mortal black hole. Gravity, the mass and energy of our souls curving space and time around us, tilting, curving the cones of our lives so that we lean back towards our past with our future frozen in the penultimate event of our lives - we observe the time slowing down and then freezing, but time continues, albeit at a different rate or curve for the person tipping beyond the black hole. The collapsing star frozen in time, in harmony, awaiting the cataclysmic end.

So let me pause there in this state of timeless emotion staring at the events of my life that are thrown together in a mosaic against the stars to give an instantaneous image of what is happening around me.

I have spent all my life in space. I was born on a ship, the same ship I now command. I'm not its captain, I'm its military leader. I leave the flying of the thing and the technical knowhow to those who have the specific qualifications in that department, I give them the respect they deserve, and in return I demand what is owed to me.

I am tall and bulky, almost a giant amongst men, and with a commanding demeanour. I'm extremely fit and fast. I'm experienced and highly trained: weapons, assault tactics, hand to hand combat, intelligence gathering, covert surveillance, recon, information extrapolation (officially we're not allowed to call it torture) - you name it I'm trained in it and so are my men to varying lesser degrees. Some might call me arrogant but the results I produce speak for themselves and no one within our government would dare contradict me or my tactics - that's why they leave me alone to do my own thing, with my own fleet, all for the glory and honour and survival of our people.

Mining is a core component of our work. We seek out the planets that can be mined and colonised, if they can't be colonised we rape them of their natural resources for the benefit of all. Many years ago in our history our people discovered a plentiful ore that we could manipulate into a metal that we would end up using in almost every facet of our society. Unfortunately mining this ore on our own planet led to its instability and we, through our foolishness, weakened its orbit and pushed our own world too far from our sun so that our home began to slowly die. Equipped with the facility to travel the stars we fled seeking a new home, and have been travelling ever since.

All that was way before I was born, and our people have scattered themselves across the galaxy as a fragmented race consumed with the desire of finding a new home big enough. A false economy of hope as those of us who travel the stars who haven't settled on one of the many colonies know full well that we are too widely dispersed and too diverse in thought and beliefs to be accepted any more as solely one race.

The ore we mine is so versatile we use it in everything. It has a really long scientific name which nobody bothers with but is generally referred to as Pa'as. When heated it can be molded into any shape, the thinner the more flexible it becomes without losing its integrity. We use it for the lining of our ships to the casing of our weapons, it conducts our power cables and encases our water supplies; every container you can conceive of is made from it, and essentially it's the base material of our exosuits, providing skin hugging yet flexible and repairable polymorphic material that suctions and molds to the wearer so that we can wear it under our more bulkier main atmospheric suit (also lined with Pa'as) providing us soldier explorers with a comfortable armour that can survive all terrains so long as our air holds out. We have these tiny triple needle inserts that plug into our temple; it's actually a surgically implanted interface, a bit like a USB port but it can also be accessed remotely like Bluetooth or Wi-Fi. The inner suit's circuitry reads our biometrics and stores enough data in each individual suit's temple implant for any communication relay and uplink to the ships computer, storing all information needed for mission parameters; if the outer suit gets damaged in any way the inner suit can still communicate our location and vital signs to anyone tuned into our systems.

Of course with greater defensive suits also came greater projectile weaponry to pierce them, so within the expansion of the arms race that all battle hardened generals gravitate to, our fighting comrades were created. Robots built in our image designed to fight for us and with us, whose programming was initially to protect us, but in whose development, or maybe evolution would be a better way to describe it, either way they became self-aware and for a while, in a climate of fear, they became the enemy until we formed a truce and an alliance so that now we live together, fighting together, surviving together.

4

No, it's ok, no more hypnotism, I can recall the rest on my own.

Stick with me for this, I'll try and tell it as it happened, as I remember it, but forgive me if I get lost in the story. A lot of water has passed under the bridge and time in my mixed memories gets confused, and the events leading up to today are confusing enough as they are! At least in my head anyhow!

Let me recap from the beginning. It was Christmas Day 2003 at 2.15 in the afternoon, that's when the switch happened. I remember the time clearly because we'd been talking around the dining table about when the Queen's Speech was due on TV, half the camp wanting to watch it, the other half not wanting to see it at all. It was as though I'd awakened from a dream. Of all days it had to be when everyone was gathered together, the whole family around me: Gemma, the kids, my damn in-laws; it couldn't have been worse timing.

It's hard to explain how it felt, it was like flicking a light on in a darkened room, only everyone else was used to the blinding glare except me. I tried to focus on the festivities and the conversation around the dinner table: the smiles and laughter as the kids pulled the crackers and Grandpa read out the jokes whilst Gemma and Grandma served the food, but the tumult of strange images and voices blurred my senses, spinning my head until I was forced to excuse myself, bile rising from my stomach as my head splintered painfully into a bright glare across my vision.

I missed lunch. Gemma kept checking on me but I was too giddy to join the others as I hurled into the toilet bowl. I laid down for a while confused at what was happening inside my head, voices and echoes, thoughts and memories merging painfully, but they weren't mine.

An hour went by and I collected my strength enough to re-join the others downstairs and casually stood to the edge of the room amidst the concerned and sympathetic looks of my family gathered for the post lunch joviality in the living room, laden with after dinner drinks, Grandpa giving in to the soporific effects of a heavy turkey lunch, collapsing on the sofa with drooping eyes barely conscious of the two young children crawling on the floor at his feet eager to rip at more paper covered boxes under the Christmas tree, he barely able to recall the Queen's message he had so fervently fought to watch. Gemma urged the kids to be patient as we waited for Grandma to bring in a tray of nibbles, as if they hadn't eaten enough.

I can't say whether it was the sight of the food or the strange audible voice in my head that drained the blood from my face but all I remember was that tipping loss of balance just as Grandma walked into the room and my body falling heavily as I collapsed, falling blank to the floor and hitting my head on the coffee table on the way down.

To some that blank day was the beginning of mental illness. To others an unfortunate accident resulting in a mild form of brain damage. Either way a lifetime of anti-depressants and anti-psychotics would follow as I was later diagnosed as paranoid schizophrenic. But never believe all that the doctors say!

This will mean nothing to you I'm sure at this point of my tale, so let me paint the picture of who I was pre-Christmas Day 2003, an issue in itself which is debatable and open to conjecture as you'll come to understand.

My name was then and is, as you have on file, John Cade, and known also as Abadd'on to some. John Cade had earned an ample living as a graphic designer for a London based magazine and had been married to Gemma for six years, having hooked up at a works Christmas party – yeah I seem to have all my life changing events around Christmas! Mia was born in early December 98 six weeks premature which made for an eventful Christmas that year, and Toby arrived in May 01. We were a happy unit, I even got on with my in-laws! My parents had moved out to Somerset in their retirement to be closer to my older sister and her husband, who having lost her first child at the age of four to leukaemia had since struggled with depression and mental illness. We had always been a close family and it affected us all. I kept close regular contact with them and travelled down as often as I could, but it was hard taking the kids and often I would leave them behind with Gemma, Samantha just couldn't cope with seeing our two when she was left with just one. It was sad, but it was a reality we lived with and my folks were great with her.

I'm a tall guy, just tipping 6'4", but I'm lean and lanky, having never really been into sports I've always struggled to put on any muscle and my fast metabolism burns off any excess, so I can consume as much as I like without having to worry about ever getting fat.

I like movies and music; sadly I have to admit that I do actually like sitting down with Gemma and watching a chick-flick. I play the piano and guitar and love listening to jazz and classical music.

In general I'm a pretty easy going, laid back, hard to stress out kinda guy – or was. All that I can watch in the distant eye of a desert mirage, all that I, John Cade, was.

When I came round on Christmas day, even Dyson, our Labrador, sensed the difference.

Dyson was a guide dog puppy but having failed the training we had acquired him through a friend. Despite his failing to meet the standards of being a guide dog he made the perfect pet: he never barked, he never made a mess where he wasn't supposed to, he never jumped up on the furniture, and he was great with the kids.

Boxing Day was the first time we experienced him having a 'mad moment'. He ran wild through the house leaping off the sofas and growling and barking furiously, and all it appeared whenever I walked into the room.

By this time I understood it, or at least I knew all was not right in my head, despite what the doctors at the hospital said – yes the latter half of Christmas Day had been spent in A&E: no major problems, slight concussion from where I'd collided with the coffee table and a couple of stitches, but other than that they could find nothing wrong with me. Of course I hadn't told them of my main complaint, my main symptom – I may be crazy but I'm not stupid!

No one knew the turmoil I was going through that day. No one saw me breaking down in tears as I lent over Toby's bed singing 'You are my sunshine' to get him to sleep, not understanding my emotions as I stared at him with a heart full of love, and yet with a head full of repulsion and disgust – I cared for him and yet couldn't care less for him at the same time.

That night I couldn't cope. That night I snuck out, desperate to see the stars. I sat out on the doorstep in the cold as though I'd been used to being in the cold all my life.

I grabbed the milkman, that alien being intruding upon my space. I meant him no harm but acted on instinct, like a lizard tonguing a passing fly thinking it his last meal. My body had shut down and was refusing to move. It was malfunctioning. I was used to the cold, but this body was not.

How many times had I spent in the vacuum of space with nothing by a Pa'as suit for warmth? Pa'as is a metal so generates little comfort when you are waiting on a barren rock for a transport detail and the suit's bio-reader has been damaged, or you are piloting a damaged Arra-tet fighter back to the ship having lost temperature controls and life support and are relying on the swiftness of time that short burst thrusters can give you to close the distance.

Those memories seem such a distance now.

When the body froze beyond normal parameters a short duration in the recoup ward would regenerate the cells to normal capacity. Being sick on board the ship was not an option, there was always too much work to do and all but the most severe of injuries could be reconciled in the recoup pods.

The recoup wards here, from what I saw when they poorly attempted to mend the cut on my head - seriously I have seen field repairs more adequate than that - are primitive, archaic even.

I couldn't make sense of it all at first, but slowly and silently I began putting it together.

It is a strange mixture of memories and emotions and thoughts merging. We are not two but one. Not two separate entities joined, but one blended, shared thoughts but differing perspectives, memories and attitudes. It is hard to compromise with yourself when you are so opposed to the different ends of the spectrum of your own personality.

I know I must try to suppress the... how do I describe it, the alien part within me? for that is what I feel I am. I feel that part of me is new here, so for now, at least while I find my feet, I must silence that side of me so that I can adjust. With a galaxy of knowledge in my head I know that this is not normal. This, as far as I know, is a first. I have never encountered a species anywhere before that can transfer its consciousness upon death. Not that I'm saying that is what has happened, for I don't feel I've been invaded by someone else, or that I've invaded someone else. I just feel... me, whole and complete, maybe for the first time. Only part of me has lived a different life.

Sorry, tenses, yes I drifted back again. You told me not to do that. Keep it in the past to see it as an observer.

I guess everyone dreams of living a double life, wondering what person they would be if they had made a different decision in life, or maybe going as far as to imagine they were someone completely new, someone famous maybe, or a spy, or someone filthy rich, maybe some have even dreamt of being aliens. But I actually am one!

I've never been one for dreaming of another life. I've always been quite content with who I am and the cards I've been dealt. I've never wanted to be famous or rich.

Although famous and powerful I have been.

It has just occurred to me that this is going to get very confusing trying to communicate my story. I am going to need a device to separate the past thoughts and personality of John Cade from that of Abadd'on Apolly'on V'hihyon. We are one now, but as hard as it is for me to comprehend, for anyone else the confusion would be too much.

Of course my next step in comprehending what was happening to me would naturally be to talk to someone about it. Gemma was the obvious person. She knew me. She understood me. She trusted me.

You know I said about dreaming about making a different decision in life and ending up somewhere else – I wonder where I would have ended up if I hadn't told Gemma.

5

As commander of my ship I've had the best of the crop so far as the women go, but never have I had the inkling to be yoked to one. Nor have I ever had the paternal instinct. I am a warrior with an ego and the stout bravado that towers with the status of my rank amongst the fleet. I am not some wimpy homemaker ready to settle down on a habitable planet to build a peace loving farming community. I keep myself to myself. My thoughts are my own. My ambitions and my fears are kept in check and locked away in the privacy of my steely eyes.

Maybe if I'd listened to that side of me I wouldn't have ended up in this mess.

I could bore you with masses of in-depth information and detail about the mistakes I made with my family: how Gemma begged me to take it all back and say I was making it all up, how her parents tried to have me committed, how my kids grew scared of me, how my parents cried at having another child with mental health issues. I could give you all the fine details I'm sure, but you're not really interested in that and you'll glean enough of the back story from what else happened.

To make a long story short, ten months after the great Christmas Day incident (as I like to call it) and I had lost everything: my job, my home, my family, and my marbles. The doctors had diagnosed me with paranoid schizophrenia and had me dosed up with enough medication that I didn't know whether I was coming or going. Hell, even I thought I was crazy! Tried all I could to get the thoughts out of my head. I couldn't distinguish who I was. I just kept banging my head against the wall – literally – hurt like hell!

So a couple of stints inside the mental health unit of the local hospital later and I'm sitting in my bedsit, a downtrodden halfway house hotel where the council housed the lowlifes that couldn't be housed anywhere else. I'm sitting there on my flea ridden bed when it suddenly occurs to me that maybe I'm not the only one, maybe there are others.

Not having a computer of my own I decided on making a trip to the library. They had a bank of them there, all the free internet searching I could get!

Nobody paid me a blind bit of notice as I sat there for hours on end amongst the students and unemployed that queued up to use the machines. The internet was slow compared to now, prehistoric compared to what I was used to onboard Apolly'on. We networked across star systems no problem. Here I had to wait ages for each webpage to load.

My initial search showed up nothing. In fairness I had no idea of where to look. I found myself logging on to pages for magazines featuring articles on bizarre mysteries around the world and their related television programs: Arthur C. Clarke's Mysterious World, Fortean Times, Myth Busters, that sort of thing.

I was surprised at how much crap there was out there. I couldn't take any of it seriously and figured I'd end up placed on a similar shelf unless I could connect with someone who could understand and maybe relate to my story.

I started looking at scientific magazines and journals trying to make sense of what was in my head. Medical journals were a dead loss. Religion and eastern mysticism probably came closest, but being branded a religious kook was far from my agenda, despite the following outrage that occurred later.

I looked to the skies, searching the heavens for any sign of my home or my people but none of the UFO encounters seemed credible and our telescopes were too weak. I scrolled back through the scientific theories and papers and saw an opportunity of making myself heard on a level with people that might take me seriously.

I was new to forums so having my words opened up to a community of scientific nerds sitting on terminals around the world was a bit too geeky for what I was used to.

But you designed on a computer, did you not?

Yes, but not everyone who works on a computer is a nerd. Besides, we are one, and Abadd'on is a man of action not science.

Anyway, I started emailing authors of articles where I saw gaps in their theories, or would propose ideas on forums and then wait for a response, hoping that someone would question my science and contact me with curiosity as to the origin of my advanced knowledge.

I know what you're thinking, Abadd'on wasn't a scientist. That's true, but I was still a commander of an advanced civilisation who had lived long enough to know without thinking the basics of the technology he used daily, those things that every child grows up with as standard, just like kids today knowing how to work the TV and DVD player, or mastering the levels of a computer game. It was basic childhood education, and we also had the advantage of the circuit boards who brought us up as their own.

I...um... sorry, I lost track of what I was saying.

Are you okay?

Yeah, just Mia and Toby flashed up in my mind.

Would you rather talk about them?

No. No, I wouldn't.

I'm glad I only had limited contact with them when the crap hit the fan. It was bad enough for them as it was, I can't imagine what it would have been like if I was still living with them.

How long was this after the Christmas Day incident?

I guess it was about eight or nine months after, no Christmas had been round again, it had to be longer, just over a year I think when I sparked some interest with the scientific community, the press got wind of it shortly after that. It was only small to begin with: local press running a local interest story, then the nationals got hold of it, and before you knew it all hell was breaking loose around me. But that wasn't the worst of it, months later after it all died down, I don't know maybe six months or so, that's when the interviews began.

Interviews?

Yeah. MI17. You know about them right?

6

The inner corridors of the basement offices of MI17 were dull and dreary and in desperate need of redecoration. There was a constant atmosphere of oppression as the heavy air, poorly ventilated from the floors above, weighed down upon the staff so eager for a window view of the world outside. The corridors ran to rooms which for the main split into two categories: working offices and storage rooms, there were a few extra rooms which were little used showing the signs of a dwindling department which struggled to maintain the justification of its funding budget. The storage rooms housed decades of paperwork: files built up from interviews and research projects containing governmental secrets relating to the department's purpose. The working offices found the largely depressed staff monotonously scanning the older files for digital storage in lieu of more pressing work. There were always rumours and activities which they could research, but mostly they were quickly debunked as unreliable; they were used to sifting the wheat from the chaff. Generally their time lacked the interest and excitement that the conspiracy theorists fantasised about.

The start of the day was dark when Louis Vost made his way through the upper floors of the old governmental building which was earmarked for closure in the next financial year, and unless something dramatic happened his department buried in its depths would go with it. He cleared the lapse security check point, the guard having his head buried deep in the sports pages of The Sun. He gave his usual smile and nod as he pushed through the door towards the archaic lifts under the flickering light at the back of the building. He knew, as usual, night would have fallen again by the time he left as he and his staff pulled the hours of daylight trying to search that extra harder to save their jobs. He had thought about installing some SAD lamps to lift the mood of his staff and compensate for the lack of natural light they were forced to suffer under, but he knew the budget wouldn't stretch to it. As the lift rose to meet him he pondered whether his own personal finances would be able to cover it.

The upper floors were normal office workers, accounting staff who knew little of the department in the basement except that they too were government based and that the lower floor was restricted access.

The military intelligence agencies had numbered up to 19 after the Second World War, but most were folded and condensed into MI5 for internal domestic counter intelligence, MI6 for external international liaison for the Secret Intelligence Service and the Foreign Office, and GCHQ for all communications related activities. Some of the old codes were gone completely and even Louis didn't know what all of them were. MI1 (Codebreaking), MI2 (USSR and Scandinavia, USA and South America), MI3 (Eastern Europe), MI4 (Geographical Maps), MI7 (Press and Propaganda), MI8 (Signals Interception) MI9 (Escaped British PoW Debriefing, or Undercover Operations - he wasn't sure whether they were separate entities or whether the latter enveloped the first), MI10 (Weapons Analysis), MI11 (Military Security), MI12 (Military Censorship), MI14 (German Specialists), MI15 (Aerial Photography), MI16 (Scientific Intelligence), MI19 (Enemy PoW Interrogation). There were other codes but like the list of those he knew of they were mostly defunct, having merged into other departments, renamed and rebranded for the changing post war world that we lived in with its rapidly changing needs of the intelligence community.

MI17 had been the Secretariat for Director of Military Intelligence from April 1943 but in the late 60's, in light of the space race and the need to cover test flights coordinated with the CIA, MI17 had switched roles to become a clandestine department handling cover stories for the test flights and investigating anything relating to rumoured or unexplained phenomena concerning all matters extraterrestrial, a department that officially didn't exist in the eyes of the general public, unlike the US Air Force's high profile Project Blue Book which was eventually canned in the late 1960's due to the lack of evidence of extraterrestrial life, despite having over 700 unexplained files still open.

In essence, Louis Vost's department employed the government's unofficial experts on aliens. Not that they had ever found any concrete evidence to support their existence. They certainly didn't attract the publicity that the Americans had drawn decades before, but their fate, it would seem, was likely to be the same.

Sadly their search and investigation, despite what conspiracy theorists believed, left the whole department jaded and deflated and scratching around trying to justify their existence in a world that accepted the probabilities of intelligent alien life-forms without the need for evidence. Science fiction filled in the blanks and there was no longer felt a pressure to cover the tracks of the airforce as the consensus was that it was generally accepted that they regularly experimented with advanced flight testing.

None of that prevented Louis and his staff from wanting to believe. It never stopped them looking.

"You might want to take a look at this," said Surjeet Kapoor, one of his most dedicated and experienced researchers who stood waiting at the lift as he stepped out of it into the corridor.

"You stalking me Surj?" asked Louis lightheartedly.

Kapoor shook it off, "I heard the lift coming, no one else was likely to be coming in this early."

"Which begs the question, what are you doing here so early?"

"I just wanted to do some checks on this." He held up the newspaper he had been waving as he'd stepped out of the lift. It was one of the tabloids from yesterday. Louis recognised it from having been laying around on the table in the small canteen at the far end of the corridor. He hadn't read it. He hadn't taken a break as he had his head buried in writing references for two of his staff who were defecting, having put in transfers to other departments.

"Give me the summary," he said without slowing his walking pace as he aimed for his office.

Kapoor took a deep breath then exhaled in a torrent of words. "Last year a London family man hits his head on Christmas Day resulting in possible brain damage, as he went on to suffer mental health issues which cost him his family. Over a year later and he is hitting the press for claiming he is possessed by a dead alien."

"Hardly newsworthy."

"That's what I thought, then I read the article in more depth." He stopped speaking to allow Louis to unlock his office and step inside. He followed him in before continuing. "He's making waves in the scientific community for simplifying their theories and having an unprecedented knowledge of astrophysics."

Louis raised an eyebrow as he put his briefcase down on the desk and took off his coat. He shrugged a shoulder with a dismissive thought.

"Increased intelligence from head trauma, it's been documented before. Maybe he's researched all his answers on the internet to back up his story. I doubt it will amount to anything. Check out the science. Dismiss what you can, which I suspect will be all of it. Keep an eye on the press coverage and suppress it if necessary. Let me know if we need to get someone out to him."

"Can I volunteer for the job?"

"You want time out of the office?" he thought for a moment, "yeah why not, if you think it's worth looking into, go for it, just keep me informed."

"Yes boss, thanks!"

Kapoor span on his heels and headed out of the office leaving Louis with budget sheets and progress reports on the records transfer, knowing full well that condensing the department's physical assets was always the first step to shrinking the department before culling the staff. Surjeet Kapoor was already highlighted on his budget sheet, being a long term experienced member of staff who was now too expensive to make it through to the next quarter's payroll.

Hope was all any of them had left but that was unlikely to save their jobs.

7

So tell me about what happened with the press.

Oh man, it was a bun fight. The local rag broke it first, I'm not quite sure how, I think someone had contacted them making enquiries about me. I know similar calls had been put into the local university and colleges trying to figure out whether I was an advanced student, an emerging genius testing out unrealised theories, or a frustrated lecturer confined to a role beneath his intellect. Of course all their enquiries came to a dead end, hence why they went to the papers, maybe thinking it was an elaborate hoax or hoping the local legs would do the running around for them - which they did. Imagine the looks on their faces when they all realised it was me flooding the scientific forums with things beyond the technological scope of the finest minds on the planet.

The papers called me up first to verify who I was. It was they who then contacted the people I had been chatting with online. Of course I'd hinted to these unseen faceless intellectuals where I lived and gave them my name but I wasn't fool enough to tell them exactly where I was staying, nor my situation. I guess I just wanted to leave them with enough to intrigue them, to get their interest, to have them focus their attention on me.

They looked for someone that I might have been acting for in the first instance, but failing that they then emailed me back directly asking for me to meet to verify the ideas and theories I had tantalised them with, dangling carrots before them, and drawing them in. There were two who wanted to meet but only one lived in the UK, and he was prepared to travel down from Edinburgh to investigate my story loaded with questions he had worked out with the other one who lived in the States.

The press in the meantime found my story unnewsworthy as they lacked any substantial information - it seemed the scientists had been purposely vague about the fine details of what I had shared over the internet so their story lacked any clout and much of my early postings had been removed by the professors as they studied my claims.

I have to admit that I'm at a bit of a loss to explain how the initial article was run, it's possible that someone from the uni in Scotland contacted them when their associate travelled down, or one hack simply wasn't deterred by the scientists' attempts to downplay the story, desperate for something to run to boost their own profile, who knows? Anyway, a local journalist turned up at the coffee shop where I met Professor Hipkiss and took a snap of us and bombarded us with questions about the printouts they had ripped from the public forums I'd frequented. They must have done some serious trawling to find what they had.

It was a bit embarrassing because at this stage I hadn't even managed to convince Hipkiss of the ideas I was putting forward. All he had been doing up to this point was quizzing me over who I was acting for. Call it professional jealousy but these guys are very protective of their theories and ideas and paranoid about someone else stealing their work and publishing it before them.

So anyway, the press vanish and I'm left alone with Hispkiss for a couple of hours - coffee and lunch, paid for by him I'm glad to say. He posed his questions, finely worked out and intricate in gauging the level of my intellect and knowledge. I answered as best I could but there were obvious gaps in what I knew: he could identify fine detail where my military mind only knew the bigger picture. I didn't tell him the whole truth. I wanted him to accept my science. I needed him to accept its realities first in order that the fracture of plausibility of the truth of origin could be explored. My fear of rejection was too great.

We agreed to meet the next day. He wanted to check things out with his colleague in the US and with friends in Edinburgh.

The next day he didn't show. I sat in the coffee shop alone for twenty minutes. Then a journalist from a national tabloid showed up. I don't know the workings of the press but clearly word was getting around quickly before the story had even been run. Maybe the local rag guy wanted to move on up to a bigger paper and was feeding the story up, or maybe he had made enquiries there, pooling their better equipped resources. However it happened it mattered little in the end.

I didn't see the harm in sharing some things with the journalist, it wasn't as if Hipkiss had instructed me to keep my mouth shut, and why should I? I owed no allegiances to anyone. I saw no harm in sharing a few of the things I'd talked about with Hipkiss. Our conversation was brief and he left, having bought me coffee and lunch. I was on a roll, who, I wondered, would pick up the tab tomorrow?

Later I found out why Hipkiss hadn't showed: the journalist had already called him, freaking him out and causing him to bail in case they had their meeting date crashed again.

Skip a day and I'd met up with Hipkiss again. He'd had time to verify a couple of my theories but still didn't believe that they came from me, so, naively, I gave him the whole story which I'd been holding back on, starting with Christmas Day.

He laughed and walked out, leaving me with the bill for the coffee and lunch.

The next day the papers ran a story that a top scientist was taking advice on theories from a schizophrenic claiming to be possessed by an alien. It was a small story and Hipkiss had clearly spoken to them trying to distance himself from it with damage limitation, insisting that he was lured down by someone who was fantasising with outlandish ideas that needed to be verified from a scientific point of view before being dismissed entirely.

I never heard from Hipkiss again but others in the scientific community whom I had been in contact with had responded to the press article stating confusion as to how I had been revealed as the mastermind behind all their communications. Naturally this led the press back to my door. That was when I found it was much easier to feed them a story of who I was and why scientists were taking my theories seriously. They didn't care whether it was true or not, it was a space filler.

It was my last ditch attempt at recognition. I knew the possible damage it could cause to me (which was why I'd avoided that route in the first place), but I'd already hit the papers so the damage was already done, and now I knew how the intellectuals were all likely to treat me. If I just gave a brief synopsis of my story with enough scientific data to make me sound credible then, if there was anyone else out there who could relate to it, maybe they would contact me - my sole aim was still to find others with a similar experience to my own.

That was the hope anyway.

It didn't quite pan out the way you expected it though, did it?
No, not quite.

8

Daytime TV - Channel 5 - The Wright Stuff

Matthew Wright: "Now here's a great little story that our wonderful researchers have pulled out from the fine columns of the tabloids. Have any of our guests this morning come across this: it's a man in London, called John Cade, who claims to have the consciousness of a dead alien living inside his head sharing his thoughts."

Lowri Turner: "You know I did read this, and what was interesting about it was the number of physicists who have been taken in by the story."

Matthew Wright: "Well, yes indeed, because not only has he claimed to have this little green man in his head but he apparently has been giving scientists revolutionary theories and calculations about space travel."

Steve Furst: "How does that work exactly? There you are sitting in the bath and *zap!* a ten tentacled alien climbs inside your head and suddenly you have a eureka moment!"

Matthew Wright (laughing): "You don't believe it then?"

Steve Furst: "No I do, I think all future space travel should be designed on this man's calculations. He should be put in charge of NASA and offered the Nobel Peace Prize. Who know's he might actually make more progress than the real thing - Rainman for the space agencies."

Lowri Turner: "To be honest with you the paper must be desperate for stories to have run this. The story says he hit his head and has since been diagnosed with mental health issues. It's not like there are any Area 51 Men In Black types hurrying to shut him up and whisk him away to a secret facility somewhere."

Matthew Wright: The science is quite fantastic though, isn't it? I mean it says here that he has given precise calculations of star systems that even top astrophysicists had a job verifying; he has given a plausible design for a sub-warp engine (sounds very Star Treky doesn't it), and has provided an equation for interplanetary space travel that has experts at all the space centres around the world, the Americans, the Chinese, the Russians, etc., all working together to try to make sense of what he has proposed."

Lowri Turner: "How much time has this guy spent on the internet researching this material before going public, that's what I'd like to know?"

Steve Furst: "I banged my head the other day and then I woke up this morning thinking I was Father Christmas, when I go home tonight I'm going to email my specs for a new sleigh to Ford and then contact Hamley's for a gift list, and then maybe I'll email Inland Revenue to see who's been naughty or nice."

Matthew Wright (laughing again): "Well there you have it. What's your verdict? Drop us a line to our usual address. Do you think aliens exist? And when they die can they inhabit our minds? We'll see you after the break."

BBC London News

Newscaster: "Now causing a stir across the capital is a story which seems to have snowballed into a bit of a religious argument over life after death. A few weeks ago it was reported that a London man, John Cade, was gaining recognition among world scientists for his insights into advanced alien technology, claiming his knowledge being the result of having lived a dual life as an alien in a far flung corner of the galaxy. Having been mostly debunked by all serious critics the story still rumbles on as it seems to have sparked a religious debate about the nature of the human soul. Nina Houssain reports:"

Nina Houssain (stood outside an unidentified church building): "Yes, here I am on London's streets to talk about an issue which is becoming a hot topic amongst the local religious community, and one that affects us all, that of what happens to us when we die. Now I'm joined by Father Paul Delaney, a local priest. Father Paul, most religions believe in life after death in some form or other but obviously many people believe that this is it, that when they die they are no more. What would you say in light of the recent claims of alien life on other planets and that when we die we inhabit other souls on other worlds?

Father Delaney: Firstly let me state that in my opinion God created us to be his people here on Earth and I don't believe there is life out there on other planets. That said, if there were it would be totally contradictory to everything the Bible says; ascending to another planet, or being reincarnated into another life-form, be it on this planet or on any other, is blasphemous. Jesus says 'in my father's house there are many rooms, and I am going there to prepare a place for you.' We are ensured a place in Heaven not in some alien body."

Nina Houssain: "It would seem that in many ways you stand united on this stance with some of the other religions in speaking out against this idea of reincarnation."

Father Paul: "Well of course. We as religious groups hold firmly to our beliefs and certainly there has been no evidence presented to deter us in that, but I can understand people wanting to get behind this story. It captures the imagination and gives people hope in there being something more, something else to live for, and for them this is more believable in our age of space travel and technology and the vivid images of science fiction that populate our cinema screens. It's easier and less imposing a thought to believe in aliens than in a god who sets a path for you to follow and gives you guidelines on how to live a better life. Personally, if aliens turned out to be real, I would still choose to follow Jesus and rely on him for my existence."

Nina Houssain: "Well, thank you Father Paul Delaney. Of course there are some religious groups who welcome this theory of reincarnation and the debate it has sparked in the public eye, so let us take a look at what you the public have been saying on this story:"

switch to VT: vox pop montage of public on a busy street

Large black woman: "Aliens rubbish, I have enough thoughts in my own head. You can keep your aliens out, I don't want none o' dem messin' in my head."

Tall middle class white male: "Well it's preposterous really, isn't it. The poor man is clearly delusional and being taken advantage of. I feel sorry for his poor family."

Two teenage lads of mixed race: "Yeah, I wouldn't mind being invaded by aliens. Just think of all you could do." " It can't all be rubbish if he's managed to confuse all those science boffins. There's only so much you can read up on, eh." "Rather that than going to hell mate."

Middle class white female: "I believe in an afterlife, sure. I believe something happens to us. I couldn't say we go to sit on some fluffy cloud in the sky or whatever image of Heaven you have. As to a god, I couldn't say, I'm not saying it sounds any more ridiculous than aliens."

Short Asian female: "Aliens? No, I don't believe."

out of VT

Nina Houssain: "Well, I'm sure the debate will rage on. Back to you in the studio."

Newscaster: "Thank you Nina. Let us know your views by going to our website and joining the debate. Now let's recap on the day's headlines..."

Written statement issued to the press from Professor John Hipkiss:

'It is with great regret that I feel I have to issue this statement. Not for myself or my professional colleagues in the scientific community, but for Mr John Cade who I fear has received more publicity than he warranted.

For my part, and that of my colleagues, we have not solicited any of the attention drawn to us but have instead been bombarded by unnecessary and unhelpful contact, firstly from Mr Cade himself, and then by members of the press.

There is no doubt in my mind that Mr Cade is suffering from delusions brought on by a blow to his head some time ago. The exact manner of his condition would be a matter for his physicians, and I, not being a medical practitioner, am not in a position to comment professionally on such matters.

I can say, however, that I and others, having received information intriguing enough to warrant further investigation, and upon not knowing fully its source, set out to discover the truth of where these wild theories had come from. Having interviewed Mr Cade I am satisfied that his lack of any fine detail about the inner workings out of his communications has highlighted a blend of science research and science fiction. His practical application was exemplary but his knowledge was questionable. It is my conclusion that Mr Cade has therefore done much in-depth study on the subjects he has proposed and added some very fortunate guesswork to fill in the blanks.

Ultimately there is nothing remarkable about any potential discoveries Mr Cade has made in his claims.

I hope that the press will leave Mr Cade and his family alone and I hope that he will receive the proper medical care and counselling that he needs.

Professor John Hipkiss
University of Edinburgh
College of Science and Engineering

9

How did this all affect your family? How did you view them throughout this time?

To be honest with you I've been torn. Ever since that Christmas I've not known how to act around them. Gemma doesn't know how to act around me. She's scared of me, scared of what I've become. She can't see that I'm the same person.

My difficulty is that I've been wrenched apart by these two opposing personalities.

John has always been a family guy. Has a heart full of love. Wants to spend all his time with his wife and kids. Wants to see his children grow up and be part of their lives.

Abadd'on on the other hand hasn't got a paternal bone in his body, the body that he had that is. He's cold and uncaring. He never married, not in the conventional sense that we know it anyway, and never fathered a child. His allegiance was to his men and his ship, his duty to his people, he lived for the excitement and the danger. He's the all action hero, but that doesn't come with a family.

I know what you're thinking: Abadd'on is my created alter ego, right? He's the opposite of me, every man's fantasy of what they wish they could be, right? So therefore I've made him up and he's a fabrication of my imagination. That's what all the other head shrinks and quacks thought too.

Do you really think I would give up my family for a fantasy? Do you really think I would let my wife and kids go through hell to satisfy some bizarre escapism? The press hounded them for months. It was bad enough that Gemma was struggling with my breakdown and us being estranged, but to then have it all spilled out in public was humiliating for her. And that's not to mention what the kids are going through: the other kids are all too young to understand, fortunately, but what will happen when they are older and they're teased for having a nut job for a father with all the other mothers sniggering at the school gate. What sort of life have I left them? Is this to be my legacy?

Do you care about them now?

You want me to look you in the eye and tell you I do? I do. And I don't. That's the paradox of who I am.

John Cade are you aware your narrative drifts into a distant zone?

I don't understand.

You speak as though time hasn't moved on.

Sorry, I get detached at times.

I see. You struggle to let go of the moment. You relive it in your mind with regret, wanting to change the outcome. That is understandable.

After all your press coverage did you ever achieve your goal?

10

"Boss!" Surjeet Kapoor slammed down his phone, pushing his seat back away from the desk as he raced to the door and called again down the corridor before the figure that had just whisked passed the office could make it to the lift. "Boss!"

Louis Vost turned, his coat only half on as his right arm fought to find the sleeve.

"It's the wife's birthday today Surj so make it quick."

"Do you remember that case about a month ago that you said to keep an eye on, the alien possession case?"

"You mean the one that caused the spike in the suicide rate." He put on the voice of an advertising commentator, "Depressed, thinking of ending your life, seeking a new existence in a far off corner of the galaxy. Why not end it all now and rejoin your split soul and live a full and enlightened life elsewhere on another planet."

Kapoor stepped forward out of the shadows, the fluorescent

strip light above him dead and in need of replacement, but like so many other things in the department was a casualty of budget cuts and a low priority as all the staff scrimped to help save as much as possible from their running costs.

"Yeah, that's the one. I let it die while the press circled it and just collected the data to check it out later. Turns out the profs were right to give it a wide birth."

"But?"

"I sent a couple of claims he'd made about constellations over to NASA. As expected it all came back negative, it was all too vague or already established published work."

Vost looked to his watch and then gave a circling gesture with his hand to hurry him up.

"I just got off the phone from Sentinel," Kapoor said, his voice rising with excitement, "one of the sites John Cade quoted was in Cygnus, just so happened they had a couple of telescopes down in Hawaii already pointing that way so they've spent the last couple of weeks analyzing the data."

"It matches?"

"And it's unpublished," he confirmed nodding, "so he couldn't have known beforehand."

"Coincidence?"

Kapoor held up papers with his handwritten notes on and shook his head.

Vost checked his watch again calculating how late he could be leaving.

"You've got two minutes," he said walking back towards Surjeet Kapoor's office.

Kapoor sat behind his desk as Louis Vost hovered over it from the other side. He laid the papers out between them comparing the printouts of forum chats between Cade and Hipkiss and the newspaper reports. In the middle he placed a rough drawing, a doodle based on what he'd been told on the phone by Sentinel.

"Here he talks about a planet which is part of a binary system about 5,000 light years away and has a pair of stars that take 7.5 days to circle each other. Only one star is sun-like, the other is much smaller and fainter. His story claims he was charting a neighbouring system to this when he died but that system was unremarkable in its attributes. This particular twin system, he claims, had settlements on it for centuries until the solar system was disturbed causing one of its moons to be flung out of orbit on a collision course with the main habitable world in the system."

Vost reached across and picked up the doodle drawing comparing Sentinel's observations with John Cade's story as retold by Kapoor.

"According to Sentinel the polarization of the two stars could have caused just such a disruption in the solar system."

There was silence for a few seconds as Vost processed the information and decided on a plan.

"Ok, follow it up. Double check it with NASA, see whether they concur. Bring him in if you have to. What have we got to lose? We're about to go the same way as Project Blue Book. We'll be closed down in six months if we don't come up with something to justify our existence."

"Great, thanks boss." Kapoor gave a broad smile eager to get some more time out of the office and have a dedicated project to distract from the constricting atmosphere of the lean department.

Vost checked his watch again.

"I've got to go. Let me know if anything comes of it. Just don't spend any money!"

"Yes boss," replied Kapoor as he watched Vost turn on his heels and walk out through the door.

11

Would you say that you were a good man, before I mean?
Yes.
And now?
You ask it as if Abadd'on is some evil spirit. I'm not possessed by a demon. You can leave that junk back at home where you come from.

I've told you, we are one, and we are good. We strive for what is right. There is no part of who I was in either life that has mastery over who I am now. I am a new person, neither one nor the other, but a new creation.

12

The press didn't leave me alone straight away. All those lunatic magazines I'd successfully avoided contact with initially were now all calling me for information. I'd already lost my family, my supposed sanity, and my good reputation, so what did I have to lose?

I gave a couple of interviews but was cagey with my answers. I guess experience makes you smarter in how to handle journalists. I was a novice being taken advantage of to begin with but I smartened up pretty quick. For fun I'd throw a few curve balls to lead them down the garden path, so to speak.

Don't worry, I'm being honest with you. You have the advantage after all.

I hadn't realised at the time but the debates I'd sparked were rumbling away around the world. Across the nations academics and theologians were debating anew the ancient wonderings over the immortality of the human soul and our uniqueness amongst the cosmos. They weren't new debates by any means, but my story was now thrown in the mix, even if my name got lost in the retelling as just 'some guy in England had this experience'.

They said my fantasies were the embellishment of an already creative mind screaming to be heard in the constraints of a conformed society.

What bollocks!

Still their arguments rattled on without most even naming or even recognising me as the origin of their dispute. Which was fine by me.

Then MI17 picked me up. That was something new. I hadn't seen that one coming at all.

13

Louis Vost looked in through the window of the interview room.

The room was bare save for the table and three chairs (two one side and one the other) which sat in the middle. It didn't need a keen observer to spot the cameras mounted high up in the corners of the room, but a harder inspection upon sitting there bored for 40 minutes would undoubtedly be enough to identify the pin hole cameras mounted in the wall clock opposite the single chair and in the smoke detector in the ceiling above the desk. There was a microphone on the table and a pad of paper and a selection of pens and pencils; so far John Cade had resisted any temptation to use any of them as he sat patiently waiting for someone to fill the other seats.

"Any trouble getting him here?" Vost asked Kapoor who stood just shy of the door to his left.

"No. No resistance. He seemed surprised but quite happy to come along. I think after being ridiculed by the media he's quite thankful for some serious attention."

"Have you checked the equipment?"

"Yeah it's all set up and working fine, I'll monitor it from the suite."

"I'll monitor it. You'll be in there."

Kapoor flicked his head surprised. "You want me to do the interview?"

"Look, I'm going to level with you," Vost turned to look him in the eye. "In six months the department is up for review. There's just too many cut backs in the public sector. The chances of us surviving the next round are less than slim. I'm pretty sure I can make a transition to another management role somewhere, I've got military background and high clearance. You're an analyst and investigator, and a damn good one at that, but the powers that be won't recognise that, they'll just see you as a budget figure."

"What you're trying to say is I'll be gone before the department closes." Kapoor looked dejected and downcast.

Vost nodded slowly.

"You're a valuable part of the team here and I don't want to see you go, but you're on the higher pay band than some of those others I'd rather lose. If I can throw you a bone I will. That's why I want you in there. Cade's likely a nutcase, but if you can spin it in any way to a positive result for the department then you get the credit and I can argue for your position."

Kapoor gave a half smile, his head nodding uncertainly.

"Take five minutes before going in. I'll be in the suite."

Vost walked off leaving Kapoor to compile his thoughts as he filled the vacated air to peer through the window at John Cade who stood staring at the clock on the wall.

"So what do I call you?"

"John is fine."

"Not Abadd'on?"

"Abadd'on is dead. The person he was is anyway."

"I see. Curious name, Abadd'on. Where did you get it from?"

"The name is Abadd. It's not quite pronounced that way, our language is more... musical, our words more hummed, with the occasional guttural exclamation thrown in. I can't replicate the sound, my voice isn't used to it."

"You've tried?"

"Yeah, it's like trying to master a New York accent, totally out of my skillset."

"But surely 'Abadd' would be used to it."

"Of course, but my muscles aren't, my vocal cords just aren't used to being used in that way."

Kapoor typed a note on his laptop. There was a direct Wi-Fi feed through to the suite so that he could relay any thoughts or notes back to Vost watching the interview on camera, and it gave Vost the opportunity to bounce back and direct the conversation should Kapoor miss any angles.

"And the 'on' of 'Abadd'on'?"

"Abadd is a common enough name amongst my people. The 'on' denotes the manner of your birth. So for me 'on' is birthed by artificial means onboard a ship. If it were 'el' it would be birthed naturally, this is unusual on a ship, so normally only terraformers hold this title. Our second name normally denotes where we are from, for example I would be John of Earth. Abadd'on Apolly'on V'hihyon. I'm not referred to in the common shortened form out of respect of my rank."

Revelation 9:11

Kapoor looked down at the screen confused, his biblical knowledge was poor, he tipped his head to the camera with a confused look. Cade didn't appear to notice.

'They had as king over them the angel of the Abyss, whose

name in Hebrew is Abaddon, and in Greek, Apollyon.'

The words appeared quickly on the screen as though Vost had a Bible with him that he was copying the text from. It was clearly something he had already thought of and had come prepared with the information ready to raise it at the appropriate time.

"And the other names mean?" Kapoor stalled for time as more words appeared on his screen.

Abaddon means "place of destruction". Apollyon literally means "The Destroyer"

"Apolly'on is the ship I was born on. V'hihyon - you may find it easier to simplify the pronunciation a bit as again it is hard to say in English, I think you'll find Furi'on is the closest you'll get, it is the name of our home world and the name of our race."

Kapoor typed back - What are we saying, that he's Satan, or possessed, or a religious nutcase?

?

his pronunciations of the names are too coincidental

Kapoor didn't feel comfortable challenging the names at this point, he needed more of an understanding of them first.

"As I said at the beginning, in these interviews we're going to be bouncing back and forth through various subjects..."

"Of course, you need to verify what I'm saying before you can expand on those subjects. I understand."

Kapoor nodded his thanks at him making the process easier to move forward.

"Before we move on, I just want to clarify your medication. You've been diagnosed recently with schizophrenia and are still undergoing tests and have been under observation at the mental health clinic at St Mary's, is that right?"

"Yes, and they have prescribed me a course of medication including anti-psychotics and anti-depressants, none of which I've been taking."

"I see." Kapoor looked down to the screen. Your medical records show that you are deemed delusional but not a danger to yourself or anyone else. Would you agree with that?"

"I can see why the doctors would think that, yes. Obviously I would argue I'm not delusional otherwise I wouldn't be here now."

he didn't answer the question fully

"Do you see yourself as dangerous?"

John Cade smiled before answering.

"Are you scared of me, Mr Kapoor?"

Kapoor sat back waiting for an answer, he wasn't prepared to be baited and was too experienced to know not to play this kind of game.

"No. No, I'm not dangerous, Mr Kapoor."

Kapoor nodded and sat forward again ready for his next set of questions.

14

What did you think of the interviews?

I didn't have a problem with them to be honest with you. The Indian guy, Kapoor, seemed very competent in what he was asking and clearly they were checking things out as they went along. I think they started it expecting it to only take a couple of hours, they weren't prepared for the long haul. Months we bashed out arguments as they grilled me. I got to stay there under guard. It was funny. It went from a low security facility to high in the space of a week. Then there was the power struggle as those in charge fought off the MOD to retain jurisdiction. I wasn't let into the ins and outs of it but you could tell there was a power struggle going on. I don't know which part of what I'd said turned heads but something obviously had, something the likes of Hipkiss had missed or hadn't taken seriously.

Did you think of your family during this time?

A little. They kept me informed of what was happening to them. They had to interview Gemma, and I'm guessing they got copies of all their medical records too, same with my folks and my sister. They went down to Somerset and spoke to them there.

I guess the worst part of the interviews was the repetitiveness of it all. Going over and over everything time and time again. I guess they were waiting for me to slip up, make a mistake, and contradict myself. But it wasn't going to happen.

15

It had been a long day, most of which Louis Vost had spent waiting in the corridors of the Ministry of Defence building in Whitehall whilst the Chief of Defence Staff and the Permanent Secretary read through the reports and weighed the value of MI17 and its worthiness to continue as a department. A separate military taskforce had submitted a bid for control of any ongoing concerns of MI17 once it was disbanded, and in failure of that to take control of any ongoing investigation with anything relating to the John Cade case, or what was now being known as the classified Project Furion. It was clear the powers that be higher up were taking the case seriously enough to consider attributing it further resources.

"Well?" asked Surjeet Kapoor following him into his office.

Vost took off his coat and hung it up and then circled his desk and sat down.

"Go get the Major in here," demanded Vost with a tired no messing tone.

Kapoor scooted off, visibly anxious for more than his boss was giving him. He returned a moment later with Major Kennedy, the military's man in charge and potential Operations Manager of MI17 to replace Louis Vost. The two men stood in front of Vost's desk waiting as Vost signed a document held within a file marked 'classified'. Kapoor still held his nervous edge, but the Major had a smug smirk riding above his khaki uniform.

Vost slid over the document he had just signed.

"These are your new orders, Major. You are assigned to the security of this facility and answerable to me."

Major Kennedy looked up with shock on his face, questioning that this was surely a mistake. He read the document carefully before responding.

"Yes sir."

"That will be all."

The Major nodded, turned and walked out without saying another word.

Kapoor was stunned. After weeks of being treated like dirt by the military who had been drafted in to patrol the corridors and secure the facility with an aim of replacing its civilian staff, with their snipes about civilians soon to be stood in line in the doll queue, the Major in particular getting a rise out of Vost by telling him he ought to be careful what he says to him as he'll be the first transferred out, after all this he was amazed to see Kennedy retreat so suddenly with his tail between his legs.

What happened?"

"Let's say it's a good job I have a military background or else he'd be your new boss. There will be some restructuring of the department but for the moment we have been budgeted for another five years."

Kapoor's mouth dropped open.

"Oh, and by the way, one of the first things I'm doing round here is giving you a promotion. Now what's the number for maintenance, let's get those damn lights in the corridor fixed."

16

'How are you doing this morning John?"

"Full English this morning so I'm good. Glad to see the catering's improved under the new management." John winked with a broad smile.

Kapoor tapped the keyboard he had just opened up on the desk and waited a second or two for it to ask his password. He typed it in and refreshed the log of where they had left off yesterday.

"Let's see, yesterday we talked again about the cloning process and parental responsibilities of the AI's. So we've established that you're a clone, of sorts, and that your race is split into two main political factions, the free born and the military clones. I know it's more complicated than that but I'm just summarising.

"Now you estimate your age at time of death to be approximately between 70 and 170 earth years."

"Yeah, it's hard to calculate as time is measured differently to here on Earth. UTC is standard across the known galaxy for space travel as you can't set a time based on any one planet's revolutionary cycle. Each planet has its own time spectrum of course, but for space it's different."

"That's Universal Coordinated Time, this fixed time zone in space, right?"

"Yes. We don't celebrate birthdays so marking the passing of years is done by the religious factions who commemorate the falling of our home world. They shun technology as being evil and the cause of the downfall of man. They led the fight against the circuit boards in the early days as being demonic and sent from the gods to destroy us. I don't go in for all that crap. I can give you details of planets, the people that live there and our attempts to survive and live in peace with one another but anything religious, including the passing of time, I just ain't interested."

"So you couldn't tell me, say, how long ago it was that you were wounded and lost your arm? Or your eye?"

"I can tell you they were repaired..."

"Regrown?"

"Regrown, and that there was about 5 or 6 years between them, but that won't help you in calculating my age. We kept youthful through advances in medical recoup pods which incorporate cloning skin grafts and regenerative limbs and organs. Although we live longer, the harshness of space and the disease of malnutrition in the general population of terraformers meant that many children didn't survive for long, and mostly those born aboard battleships were purpose bred as soldiers or technicians through the cloning process and reared by nurturing circuit boards who were supposed to show more interest in the developing, educating and caring of us growing lifeforms."

"You've given me a hundred year window, care to narrow it down?"

Cade shrugged his shoulders and answered non-commitally, "Probably somewhere in the upper end maybe."

it's too vague. move on.

"One of the things I don't understand John, if you could explain it to me, how can a soul exist in an omnipresent state?"

"Omnipresent? Do I sound like a god? Do I look like a god? I make no pretense to be one, nor do I wish it. You may have a desire of omnipotence but I desire to be worshipped by no one. Like I said, I don't go in for the religious stuff. "

"Maybe omnipresent was the wrong word to use."

Cade sat back and fixed Kapoor with a steely glare. "Careful with your words and phrases, we need to understand each other clearly, do we not? I never said the soul was omnipresent."

Kapoor raised his hands defensively. "Ok, in a parallel plane, or however you want to term it, basically what I want to understand is how can it exist in more than one place at a time?"

Cade thought for a moment, his eyes searching an empty space before him.

"Maybe the simplest way to answer that is to ask you a question: when you are in your car and you turn on the radio and you listen to a song, where is the song? Is it in your car, in the broadcasting studio, or floating above the streets being beamed through the air? One song. Same song. Different places at once."

Kapoor sat back in reflection and turned the corner of his mouth skyward in appreciation of the answer.

smug answer - move on.

"In one of our discussions you mentioned the planet where the moon was knocked out of orbit. Tell me again what happened there."

Cade let out a long sigh as though recalling a painful memory.

"Did I tell you I was pierced by a lance in that battle?"

Kapoor shot his head up curious.

"I thought it was a natural catastrophe not a battle."

"It was. The people on the settlement fled and broke into factions. Those wealthy enough to gain access to the fastest and better equipped ships bought an allegiance with the marauding fleets that travelled the galactic highway through the system, this left the poorer people to risk a lottery over who would survive, many having to fight each other for survival – it quickly became a battle of the survival of the fittest, creating a race of battle hardened and hate filled warriors seeking a home but being hounded and persecuted by their own people who hunted them down out of fear of reprisals. It wasn't that uncommon a thing to happen on a failed terraformed planet, when the social structure collapses all hell tends to break loose, so to speak. Anyway, mine was one of the outfits charged with hunting the splinter groups down and restoring some sort of order to the sector. You can't have violent factions fleeing through open space, they end up landing on an already occupied planet with a peaceful population and next thing you know you've got a war. The people have to be controlled. Yeah, you could argue that the government provokes a lot of it, in some cases inciting rebellion so that it can exercise military control, but usually it's for the greater good, for the good of our people as a whole.

I boarded a rebel ship and ordered them to surrender all the refugees from the lower caste that had fled the planet. I didn't get a good reception. A fight broke out and then some genius thought it was clever to blow a hole in the ship. Fortunately I was wearing my exosuit so my life support kicked in when I was blown out into the depths of space. Unfortunately a slice of the ship's hull blew with me and a jagged poll tore through my back propelling me towards the Arra-tets of my own ship. I got picked up, but man it hurt like hell."

"What happened to the ship you boarded?"

"As soon I was clear of firing range I ordered it destroyed."

"Ah come on, don't ask me about probabilities and quantum science again, I told you I'm a commander not a bloody mathematician or physicist."

Kapoor raised his hand in defence. It had been a long day and both of them were tense and getting tired with the endless repetitive questioning. He wanted to call it a day but Vost was still feeding him questions from the other room.

"We're just trying to ascertain the precise location of your home planet. It's not on any charts that we are able to see with our telescopes."

"Then maybe you need to build better telescopes."

move on. we can pinpoint it down to the Constellation Lyra for the moment. try him again on religion. he's tired, see if we can catch him off guard. switch back to Ki'La.

Kapoor thought quickly recalling earlier conversations. He scratched the light shadow on his cheek as he stared across at the tall figure sat lurched over the table with his shoulders hunched and a light gingery beard gracing his square jaw. John Cade looked worse for wear. He may have been enjoying the attention of the early interviews but now they had got down to the hard line aggressive interrogation as they tried to pull apart everything he had told them the strain was clearly beginning to show, yet despite that he still hadn't slipped up.

"You said you thought there might be others here, split souls like yourself."

Cade's head jerked up expectantly.

Kapoor shook his head.

"There's no more news on that score. I'm interested to hear more about the religious aspect of what your people believe. Are their religious beliefs similar to ours? Hinduism, Buddhism, Islam, Christianity? Are there aspects of the Bible, for example, that are in parallel? Do they have an end time prophecy like in Revelation?"

Cade took an exasperated deep breath and sat back in his chair.

"Honestly I know very little of religion here; I've never really taken an interest in it, never owned a Bible and sure as hell never read one."

Kapoor gave a casual look to the camera.

"Ok, so how about your people's religion, how about there being other split souls like yourself amongst your own people?"

"Sure, why not.

"What I travelled through felt like a sort of wormhole. Our people have long thought that upon death we would travel through the stars to the void beyond the universe where our souls communed as one collective being, harmonizing with that which existed at our creation and destined us to be the eternal entity to reshape all that exists.

"Not all souls make the journey to Qcht'bar, some are sidetracked..."

"Sidetracked?"

"Ki'La. The ancient priests believed we were all destined for something greater beyond life. They didn't believe in the longevity brought about through science, therefore they shunned reanimation and organ transplants and viewed cloning as an abomination."

"They were peaceful in their protests?"

"No, they were barbaric, viciously violent in their opposition. They waged war on the government and on the scientific community."

"Did they have many followers?"

"Plenty. Whole colonies hung on their every word. The religion was a cornerstone of our culture which many thought was being lost for the financial gain of the conglomerates that were propping up the central government. Not to mention the fact that it was our people's greed for technology that shattered the very core of our home world to begin with; this alone had ensured a lasting legacy which the priests were ever ready to echo in their rhetoric.

"But the war with the priests was a short conflict which dwindled their numbers down to an elite few who would travel preaching their message until they found a willing flock they could shepherd to live out the faith in community. In time their number grew again but they knew they could never amass enough of a following to outweigh the rest of our people who equally had multiplied numerically."

"Why was their war so short?"

"Many of them were master warriors but their beliefs prevented them from taking advantage of those very things that kept us alive and able to reenter the battle field. They lived a relatively short lifespan and welcomed their mortality as they reached beyond to Qcht'bar."

"You've spoken a lot about the different conflicts of your people. Your race seems to revel in violence."

"And we don't? Our conflicts here on Earth are no more diverse nor violent. We rage war over religion, over property and land, over resources, over sex, and over a general dislike of our neighbour. Who are we to take the moral high ground? Who are we to stand in judgement over another race struggling for survival? Yes, there are many conflicts amongst my people but we have had many obstacles to overcome, and I think on the whole we have remained united as a race despite our factions of cultures and beliefs."

get him back on track - Ki'La

"You mentioned Ki'La."

"The belief that some souls were destined to greater things by living a more experienced life as another creature within another civilization, thus attaining an elevated seat above all others in Qcht'bar. The Ki'La are ordained split souls coexisting in the universe but never complete until death."

"So you're saying you are destined to be some sort of god?"

"I never said that. I've maintained all along that I've never believed in the religion of my people."

"Yet your experience would tally with their beliefs?"

"Arguably, yes, I suppose, but I do not believe in Qcht'bar or heaven, or Valhalla, or whatever you want to call it. When we die we die, and in the meantime I rely on science to keep me alive and in one piece."

"So you accept that your life won't be prolonged now that you are just John Cade?"

"What?"

"You're not Abadd'on. You're not the Six Million Dollar Man. We have no technology to rebuild you. When you die here, or suffer a mortal wound, or terminal illness, you die for real - permanently."

Cade looked to his hands, his face downcast.

"Of course, I know that."

"So do you think you'll transfer to another body, whisked through another wormhole to possess someone else or, as you just stated, when you die you die?"

Cade shook his head but didn't answer.

"Do you think Ki'La have travelled from here to your people? Do you think that is how your religion started? Split souls from Earth? Maybe *we* are the origin of *your* people."

Cade looked up with vehemence sparking through his eyes, his nostrils flaring in rage at the apparent insult thrown at him as though it were a bucket filled with sewage, and for a moment Surjeet Kapoor saw a glimpse of something that hadn't been there before: for a brief second he saw the spirit of Abadd'on staring at him from within with hate filled merciless eyes.

17

"How long do we have to keep doing this?"

John Cade slumped down on the floor beside the treadmill which still whirred its dying cycle as its rubber slowly braked. The gym still smelled of the white paint which was newly coated to the walls of what had been one of the storage rooms.

Eric Rosen, a military doctor, had been drafted in to assess the subject's physical state and wellbeing. He read the results off the machine readout and punched the data into the handheld console which was connected via a coiled grey cable generating a progress chart. The subject had remote sensors attached to his body which relayed additional information such as heart rate and blood pressure. So far everything seemed normal, insomuch as John Cade was a 6'4", 196 lb, slim asthmatic with poor posture and ingrown toenails. He had no allergies, and so far no allergic reactions to anything that had been tested on him. His legs were sturdy enough but his upper body strength was weak through lack of exertion, and by his own admission the most exercise his muscles had received in recent years had been the lugging about of his two children, Mia and Toby.

For two weeks straight Dr Rosen had been putting John Cade through his paces as he tested his stamina and endurance, his body strength, and his tolerance to pain. He ran his bloods and ran every toxicology test the lab could cope with. The hematology report came back clear on every aspect: no disease, no abnormalities or defects, no narcotics of any kind in his system. ECG and CAT scans all came back with negative results. His psychiatric report came back surprisingly on a par with what he would expect with any average person not suffering an extended episode of delusional paranoia. Everything about the man said he was normal.

"These damn sticky pads itch like hell. I so much prefer the Pa'as suits."

Normal that was except for the comments about the alien hardware.

"So you've said before. John, please don't take them off. I need the data and if you take them off I'm just going to have to make you run for another twenty minutes."

Cade stopped scratching at the pads which attached to the small electrode-like sensors on his chest and temples that were beginning to react to his sweat. He pulled himself up into a stood position by grabbing the handrail of the treadmill and started moving over towards the rowing machine. He knew the drill: ten minutes rowing followed by bench press and shoulder press, then back to cycling and leg press before cooling down on the treadmill again. It was exhausting, but he guessed that was the whole point. He wasn't dumb to what they were doing: wear him out, make him feel the strain, then interrogate, followed by minimal sleep under controlled lighting conditions and then up early again the next day to repeat it all again. He was impressed. It wasn't the way he would have done it, but he admired the approach nonetheless.

Dr Rosen reset the readout on the rowing machine as Cade sat down on the sliding seat, it was an air resistance machine so it made a hell of a racket as he grabbed the T-bar and pulled back on the cable. Dr Rosen studied the ripples on his graph as he held his tablet before him knowing that Cade was eying it from the corner of his eye each time he pulled back from the machine.

"You know the Pa'as suit..."

"Implanted directly and fed back the stats and registered and maintained body function, yes I know, you told me already."

Dr Rosen had heard it all before and was getting fed up of it and was beginning to let it show despite the warnings of Major Kennedy. He didn't believe any of Cade's story, why should he? It was preposterous. He couldn't make out why the MOD was spending so much money on studying the man when he was so clearly making the whole thing up.

18

"So what's the topic for today Mr Kapoor?"

John Cade had an energy in his voice that was deceptive of the weariness that lined his face. It was a brave front he was clearly struggling to maintain.

Kapoor was equally tired, well maybe not to the extent of the prisoner, not that anyone called him this aloud; technically he was free to leave at any point he chose but the pressure and emphasis in the language and mannerisms of the soldiers that now manned the corridors were incentive enough to deter any thoughts of freedom. Of course they would let him go if he became stubborn and totally uncooperative and insisted on leaving, but so far it hadn't come to that.

Kapoor was glad he didn't have to endure the trials of sleeping on site. He had done it once or twice out of choice as he'd stayed late reviewing tapes and researching answers, and on occasion awaiting call backs from across the globe, but he made it a point to escape home daily; despite the new office makeover it still felt oppressive. He was grateful for the comfort of his own bed and the daylight he could enjoy as the day lengthened outside. The things that energised him were all the things that John Cade was purposely being deprived of in order to get him to crack.

"How was your lunch?"

"Not long enough. You do know that Dr Rosen is a sadistic bastard?"

"Are you talking about the exercise or the diet he has you on?"

"Both. No actually the food's ok."

"He's wearing you out is he?"

Cade rubbed his face as if trying to wake himself up.

"A little."

"How do you feel about me, about our talks?"

"I'm cool with it. I quite enjoy it. I like talking about the old life. When else can I get to boast about all my achievements? There's no one else alive to revere me."

"You think they're all dead then?"

"My people? I don't know. Who can tell the time that has elapsed; hundreds, thousands of years may have elapsed. You know I was always so consumed by the moment, living the mission, planning the next one, thinking I'd live forever, that I never stopped to think about who would ascend to command after me and continue the survival of our people. There are a couple who could rise to the challenge but they'd have big boots to fill."

"You thought you were immortal?"

"No, not really, just kidded myself that I'd always beat death. I guess I got lucky so many times I began to believe my own hype."

"When you talk about the survival of your people you always seem to narrow it down to your ship and not the people as a whole."

"Our people are too vast for me to be concerned about each colony. That's the role of the central government and the MCU.

"MCU?"

"Military Command Unit.

"My ship is my family; they are my primary concern. What we do as a ship, as a fleet, benefits the colonies and the central government, but firstly we take care of ourselves and ensure we look after the interests of the ship and the fleet I command."

"You look after number one."

"Survival of the fittest."

"Is that what your people are all about?"

"It's what I'm all about."

"You don't see John Cade as weak then?"

"We are different personalities I'll grant you that, but we, I, are not separate in our views."

"Do you have counsellors in your culture?"

"No, everyone has too many issues to be analyzed. They would not be taken seriously. The closest we would get would be the circuit boards who tend to try to rein us back and instill an air of comfort as they take the moral high ground, but that is just an attempt by them to peel apart the layers of the human psyche so they can emulate us."

"You don't think their compassion is genuine?"

"No, I don't. We created them."

"How would you feel about speaking with a counsellor?"

'They tried to make me do that at the hospital - didn't work out that well."

"Maybe you could give it another go."

John Cade shrugged his shoulders.

"Maybe we could arrange one for you when you leave here and go home."

Cade didn't answer but instead looked down at his fingers.

keep him talking. don't let him shut down. speed it up, get his responses quicker

"Talk to me about the wormholes."

Cade tilted his head up and a slight smirk broadened his face. He lent forward a tad, his hands resting on the table for support.

"Like I said before I don't know the exact science so don't beat me up if I get the lingo wrong, ok. We don't use them much, mainly for two reasons: 1 - the maths involved in calculating them is too complex, I wouldn't leave it to a human; it's probably one of the few things I'd trust to a circuit board, and 2 - they're way too dangerous."

"How so?"

"Well let's say you calculate it right so that one opens where you're expecting it to and it opens up at the other end where you expect it to and not in the middle of an asteroid belt or on the edge of a black hole somewhere, all being good you then have to get through its mouth without being spun off to the edge so you need to hit it dead centre; it might look stable but the whole damn thing is spinning, you know like one of those toys you spin on the table, not that you can tell from looking at it - it looks calm and serene, smooth as glass but don't be fooled by appearances. Eventually the damn thing stops spinning and when it does do you don't want to be anywhere near the mouth when it closes 'cause it will just rip you apart. Then imagine you get through the mouth, you still need to navigate a central path, remember the damn thing is still spinning, you're like a rat in a ball you have no control over, it rolls straight so long as the legs of said rat don't touch the ground, but now you've got the extra velocity as it pulls you through space with half the gravitational pull of its parent black hole. As a pilot you don't want to be in that situation unless you don't have a choice, and as a commander you don't risk your ship like that unless the alternative is already utter destruction."

"Have you been through a wormhole?"

"Once or twice. Believe me, not many can make that claim."

parent black hole?

"You referred to the black hole as its parent, care to elaborate on that?"

"Wormholes are essentially tunnels through space-time that connect black holes. They're not as dense and therefore can't crush and swallow with the same sort of power. Where a black hole is stable, to a certain degree anyway, a wormhole is kind of like a string of spaghetti spat out from a toddler having a tantrum. The black hole spits out bursts of energy once it's digested something - something goes in, something comes out. The energy that comes out jumps from one part of space to another as it folds the matter around it."

Cade picked up the pad of paper and tore off a page and folded it three times.

"It opens here on this side of space and leaps through to the same side by taking a short cut through the folds rather than taking the flat route."

"Wouldn't that analogy imply it could open up on the other side of the page?"

"The flip side of the universe? The circuit boards think so, that's why they always want us to use them. You could call it their religion. They're always seeking the unknown. I like taking risks, but that's ridiculous. I stick to what I know."

"What about it being Qcht'bar?"

Cade shook his head with a snigger.

"I'm not a priest, you'd have to ask one of them."

"Can the AI's really calculate where they will appear?"
"Yes."
"So what's it like going through one?"
"Like being thinned out in a volcano, hurts like hell but then you come out on the other side and it feels like you're submerging in a cold bath."
very descriptive and fast response! replied Kapoor.

Kapoor thought for a moment. John Cade was being energised by the conversation but he didn't want him energised, he wanted him confused and tripping up on his own theories. He needed to complicate his thoughts by stretching his imagination and make him work out the science.

"Much of what you've said is very Star Trekky."
"How so?"
"Come on John, even you have to admit that a lot of this could have been pulled from science fiction films. But my point is this: with similarities between warp drive, vipers, and wormholes, why have you not spun in teleportation?"
"Battlestar Galactica."
"Pardon?"
"Vipers. They're from Battlestar Galactica not Star Trek. They only have shuttles in Star Trek."
avid fan obviously!
"I stand corrected. So why not teleportation?"
"The technology exists, but again we don't like to use it."
"Too dangerous?"
"Again it's complex maths. Yes the circuit boards can handle it, even our best navigators can do it, but you have to take into account such variables as moving objects, weather, solid walls, etc. It's basically trying to place yourself somewhere you can't see. Plenty of people have died ending up somewhere they hadn't expected. As well as that all it takes is a power outage or surge in the system and you're gone, disseminated into a billion particles never to be integrated together again, just lost to the elements of space.

"Then you've got the moral argument. This is the one the religious nuts argued when the technology was first developed."
"What's the moral argument in teleportation?"
"They claimed that if the soul is spiritual then it is not cellular,

so cellular dissemination would not happen on a spiritual level, body and soul would have to travel whole for the entire person to arrive at the other end, so disintegration of the body as a cellular form is plausible, but not the entire being."

"So does that mean that disintegration is only possible for inanimate or non-spiritual objects?"

"That's what they argued initially. You think I caused a stir and started some religious debate, you should have heard what echoed around my planet, playing out on screens globally."

"This was before V'hihyon was destroyed?"

"You've been working on saying it, I can tell. It wasn't destroyed, it died. There's a difference."

"Your people killed it."

"My people's lust for technology killed it, yes. Again you see how religion was able to propagate within our culture. There were those who hated technology with religious vehemence, and then there were those who argued that it was technology that saved us, enabling us to reach out to the stars.

"Teleportation technology developed in the years when we knew our planet would not survive but before we had drawn up a plan to escape our doom. There was desperation amongst the governing bodies to try every scientific way of ensuring our future. Many new advancements were made in those days, but in the rashness of time restrictions not all necessary care was taken to ensure safety of the experiments. Many people died. Teleportation was but one of those failed experiments as they looked at how to evacuate large groups on mass to off world space stations and neighbouring moons which had been terraformed.

"Illegal beaming platforms were sold on the black-market, as with most abandoned tech, all of which eventually merged into an open market as law and order collapsed and differing factions sought for political control of what was becoming our slowly spreading empire throughout our corner of the galaxy. Of course all modern tech is bastardised and individualised for each ship's needs. There's no quality control or patent on anything. A ship's commander relies on good acquisition hands who know their tech and top notch mechanics to keep things running."

"What about the AI's, do they not fix things?"

"Not on my ship. If they do I have it double checked.

"Anyway, the spiritual question always kept people skeptical of using the platforms for anything other than transporting cargo and weaponry down to a planet surface. The debate just raged on: can the non-corporeal consciousness separate from the physical cellular body, transporting separately? If so, does this take the spirit outside of the normal space-time continuum as we know it into an alternative plane of existence? Of course questions like this led to people questioning whether attaining such a feat equated to 'ascension', and if so where exactly do we ascend? You see where I'm going with this?"

"Another religious war?"

"Not so much as a war, more angst and a split in theology from the mainstream church, only this splinter group drew attention due to the number of circuit boards who wanted in on the action."

"They believed in Qcht'bar?"

"Qcht'bar, God, ascension, a higher purpose, the works. Basically they wanted to believe in anything that took them out of the idea that they were just a bunch of circuits we'd put together. That kinda made them good cannon fodder as they were more prepared to die than we were."

"Was there any safe way to teleport a human?"

"Not really. There were theories, theories that said it wouldn't be possible unless you were encapsulated in an inanimate bubble of sorts, ensuring solidity through some sort of wormhole. Frankly, mixing those two things together doesn't float my boat much."

19

"Well, he seems to have an answer for everything."

"Boss I'm shattered. I can't keep up with him."

"It's tiring just watching you guys. Seriously Surj, you're doing an amazing job in there."

They both looked out the window of Louis Vost's office as Major Kennedy strutted past.

"What's eating him?" asked Kapoor.

"A few things that Cade has said have rattled both Whitehall and Washington. He's talking about things he shouldn't know about. Not so much alien stuff but more experimental tech, which has got them worried they have a mole somewhere."

"Even if that were the case, how the hell would John Cade have gotten wind of any of it to begin with?"

Vost held his hand up in submission. "I know. I know. But it's the only reason we've still got him here."

"How are linguistics getting on?"

Vost laughed before answering. "I'm no musician but I do speak three languages so I'm used to being able to translate one from another, but the contortions on these guy's faces is a real picture as they try to harmonise what Cade has provided as an alphabet. Let's say it's tuneful and not particularly wordy, and that's just on the one dialect he's given us."

"But do they think it could be a language?"

"That's the worrying part. They think it is, but it's not made up of any language spoken on earth. It's closer to something whales do rather than humans. And we've played back the tapes, he's consistent, when you've asked him over time for specific words they've matched what he previously said. So either he's worked all this out beforehand, or he really can speak both languages: English and Furion."

Kapoor rubbed his head. This was all getting too much for him. When all this was over he planned on taking a long vacation.

"Go home Surj. We'll have another crack at it again tomorrow."

Kapoor nodded already walking for the door. "Yes boss."

20

"So where are you?"

He looked around his room. The low bunk he sat on, the filing cabinet he utilised as drawers for his clothes. The washroom was down the corridor where he was observed journeying to each time by the guard on duty in the corridor. He had tried to tell her on a previous call that the government was interested in his story and was questioning him, but he could tell from the exasperated tone of her voice that she didn't believe him.

"To be honest I don't really know. Central London somewhere I think."

Their conversation rode out in long hesitant pauses as they both felt they were walking on egg shells trying not to offend the other and provoke a hostile emotional response.

"I spoke to your folks, they're worried about you. They said they haven't spoken to you in months."

John rubbed his head in anguish.

"They've got enough on their plate dealing with Samantha. Did they say how she was doing?"

"She's good. Doing better than you. She and Michael are working on things."

There was a long silence above the murmured hiss of the open line. She was the first to break it.

"We could work on things." Her voice was pleading. She was holding back the tears, and barely able to get the words out.

"Gemma no. You can't accept what's happened to me, who I am now."

"I can try."

"But you'll always see me as a mental health case."

"The children miss you."

"How are they?"

"They're good."

"Can I speak to them?"

"They're not here at the moment."

"Of course not. And if they were?"

"John... please."

"It wouldn't be appropriate. You're scared of me Gemma, and you won't let me speak to my own kids because daddy's had a mental breakdown and got himself sectioned. Daddy thinks he's an alien so keep away from him."

He could feel the anger rising in him. He tried to rein it in, fully aware that his time was short and other ears were listening on the line.

"Are you eating ok?" she asked in an attempt to change the question.

He didn't answer. He was thinking, trying to picture her sat on the sofa of their family home, tissues in hand. He could also picture Kapoor and Vost sitting in their den listening in with Cybermen headphones; it was an image he could only imagine, he'd never seen the inside of the room where he suspected all the cameras and mic feeds fed into, but in his paranoia he suspected every breath he took was under observation.

"Don't you want to come home?"

He thought about it. In the early days he was desperate for her to ask that sort of question, but now it was complicated. He was a different person now, having to form his own way in life, and he wasn't sure where the old ties fitted into who he was now.

"Of course," he lied, "but it's not going to be that easy."

"I know."

She sounded relieved as she grasped hold of his words with a sense of hope.

"I still love you John."

He grunted a wordless response, almost tailing off into a hum.

"How's Dyson?"

She choked back a stunned response.

"Dyson? He's here, he's good," she sniffled.

"I have to go, they're coming for me," he lied.

21

"Tell us again about the day you died, but this time take us back a day or two."

"You want me to set the scene."

Louis Vost nodded from across the table. Kapoor was monitoring, having opted for a change of scenery. It wasn't a change Major Kennedy was happy about as he made no qualms about letting his feelings known that he wanted a crack at interviewing Cade. Vost's rationale was that the situation would be too volatile if he let Kennedy in the room on his own; he may be a good soldier but he was a lousy diplomat, and he didn't want to risk getting Cade's back up and have him clam up, or worse, walk out.

John Cade arched his long back as he rolled his shoulders

towards the wall behind him. He tilted his head to both sides cracking his neck as his eyes drifted off to another world a lifetime away.

"We had a communicae from the MIU's permanent land garrison posted on K'avar, a planet with quite a diverse eco system which served as a training ground for military exercises and allowed terraforming assault teams to practice setting up excavation pads in ever changing climates. It was similar to Earth in many ways but it was uninhabited save for the usual wildlife, which included some nasty arachnids and some sharp taloned birds of prey which gave sport for our soldiers. I had served the best part of a decade in exile on K'avar so knew the workings of it well. It was a political hotbed. Political factions were always vying for an allegiance with the strongest military base in the sector; whoever controlled the base controlled a dozen star systems and the colonies that dwelt within. As a result these were the toughest and most robust soldiers in the core, they had to be, always on alert and expectant of an attack, which occasionally the foolishly brave would try."

"Why were you exiled there?"

Cade shrugged his shoulders as if to say it was no big deal. "I beat some of the crew and tried to take the ship."

"The Apolly'on?"

"Yeah. I disagreed with the commander's leadership so challenged him for it. Mutiny for the right reasons is respected not looked down upon. The commander saw I had potential to lead but needed training. K'avar was my punishment and my training. When a later attempted coup resulted in the ship being leaderless the fleet sent for me to take command."

"So as commander of a military fleet you receive your orders from the military base at K'avar?"

"Correct. So we had been tasked with setting up new settlements for the exiles from Hadar, I think I told you about that planet before. The poorer groups that needed resettling, it was decided, were to be separated and placed on various worlds as part of a social experiment. It was nothing new, the government was always toying with society as it tried to improve the race and weed out the weaker factions and seek ways of controlling the will of the stronger ones. They figured that if they could keep individual societies sparsely populated over a wide area then they wouldn't develop technologically but would remain as primitive hunter gatherers and farmers trying to survive off the land and not expand in knowledge as there were fewer people to share ideas with. It also made them easier to invade if needed, as the strongest will and insurgence remained with those whose population was condensed into a mass where ideas and strong wills could thrive and ultimately object..."

"To the authorities you mean?"

"All governments would like to keep their people dumb and submissive."

"What about the will of the people?"

"What about them? If they wanted something then they would have to go get it, like the rest of us."

"Fight for it you mean?"

"It didn't do me any harm. Survival of the fittest. Isn't that how evolution works?"

"Sounds very Spartan."

"Our navigational systems had been charting a new system. The primary planet in the system was a huge red gas ball. There was no chance of changing the atmosphere or landmass of such an orb but it had a number of moons worth investigating. We had abandoned two which were too close to an asteroid field and were too icy, the third looked promising: a rocky moon just far enough out from the planet to be protected from the asteroid belt and receive enough sunlight on rotation from the sun. I judged we could land an excavation pad and set it drilling foundations of a domed settlement. We would secure the rock with a small cohort of caretakers before moving on to investigate the other planets in the system. Setting up the dome takes a while and equalising the air filtration system takes even longer. We would return at a later date to leave a supply and maintenance team with their own ships from the fleet to begin the land transformation before any of the exiles from Hadar could be transferred over."

"How does the land transformation take place? You said it was a rock."

"Normally if the planet or moon is large enough and its atmosphere acceptable, within the minimum percentiles to be adapted for human consumption, it would take between what would probably be six months to two years to fully convert the outside to be breathable for settlement, and a further six months to establish a core settlement base and military compound. If there is no natural fresh water supply, as it was here, we would transfer ice from the neighbouring moons, or in this case the asteroid belt, to create lakes in the craters and then we artificially introduce lab created soil and plants. But before we can do this the external ioniser needs to be built. The simplest way to describe it is that this acts as an atmospheric sampler, the chemical compound of a desired atmosphere is fed into the computer and it is replicated on a global scale.

"I thought you said before there were lakes and rivers on this moon?"

"Yes, but the water content was full of impurities and not suitable for our needs. We needed a source we could use for growth, the samples we took from our scout were just incompatible.

"To maintain the atmosphere the land forming needs to be precise, timing is everything for both the atmosphere and the growth of the land to complement each other without killing each other off prematurely. Obviously the smaller the planet the better, which was why this moon looked ideal."

"But it didn't all go to plan."

"No. Like I said before, it had looked uninhabited. I had gone down with a scout team to look at what appeared to be some old decimated structures of an abandoned civilization but when we landed there was nothing there, just misshapen rocks that were deceiving from above. The following day we prepped the excavation pad and parked up the fleet nearby ready for the relatively short stay of the initial setup. So two days after my initial scout we went down with our main landing party."

"Do you always go down with your landing parties? Isn't that a bit irresponsible as commander of the ship?"

"What can I say, that's just the sort of commander I am!"

he means to say that he was an asshole!

Vost ignored the comment but internally wanted to snigger in agreement with Kapoor's quip.

"Continue."

"The rocks we had seen from the ship before weren't there on our scout because they had moved. They must have done. The more I think about it the more I'm convinced that the rocks were a pure form of Pa'as, I think they baited us. They waited till our entire landing party was down and then they attacked. Maybe they were looking for a way off the rock, maybe they just wanted to feed off us, maybe both.

For my part it was a tactical error, but not one that could have been predicted, and my men would learn from my mistake."

"How do you feel about that, them moving on without you?"

Cade shrugged his shoulders, he was clearly in a nonchalant shoulder shrugging mood.

"Life goes on. It's not my concern anymore."

22

"Do you honestly believe it?"

There was bite in Major Kennedy's voice as he tried to verbalise the doubt they all felt, but Kennedy was trying to tear a hole in the fabric of the character, and he was succeeding, but in fairness he didn't need to try hard.

"I think we can all agree the character of Abadd'on is one none of us would readily befriend," admitted Vost.

"Selfish, proud, arrogant, racist, violent, male chauvinist, do you want me to go on?"

"He has portrayed some poor character traits I'll admit," protested Kapoor, "But I think we need to put it into context of his position: he's a commander of a warrior fleet, how else is he supposed to act. Besides all that, he has shown some good qualities too: leadership and responsibility, resilience, a care and concern of his men."

"Egotistical, insubordinate, mutinous..." argued Kennedy before he was cut off by Vost.

"We are talking about Cade and not you, right?"

It was a comment only Vost could have got away with, and one that caused Kapoor to dip his head to disguise the smirk riding his cheeks.

"Let's face it," continued Vost, "he's not that much different from us, and were we placed in the same situations within the same culture we would no doubt have our own equivalent, only magnified in such extraordinary conditions. But being so alike in character only emphasizes the fact that he is, or could be, simply a manifestation of a creative and well thought out mind."

Major Kennedy went to speak but Vost beat him to it.

"Major, take a breath before you speak."

Kennedy did just that, seemingly swallowing the words he was about to mutter and then holding up a hand to show he was complying.

"We need to draw out his true character, not the brash boasting that he's made up to big up his story. He claims he's a military man, let me in to question him soldier to soldier."

"I've been military," Vost objected.

"Not combat though, unless I'm mistaken."

Vost made no reply.

"Let me in there, I can ask him things you two can't relate to."

Kennedy sat there with a pleading expression on his face. Kapoor sat there with an equally pleading face but its intention was the opposite, but Vost purposely didn't look to him as his mind resulted an answer, chipping away at the rough edges of his argument of why he didn't want Kennedy in the room with Cade.

There was a long pause before he spoke.

"You get one shot, make it count and don't screw it up."

23

John Cade looked nervous. He'd been sat waiting for forty minutes, Kapoor was never this long, even Vost only kept him waiting ten minutes. Either there was something drastically wrong or there was a new game plan.

Weeks of tireless examination was beginning to fray the edges of his extremities. Abadd'on on his own could have coped with much more but Abadd'on was part of John Cade now, and John Cade was a weaker mortal. The human body which housed the twin soul of the Furi'on and the Earthling was unprepared for the prolonged and yet subtle torture. John Cade had never physically worked his body, except for maybe the school yard where he saw his physical education the same way he saw it now, as punishment and torture. Nor had John Cade gone for great lengths without sleep – granted he had two kids, but the nights he had mostly left to Gemma so that he could focus on being creative at his desktop during the day. Even in the realms of job interviews John Cade was a novice, having fluked and blagged the couple of jobs he'd managed to secure in his short career, so sitting for prolonged hours having to concentrate on giving the correct answers each time was wearing thin.

All in all John Cade was ill prepared and ill equipped for the ordeal he had voluntarily submitted to.

John Cade's nerves didn't subside any as the military weight in full uniform burst in like a tornado and plonked himself aggressively in the chair opposite, a stern glare piercing across the room. John gulped visibly and his face flushed a little as he felt the nerves rise to drown him. He interlocked his fingers to stop them from shaking. Major Kennedy looked down at the motion and smiled a satisfying half snarl.

"Cade, you don't mind if I call you 'Cade' now, do you?"

"My name's John," he replied timidly.

"So Cade, for the next few hours you have the pleasure of entertaining me with your bullshit. Be clear about this son, I don't believe you. I think you're making the whole thing up. So you're going to have to work damned hard to convince me."

"I can only tell you the truth of what I know."

"We'll see about that, 'cause what you know is a little too convenient for my liking and I have every intention of tearing you apart and getting to your sources."

Kennedy opened up the laptop on the desk and typed in the command prompts and passwords.

Great start. Nice to see you're going easy on him to begin with!

Kennedy suppressed a smile, he had no intention of taking the gloves off.

"Yesterday you told Louis Vost about the terraforming on the moon where ultimately Abadd'on was killed."

"Yes."

"In your account you described the events in the course of days, and went on to express the regular operations of terraforming in periods of months and years, yet previously you have failed to convert time periods to an earth standard."

"Yes, but that is when discussing the turning of time in relation to any one planet. If you go back over our previous discussions with Mr Kapoor you may recall that I have also commented on the stretching of time as not constant from planet to planet and that within space we developed a constant time standard."

UTC

"My comments yesterday are born out of this standard. We call it UTC time. All the ships computers are calibrated to it so that we have a structure of day, work and rest periods that the whole galaxy can operate on."

"Forgive me for being blunt, but you come across as being a right bastard."

"I'm not sure I understand your meaning."

"You're a hard task master. You like blowing things up. You like getting into fights and risking the lives of your men. You treat other life forms like they're a piece of dirt. Everyone is beneath you. You're an arrogant, racist, egotistical bastard!"

John Cade gulped audibly and remained silent. This was not going well. For the first time since being embraced by MI17 he found himself unable and unsure of how to answer.

"Redeem yourself in my eyes Cade, tell me, how do you view the poor and destitute?"

"I don't understand."

Cade waited for the Major to elaborate on the question but only silence and a stern glare responded. Hesitantly he tried to reply.

"I always used to sit down with Gemma and watch the Children in Need and Comic Relief programmes on TV and we would always phone up and pledge something. We would sometimes give to a disaster relief fund. We're not rich so we could never give much but we liked to think we were making a difference."

"How very noble of you," Kennedy grumbled sarcastically. "It wasn't really John Cade's views on poverty that I was referring to."

"Oh."

Cade paused for thought but Kennedy cut across the train that was just pulling into the station.

"So far you, and your people, seem to have a dim view of the poor and displaced, an everyman for himself sort of attitude, how does John Cade reconcile with that, or does John Cade not care?"

"You're talking about a culture difference. What applies to

Furi'on's doesn't apply to us. Besides, we don't always treat the poor well and with respect. We're not exactly doing well at sharing out the riches and the food, are we?"

Keep him going – he dropped his usual pronunciation of Furion!

"But have you opened fire on those poor defenseless people? Have you butchered whole colonies simply because they don't fit in with your ideals?"

"They're not my ideals. I'm a soldier, I do what I'm told."

"But I thought that you were the commander of your fleet, and you served the interests of that fleet?"

"Yes, but I am still under orders. I still have to work within limits. If I am ordered to sort out a dispute on a planet then that is my job."

"And who dictates how you go about that? Who gives the specific orders, you or your government? Do they say go sort it out, or do they say go open fire on the weaker faction?"

"You're twisting what I've said. The stronger must survive or the weaker will become a drain on the whole of society and more will suffer and die as a result."

"But is that up to you as to who should live or die? Is it up to you to play judge and jury, playing God by ordaining who should be massacred?"

"No! It's not like that!" Cade leaped from his seat in protest and stamped his fists on the table. "You're twisting my words! I want to see Kapoor. I demand that either Mr Vost or Mr Kapoor come in here."

Major Kennedy slowly rose to his feet in a controlled manner. John Cade was tall but so was Kennedy, and Kennedy had the bulk to go with it, he also carried an authority in his personage that overshadowed the decorations of his uniform.

"Sit down," he said calmly. "You're not in a position to demand anything."

Cade took a gulp as the colour drained from his face and he leaned his legs back looking for the chair he knew he was going to have to slink back into. Cowardly he made his slow retreat as the snarling Major Kennedy towered over him.

Inside the control monitor suite Vost and Kapoor were sat with bated breath, passing the occasional glimpses to each other without saying a word, they didn't have to. They both felt the tension in the interview room, but to their surprise Kennedy was drawing out a hesitant and insecure side of John Cade that none of them had seen before and both of them were surprised that the Major was making headway so fast.

The two men stared at the monitors with renewed eagerness as Kennedy spent the next hour grilling Cade on the religious and moral reasons behind the way both his government, and he as an individual, acted towards the lesser classes of society. In the end it always came down to one thing: the survival of the fittest.

ok, change tact, see if he can show us that he's not such a bad guy.

"Your friends in the other room want you to convince us that you're not such an asshole."

Cade looked confused but was visibly relieved to be changing topic.

"Give us some examples of how you have helped people."

Cade sat in silence for almost a minute. A minute in a still room with an apparent enemy staring at you, waiting for you to deliver the correct responses was more than intimidating for Cade as it warped time beyond the realms of what felt natural. To Cade the visions of drifting from death on that Christmas Day a year ago into the mind and body of John Cade came flooding back as he stood a panicked Egyptian soldier caught in the closing breach of the Red Sea. Eventually he surfaced for air, treading water as his drowning mind began to refocus and he found a rock to stand on to keep his head above the lapping waves.

Abadd'on took over with a clarity of mind that squeezed out the spongy murky waters.

"We have remote drones that we send out to scout habitats before we send out the circuit boards to scour the surface and terraform…"

"Circuit boards? You send the robots to scout?"

"Mostly, yes, but not always."

Contradiction! His landing parties were previously human.

"As we go through space we generally travel through the tail of the interstellar plasma. The best way to describe it is like getting within the tailwind of an aeroplane or the drag of a boat, the current is smoother with less resistance from what's gone ahead. It's the same with space; the planets create a jetstream we can travel along which cuts out a lot of the radiation interference from other stars and reduces the likelihood of encountering obstacles and space debris in our path."

"Get to the point!"

Don't do that! Let him ramble if he wants, it's valuable!

"We send out the drones before we reach the planets, letting them catch up through the jetstream and into the heliopause and into the heliosphere."

"The what?"

"Each planet as it moves creates a protective bubble of headwind which then trails behind. There is an atmospheric change when you burst through the outer lining (the heliopause) into the bubble itself (the heliosphere). We always try to obtain an orbit from the heliosphere, approaching a planet from the rear to adjust for winds and gravitational pull; it just makes for an easier approach and is less taxing on the ship's hull and our instruments.

"One time we sent out drones to a small desert planet within the habitable zone of an uncharted system. As it burst through the heliopause we lost contact with the drone. It happens sometimes, especially if we have no clear line of sight or the distance is too great: a drone hitting an asteroid or a circuit malfunctioning was not uncommon. You deal with it and move on. We wrote it off as damaged and sent out another. Information from the drones is instantaneous, especially if we are lined up with it in the slipstream. Naturally we sent it on an alternative course just in case it had collided with something we couldn't see. The images that came back were of another vessel, a warrior class destroyer out from K'avar. The drone had hit its engines and caused a chain reaction throughout the ship. She was badly damaged and the crew were evacuating in shuttles and Arra-tets.

"Seeing their plight I ordered the Apolly'on to make haste to the location. I hailed the evacuating crew and warned them of our approach. The shuttles and Arra-tets are short range vessels so they wouldn't have lasted long unless they had another ship in the vicinity, but from what our scanners could tell they were the only ones out there. We picked up the entire crew except for the commander and a handful of staff on board. They refused to leave, insisting that they try to regain control of their ship. The circuit boards confirmed that the ship was likely to suffer catastrophic engine failure as its power core was fatally damaged. Basically it was about to explode and the commander had ordered all crew to flee, which included the circuit boards who were probably the only ones that could have told him of his futile attempts at repair. Risking my own life, I had a circuit board calculate the swiftest route onboard the dying vessel. I took an Arra-tet and boarded by the hanger closest to the command centre. We got out moments before the whole ship blew."

"You rescued the entire crew?"

"Yes."

"Risking your own life?"

"Yes."

"Very commendable."

Why do I feel a 'but' coming?

"You're quite quick with coming up with scenarios, aren't you? I bet if I asked you for more examples you could spin them out with only a moment's pause for thought."

"It's not like that."

"I'm sure. I have a few issues with your story."

"And they are?"

"Why didn't your drone see the ship before it hit it, and why couldn't the Apolly'on's sensors see it either?"

"It was doing tests on sensor avoidance. The crew that were still on board with the commander were a scientific detail attempting to salvage the hardware from the experiment."

"Did that contribute to the ship exploding?"

Cade hesitated with his answer.

"Why are you reluctant to answer? I could understand a military secret and not revealing classified details, but you're under no obligation. Not unless you're revealing any of our classified details and then this becomes a different interview altogether."

"I haven't revealed anything I shouldn't know or haven't been given open access to."

"So who told you about the Talos suits?"

"The what? Honestly I don't know what you're talking about."

Kennedy sighed then held up his hand as if telling himself to have patience. He clearly wanted to pursue another line of enquiry regarding who was leaking Cade government information but he hadn't yet satisfied his curiosity about the story he had just told. His military mind could see omissions in the story but he couldn't work out why Cade had alluded to them in the first place nor why he hadn't expanded on them.

"Why didn't this ship have any defenses? Surely a military battleship would have been aware of an incoming drone?"

"Its shields were down and so was its tracking array. That was necessary as part of the experiment. They were within the heliosphere of the planet to reduce all activity and interference; all non-essential systems were shut down temporarily. They didn't see us, and we didn't see them."

"Their experiment was a success then?"

"Yes, until our drone knocked them out of the sky."

"You get in trouble for that?"

Cade didn't answer the question directly and all three of the observers noted it.

"They were on a black ops mission. I wasn't to know they were there. By nature I don't advise my superiors if I decide to investigate an uncharted zone."

"You 'warned' them of your approach. You didn't 'advise' them."

"What are you implying?"

"That even though you fly the same flag you are still hostile to one another. You felt you had to warn them you were coming to rescue them not attack them."

"It would have been a fair assumption considering our drone just took out their engines."

"Lucky shot."

"Indeed."

"Tell me, considering the trouble you might have been in, once you realised the gravity of their mission and your faux pas, how many of the other ship's crew made it back to K'avar?"

"All of them."

Kennedy noted the defiance in Cade's eyes as he delivered his gritted response. John Cade was lying he was sure.

24

How did it make you feel when the Major questioned you like that?

It was like being back in training on K'avar. Having your every decision questioned and having no authority to even take a dump without being scrutinized. I just wanted to punch the guy.

Were you able to give him other examples of your good character? As Abadd'on I mean.

A few, not that he was interested. I think he had made up his mind that I was a bad guy and he couldn't reconcile the two characters, so in his mind I had created an anti-hero in Abadd'on.

Anyway, what do you care? You're just filling in the blanks of what they missed back then.

That's not true.

Who you kidding? Are you seriously trying to tell me you don't report back to Vost?

I've told you before, there is no record of a department MI17.

And I've told you that's because it's a clandestine department that's not on the books.

John, this isn't about them. I'm here for you. I'm your counsellor and what you tell me is in the strictest confidence. I know you feel let down by your family, the medical professionals, the government, and all those you've contacted about your condition have either scoffed at you or abused you, but I am here for you - I am genuinely seeking to help you be the best person you can possibly be.

But do you believe me?

As I thought, your silence speaks volumes.

John, don't give up on our time together. You have much more to tell me. There is much more I'd like to understand. And you know you want to talk about it - who else have you to tell?

25

"Narcotic drugs are unregulated. They tried to bring in laws in the early days but it was unmanageable. The greater our spread through the stars the wider the supply. New and creative drugs appeared on the scene with each new planet experimenting with an ever diverse and expanding plant life and chemical process; basic labs could be found in children's bedrooms it was that commonplace. With advances in medicine and cell regeneration most drugs such as antibiotics became redundant and only stored for emergency cases for terraformers who generally went without all the most sophisticated equipment. It tended to be the ones with the basic stocks of lab tech that went old school in drug experimentation. It didn't take long until the black-market of drug supply was coming from the terraformers. Some of them used this to their advantage to bargain for power and riches with the ruling classes, but unless they had a good planetary defence or influential allies they left themselves open to being invaded and controlled for their supply, their usefulness only being secure so long as they kept up production. So you see there was great incentive for roaming fleets to investigate and occasionally invade settlements.

"Many of our vessels were adapted of light Pa'as elements that we would scavenge for, the lighter the craft the less noise it makes pushing through the sonic boom, an all important stealth practicality for a raiding party trying to manoeuvre across a landscape for that element of surprise, even when cloaked they knew we were coming because of the boom."

"Cloaked?" Kennedy noted.

"Ripped off hardware from the government experiments hit the shipping trade quite quickly as word got round that there was something to hide our ships. Replicating the hardware wasn't too difficult once it got out."

don't probe him on it now, let him tell his story!

Kennedy bit his lip, sticking to the plan and resisting his instincts.

"The heavier the vehicle the louder the boom as it passed through the sound barrier. Of course it didn't apply to the vessels once they reached the dizzy heights and speeds of an off world atmosphere, or rather lack of, as the engines blasted out into the lonely darkness of space where no one would hear nor care. No, the only real worry, other than being slightly over calculating on the err of caution, was alerting the colonies to the adjustments that would need to be made and quickly.

"There were ways around the sonic boom but they were impracticably expensive and unpredictable and installed in older crafts we could no longer trust. It was all about the way the engine drive's superheated the temperature to refracting the shockwave that created the sound. Again it was down to size and speed and the resolve of the ship's crew. They could of course fly high and slow to avoid it all together, but that allowed none of the pleasures of thundering over them and lording it as gods if they could - the whole debacle was a contradiction on both the pilots and the engineers side but no one else seemed to care so long as they had both the option of stealth and of scaring the crap out of someone with a flyby. Truly they were just a bunch of immature egotistical jarheads who reveled in being feared and having a reputation that would go before them."

"Achilles," Kennedy muttered almost to himself.

"Precisely. Anyway..."

"You like that word don't you?"

Cade ignored him, trying to focus on his tale and not be bated.

"Anyway! They had too much testosterone pumping through their veins along with whatever narcotic the commander and crew were accustomed to feed off. Was their judgement impeded? Yes. Did it affect the pilot's ability to fly? Yes. It made for reckless and self-absorbed rogue fleets."

"Pirates."

"Pretty much, yes."

Is he describing himself?

"Now I didn't run my ship this way; we were clean. No drugs. I'd seen what they did to people. I wanted my men clear headed."

Not a druggie, just a genuine asshole! ;)

"My men saw me as their friend and guide, not just their commanding officer, and it went both ways. You always went back for a friend, for family. Family protect each other and make sure they don't get wasted on drugs that will get us killed for false glory."

Kennedy made a face which was picked up on camera.

Don't cut him short, let him tell it!

Kennedy relaxed his face, the tension of being bored loosening his features as it waned.

"There was a colony we had been to before, they were clean, they didn't deal in drugs, but we traded regularly with them for food and spices that we couldn't replicate in the machines. One time on approach we knew all was not right - we knew the signs, and we knew the best tactic was to retreat and not get involved in another fleet's business.

"We pulled out to a safe distance and signalled the marauders that we weren't a threat and that we'd be moving on, but then we received a half muffled signal from the surface, a small compound to the east of the city had a transmitter; usual practice was to disable all communications so transmissions out of the city would have been blocked and the main relay for the governing elders would have been disabled, sometimes manually so that it could be salvaged for parts afterwards but often it was just fired upon in the initial assault. The transmission we were receiving was coming from just outside the city boundary, you could liken it to a small suburb just outside of the M25, only this was more a small hamlet of only a few structures. They obviously had an emergency set in case the city fell, or else it was an illegal acquisition for smuggling, either way it cost them their lives.

"As we tried to tighten up the signal to make a reply the structures were raised to the ground, the attacking fleet having moved swiftly into position upon our arrival and fired from an orbital position above the planet. It was a show of strength. They had lain hidden on our approach, maybe hoping to ambush us when we landed, but now we each knew of the other's existence we faced a standoff. The smart thing to do was to abandon the planet; we had no claim on it, nor did we owe them any allegiance. The marauding fleet was smaller than ours but better armed: all their ships were fighting ships, whereas ours were compiled of medical, biodiverse pods, mechanised production ships that manufactured our hardware and maintained both the fleets and the terraforming needs, and then there were all the independent habitats that tagged along under our protection. We were a large fleet and anyone knew that if the flagship Apolly'on was around the rest of the fleet couldn't be far behind. You see when the Apolly'on went scouting or detached from the main fleet for any reason the fleet then became vulnerable. There were, of course, other ships to defend it, but the ship and its commander had a reputation, so the fleet would always be parked up at a relatively secure location nearby ready to make speed if attacked. These were our protocols set in place to protect our people.

"You see my dilemma, go back and protect the rest of my fleet knowing that the aggressors would always be scanning for them, or stop and help a doomed people against the odds and risk losing all."

"And your ego won out?"

"Why do you feel the need to twist my every intention? It wasn't ego, it was compassion."

"So battle stations then I take it?"

"I gave the order, yes. I sent a communicae to the marauders on the surface informing them that I, Abadd'on Apolly'on V'hihyon, was here to defend the people of the colony and that if anyone dared harm anymore of the dwellers then they would not be leaving the planet in one piece. I then set my guns on their flagship and opened fire and set my ship on a collision course."

"Why a collision course, that sounds like a bit of a dumb tactic?"

"It was, but I had a reputation which preceded me: I do rash and risky things, when angered I am vicious and relentless; most marauders know this. By aiming my ship at theirs I wasn't giving them time to think or reason as to my actions or intent, I was only giving them time to react and get them on the back foot. It worked. Their ship took on major damage to their rear as they turned and fled, they were listing with port side engine failure. They were too distracted by their damage and the surprise assault to realise that they still had us out gunned. We launched Arra-tets at their other ships and at their forces on the ground, engaging all their batteries to keep them busy whilst I once again launched the Apolly'on at their lead ship. Their surrender was swift and their retreat from the planet was unconditional. There were few loses on both sides, but it could have been much worse if their commander had had his wits about him. It was a gamble that paid off, but I didn't do it for my glory, I was trying to save the people on the surface. To this day those people live in peace and all know that they are protected by the fleet of Apolly'on."

an episode from Star Trek or some other sci-fi? we'll see if we can cross reference it with anything. He's used a lot of common terms, moving away from some of his usual Furion eloquences, ship terms and battlements all too 'earthy' today, maybe he's too tired to string it all together.

"All very interesting John, but I'm still not buying it."

Kennedy observed Cade shifting awkwardly in his seat.

"Do you need a break?"

"I could use the loo."

"Sure, 5 minutes, no more."

Before Cade stood and headed for the door Kennedy quickly typed: *Going to take a break. Lock all the toilets as out of order and sound a door alarm along the corridor.*

Cade reentered the room agitated, rubbing his temples and shaking his head. He smiled wanly at Kennedy as if to say 'I know the game you're playing' and then sat down sternly.

Between the three of them: Vost, Kapoor and Kennedy, they previously were able to come up with a number of questions that played on Cade's fantasy but hopefully would trick him into merging reality into his tale unsuspectingly to give them insight into how he obtained his knowledge. It was a satisfactory approach for Kennedy who had been tasked from on high with obtaining the source of Cade's intelligence. They didn't care too much about the delusions, they simply wanted to protect their secrets and plug the hole from a leaky department. Now he felt Cade was tired enough to sway the conversation his way, and he had placated Vost enough by letting Cade tell his tale. It was time to turn the tables.

Kennedy pulled down on the sleeves of his mustard uniform shirt, sat back and cleared his throat.

"Tell me more about the experiments your authorities were conducting. How sensitive were they? How advanced were they? Who knew about them and how?"

John Cade yawned and dropped his head into his hands. He was more than tired. The break hadn't been long enough, barely long enough to stretch his legs, or so he thought. In reality it had been almost twenty minutes, much longer than he'd been originally promised, but after the relentless bombardment by Kennedy he was feeling drained, having had all his mental energy flush out through the plug hole as he was forced to adapt to the new interview approach. It had passed through his mind a number of times that he shouldn't put up with it, that he didn't need to, he could simply walk out; it was Abadd'on's prompting and training that forced him to stay, to stick it out, to persevere and not give in to their taunting. He had waited outside the interview room, having found it locked with an alarm sounding in the corridor and had sat on the floor with his legs crossed and his head in his hands trying to block everything out. Now the fluorescent bulb above his head in the room hurt his eyes as he peered narrowly down at the plastic beaker being filled from a jug which had been placed on the table. Kennedy didn't offer him any, he guessed that would come later when he thought his bladder couldn't take any more.

"Everything can be sold for a price."

"Government secrets?"

"Especially, but it was military secrets that were valuable on the black-market. Tech was always in demand and the military was always developing more."

"Like cloaking and radar avoidance?"

"Tractor beams and lasers, missiles, engines, you name it it would be bought for a price from someone on the inside."

"So who did you buy from?"

"What makes you think I bought it? I was a military commander of a military flagship with a governmental assignment."

"You're saying you were issued with all the latest tech?"

"Most of it."

"And what you weren't supplied you simply acquired."

"Sometimes. It doesn't pay to let the enemy have the upper hand."

"So who did you buy from? What did you trade?"

"I had a few trusted insiders."

"Who? I want names."

"Why, are you going to go arrest them? Good luck with that."

"Who sold you Talos?"

"What's Talos?"

"Don't play dumb with me. Who's the mole in our defence projects?"

subtle!

"I don't have to tell you a damn thing!"

"You listen to me you little shit, I can keep you in here as long as I want and you will eventually tell me what I want to know."

"Go to hell!"

Kennedy poured another drink and passed it across the table. Cade smiled as he pulled in tight on his core muscles.

What are you doing? This is not the approach we agreed!

Kennedy closed the lid of the laptop and leaned forward.

"Drink it!"

"I have rights."

"You have nothing. No family, no home, no marbles. No one knows you're here and no one believes your crap. We can keep you in here for the rest of your life 'grilling' you with this routine every day, and believe me the 'grilling' won't get any easier."

"What, are you afraid to call it what it is, torture?"

"Just give me a name and you can get out of here. Tell me who leaked the information and why, and then you can walk."

Cade laughed. Kennedy's performance was too unbelievable and only a demented fool would believe it.

"Go to hell!" he repeated with slow and deliberate viciousness in his voice.

Kennedy picked up the plastic beaker and flicked it forward splashing water over Cade's face and the desk.

Cade didn't flinch but he could feel his bladder weakening.

Kennedy pushed his chair back and stood, undoing his cuffs and rolling up his sleeves as he rose to tower above Cade.

The door burst open and Vost and Kapoor both rushed in. Kennedy stood back like a child caught with his hand in the cookie jar. Cade, who had tilted his chair back in fear, now tipped back, over balanced and fell to the ground. He stood clumsily but rapidly to his feet and slammed himself back to the wall opposite the door, exposing the damp patch at his crotch.

"Kennedy, out!" barked Vost. He looked worriedly at Cade cowering opposite him. "Surj, go get Rosen."

Kapoor scooted off, followed by Kennedy who slinked out reluctantly with a scowl to Vost who shut the door behind him.

"John, I'm sorry. That shouldn't have happened."

A tear began to roll down John Cade's cheek as he slowly began to slide down onto the floor without saying another word.

26

A week had gone by and tensions had eased with all, except that was between John Cade and, well, everyone else. Cade, predictably, had clammed up and was refusing to talk and was refusing to engage in the physical activity. There were many more questions they wanted to ask him but Louis Vost was forced to rethink his approach as Cade grew more adamant in his complaints about being released to go back home.

Major Kennedy had been reprimanded in no uncertain terms and Vost had lodged a formal complaint to his superiors which had fallen on deaf ears; it appeared that even the higher ranks agreed with Kennedy's view and considered the department's approach was too soft. Middle ground was then sought as the Major had to concede that his tactics had backfired and left them unable to proceed in fear of a potential legal process that could threaten to derail them as the reality hit home that they all stood on shaky ground with regards to abuse of the human rights acts, and with a government that was sure to wash its hands of the department as a rogue element if things went awry. The fantasies of military detention, torture and interrogation were just that; the reality in the real world away from Hollywood was that rules still applied and the average citizen still had rights.

Both sides, the Kennedy camp and the Vost camp, agreed it was a hard balance to strike; they were dealing with a mental health case which they couldn't approach with the same process as any other mental health issue as they had security questions to tackle, and they themselves weren't counsellors but interrogators so lacked the relevant training to deal with someone with the extensive psychotic delusions they suspected Cade suffered. Dr Rosen had a wealth of experience in such matters but even he would have preferred to defer to the expertise of others given half a chance, complaining on more than one occasion that their prisoner was a uniquely sick patient who needed proper care, medication, assessment and counselling. Vost argued that he had already been offered all that in the months leading up to Cade's story breaking in the press and that they couldn't be held responsible for the failings of the NHS. If things went wrong it seemed everyone was prepared to point the finger of blame elsewhere.

In amongst the harsh words and debates and the silence from

Cade they were left with no alternative but to review all that had gone before.

"Is that all you have to say about Ki'La?"

"Meaning?"

"You told us of another belief before."

"Yes, but that is not Ki'La. Some believe in lords of legend who through history have risen up and saved their people with great strength and wisdom, they are people who have brought the people into a new age and a new chapter of their history. Some have attributed the Ki'La theology to such great men."

"But you do not?"

Cade shrugged his shoulders.

"Pause the tape."

The image on the screen held with John Cade's hunched shoulders, a half dumb snarl across his face which distorted the real dejected emotion he'd been displaying as he suffered the sleep deprivation and lack of control one would normally have in conversation.

"Considering what we've put him through he's held up remarkably well," noted Louis Vost to Major Kennedy with a convicting stare as they reviewed a previous day's recordings.

"We can't hold him forever, we need an assessment report." It was the Major who was getting edgy. He knew he was surplus to requirements and that there was no real, imagined or apparent, security risk from their subject. The assignment was shaking his confidence and had the potential to unhinge the door of promotion he was angling towards. He was itching to get away to another detail as soon as Vost had submitted his summary report and the green light was given for Cade to be released.

"I think the general consensus within the department is," offered up Surjeet Kapoor, "that he is a fraud at worst and mentally insane at best."

Kennedy nodded his agreement. Vost tilted his head in internal debate with himself.

"You say that, Surj, but you don't believe it yourself."

"True. He comes across as sane and rational. His arguments are logical. His science and understanding of the universe is outstanding. His theories revolutionary."

"But," prompted Kennedy.

"But, his in-depth knowledge of the specifics of his theories and science is lacking, yet he can explain this away creatively in the personality he alludes to. Months, possibly years of research into the various aspects of his claims could have resulted in a combination of known or imagined science merged with his creative mind. The problem with that is it stinks of premeditation which is illogical when considering the cost, it would mean he planned all this knowing he would lose his family in the process. There is absolutely no gain to him."

"Where are we at with checking Lyra?"

"NASA are on it but you could be years away from an answer" replied Kennedy.

"Tick off the theories, where are we at?"

Kapoor reached for his notebook where he kept all the things written down that niggled at him about John Cade.

"Cosmos inherently unstable and expanding at a vast rate. Scientists concur. The slowing of light and the rapid travel through a moving space. Scientists concur - it's already a working theory with tests being carried out searching for the Higgs Boson, but theoretically possible. Cloning and cellular reanimation. We know that's already possible; it doesn't take a huge leap of the imagination to get to this point in the story. Same goes with the hibernation cryogenics for deep transit: it's the long haul flight in cargo hold basically, but he's adapted known cryogenics to the hardware of his fantasy. Which brings us onto the core point of the technology: Pa'as."

Kennedy quickly butted in. "The US Army has been working to develop a "revolutionary" smart armour that would give its troops "superhuman strength". It is calling on the technology industry, government labs and academia to help build it. It's an exoskeleton that allows their soldiers to carry large loads into the field. It's still on the drawing board but the Yanks are eager to get it made and test it. They're calling it a Tactical Assault Light Operator Suit (Talos). It would have layers of smart materials fitted with sensors to monitor body temperature, heart rate and hydration levels. The exoskeleton, which could be attached to arms and legs, would likely use hydraulics which potentially could increase the strength of the wearer. The suit would also need to have wide-area networking and a wearable computer."

"So what are the odds that Cade's heard about this?" asked Vost.

"It's a classified project, but word is out there as external non-military companies have been consulted on it. However, having done background checks on just about everyone he knows, Cade isn't connected with anyone who could have shared that information with him. So either he had someone feeding intelligence that we don't know about or he's got lucky with his guesses."

"Tell him about the metal?" Kapoor said excitedly with a keen expression of really wanting to tell it himself.

"An MIT team is currently developing liquid body armour - made from fluids that transform into a solid when a magnetic field or electrical current is applied. It's based on a new shape-shifting metal they've discovered and have been toying with. They call it a 'martensite'. It's a crystal that has two different arrangements of atoms. It can change shape tens of thousands of times when heated and cooled without degrading. It has 'shape memory' so it can remember its shape even after being bent and will return to its original form. They think they'll be able to use this stuff in everything from the frames of your glasses to bone implants, to mechanical engine parts, to combat vehicle armour and even the outer hull of a space rocket."

"Shit!"

"Exactly."

"I'm guessing that's what you've been holding out on me?"

"That's the top prize. That's why you were given the funding. That's why I've been kept on and why you guys weren't given the full picture until now. There should be no way for him to know this stuff."

"But he does," said Vost questioningly.

"Yes, but I'm convinced someone told him, we just don't know who. Maybe we'll never know. What we can say though, is that we have evaluated him fully and have found him to be unremarkable and yet intolerably insane. No one is ever going to take him seriously and we can keep tabs on him to ensure he doesn't get any more press."

"Are you good with this Surj?"

"Honestly? No. But I can't prove what my gut says. I mean there's all this other stuff: the uncharted star systems that no one's spotted before and the wormhole entanglement solving the black hole paradox. Then there's all that stuff he said about Fermi's

Paradox and the geometry of space time in relation to Einstein's theory of special relativity. The wormhole stuff alone was mind boggling. I can't begin to get my head around some of it, which is fine, but then some of the top astrophysicists of our age are struggling to keep up with it also, which begs the question of where the hell has he got it all from."

Kennedy gave him a knowing look. From Vost's position he could tell that the two men had clearly had this conversation without him present and Surj had come off the loser.

"Ok, then you've got the other stuff," Kapoor admitted. "You can trace a lot of what he's said back to science fiction, most telling, and really the thing that gave it away and tipped us off was his references to Furi'on, or V'hihyon," he spat out the word in a weird distasteful pronunciation that was a poor imitation of Cade's attempt at the word. "He's clearly influenced by movies such as Pitch Black and The Chronicles of Riddick where the titular character is a Furyan from Furya, his decimated home world. Even some of Abadd'on's characteristics could be taken straight out of the films."

"The idea of the metals and the circuit boards could all be from The Terminator, I guess," offered up Vost thoughtfully.

"And let's not forget the Biblical references."

Kennedy looked at Kapoor curiously as though he'd missed something but Kapoor didn't elaborate assuming the Major knew to what he was referring.

"Louis," the Major addressed him calmly and with the respect of his senior officer, "we're talking about this as though it's all fresh news but we've been over this a dozen times. We're at crunch point. You have to make a decision. We can't hold him indefinitely."

"I know, and you're right. I'll write it up tomorrow and make the call."

"Finally."

Having what he wanted Major Kennedy turned on his heels and made for the door without another word.

Kapoor hung back waiting.

Vost stood staring at the hunched image of John Cade on the screen. "Something's not right with this Surj, and I'm trusting your instincts on this. When we let him go," he said turning to stare his colleague head on, "keep a bloody close eye on him."

Kapoor nodded agreement. "Yes boss."

Part Two

The Age of Depression

Cogito, ergo sum (I think, therefore I am)
Abadd'on Apolly'on V'hihyon, the thoughts of the disengaged soul.

1

Hawaii - Mauna Kea Observatory:

Julie studied the email for the hundredth time. It was official confirmation of the phone call she'd had earlier just after Marcus had left for the 20 minute clear run down the mountain to the convenience store. With a 20 minute return trip and another five to buy supplies, which left him gone for the better part of an hour.

She chewed on her nails as she waited. He wouldn't be happy, and that was an understatement.

The hour went slowly as she watched the second hand tick slowly round the clock face on the wall.

She saw the 4x4 pull up on the gravel in the parking lot and then watched him disappear out of camera view as he let himself into the control hub. Seconds later she heard his footsteps echoing along the corridor outside.

Marcus swept into the room in a jolly mood.

"Milk, biscuits, ground coffee and PG Tips! I even managed to get some chocolate and a newspaper. How good am I?"

Julie hadn't turned her chair but kept her pose fixed firmly on the screens before her.

"We have to move the scopes," she said bluntly.

"Which one?" he asked walking casually over to the fridge.

"Both."

"The Twins? Why, are they out of alignment?" he was curious but gave no hint of concern in his voice. The telescopes occasionally needed realigning as they fell out of sync with the command module, the computer which sent signals to instruct the two machines where to look, a mechanical hitch or birds messing up the dome cover were prone to cause lag, not much but enough to cause too great a distance variable when calculating the stars. Lag threw out the maths so everything needed calibrating and realigning along with the dishes so that all the data could be synchronised to the same far flung dot of space.

"No, they're where they're supposed to be but Sentinel wants them moved."

There was a beat of hesitation in the room. She waited for the response she knew he was processing behind her. She didn't hear the fridge door close; he'd left it open as the lit fuse burned up within him.

"I thought they wanted us looking at Cygnus. They were happy we were concentrating there. They even gave us an extra analyst to speed up the data."

"I know."

"Where do they want it moving to?"

"Lyra."

"What! You have got to be joking! No way!"

"Marcus, calm down."

"Who the hell do they think they are? I hope you told them no."

"They called and said it was imperative that we now focus on Lyra. They want both Keck I & II looking up there. They said it's only temporary until they launch Kepler, then we can go back to looking at Cygnus. It's really not that much of a deviation," she reasoned, "at least it's the same section of sky."

"Did you get a name? I'll call them back and tell them where to get off. They have no authority over us. Bloody Sentinel, they think they can just boss everyone around. NASA will have something to say about it, I'm sure, or has Sentinel forgotten that they have a stake here too?"

Julie could hear him taking deep breaths behind her trying to control his temper. He then went quiet. A few seconds later he moved back to the fridge and shut the door. She let out a breath and sighed relief. His temper was so much better these days since he'd seen the counsellor to prepare himself for years of being cooped up in a confined space with only her for company. They got on great together but his tantrums used to scare her, and so she'd insisted they were forearmed with coping tactics before moving to Hawaii. She turned slowly to face him.

His face was flushed and his eyes were watering. Moving the telescopes was a big deal. It was their project, their research, their long term study. To abandon it now would lay waste to all they had achieved so far. They were tracking comets; they were identifying stars with orbiting planets around them never before seen; they were making a detailed map of that sector of space.

"Can we even see Lyra from here?"

"Marcus, clear the red mist from your brain, of course we can, they're pretty much right next to each other. I've calculated it.

There's not that much of a deviation on the angles and so we shouldn't have to change our hours, so yeah we can do it fairly easily."

He shook his head frustrated but his face recognised the simplicity of it despite his reluctance. "Can we move one and keep the other fixed?"

"Sentinel sent an email from the U.K. confirming it as NASA's request. If we don't do it we lose our funding and NASA will send their own guys down here to man it."

"Why has Sentinel agreed to this? That makes no sense. They've invested hugely in this research, and besides, NASA already has their own scope staring at Lyra."

"Apparently it's not strong enough for what they're searching for."

"Wasn't that a Sentinel backed project anyway? Who's really pulling the strings on this?"

"The email doesn't name the NASA source but my guess is NASA has something more pressing and they'd rather Sentinel took the flack for it."

"Or the whole thing has its genesis with Sentinel to begin with and all the pushing is coming from them. I wish we'd never signed their contract."

"Marcus, this might not be such a bad thing. There might be something to see or hear in Lyra that we haven't yet found in Cygnus. It's not like we haven't strayed off course and focused on other systems of our own accord; we're always redirecting the twins to look elsewhere if we're curious about somewhere else." She tried her best to paint a positive picture but she could see the disappointment on his face.

"As true as that may be, I don't like being given a directive against our project parameters."

"You mean you don't like being told what to do."

"But Julie," he sighed, "whatever we find there we won't have a claim on. If NASA are requesting this then they will stake their flag on it, it will come with a NASA label stamped across it."

Julie nodded. He was right. This had always been the gamble of being under the control of a big corporation like NASA or Sentinel, if they had their own agenda then there was always a chance of them being squeezed out of the results. If NASA took control then this could well be the end of their dream.

2

You dropped off the face of the earth for a while. What happened?

Yeah, I wandered about for a bit, not knowing who I was or where to go. I went to my parents in the end. MI17 messed me up and no one would believe me that the government had me locked away for months, and I of course had no idea where the facility was so I couldn't prove a damn thing. Every time I'd been transported there they'd place me in the back of a van so I couldn't see out. To everybody else it was just another delusion which endorsed my paranoia.

Tell me about your memories.

Which ones, John's or Abadd'on's?

You decide. I'm interested to know what stayed with you in the years after the Christmas Day incident, after you left MI17.

You know it's funny when you think about things that have affected our past and how our past moulds our future. There's that line of our past, our history, and you just know that if any one thing had gone differently then that line would have deviated and you wouldn't be who you are now.

You have regrets?

One of us does for sure. I was somebody. I was the dog's bollocks! Everyone looked up to me. Now look at me, I'm nothing, even my own kids act weird around me.

Did she ever remarry?

Gemma? No. We never divorced. I think she's been holding out that someday I'll come back having given up on my 'double life'.

How old are the kids now?

Unbelievably Mia's now eighteen, she's going to university from September, she got into Exeter, not that she told me that, she doesn't give much away when we speak.

How often do you speak to her?

Rarely. She's a fun kid, and good looking like her mum. I get on with her better than Toby. I guess being older I had more time to bond with Mia and she still remembers a little of the old John. Toby was only two so we never really had a chance to connect. He's doing his GCSE's this year so he's using that as an excuse to avoid me.

Do you care? No John, don't just shrug your shoulders, it's an important question. Do you care about your family?

Of course I do. It's just that we're so estranged. They don't get me anymore. They don't know me and I don't really know them.

I can understand that with your children, you haven't been there watching them grow up, but has Gemma changed? Surely you still know her. Do you still love her?

The old John never stopped loving her. She was my world, but then I discovered there were many worlds accessible to us. Do I still love her? Yes, of course I do, but my mind is constantly busy with the memories and desires of two lifetimes that it's hard to focus on the emotion of the life I once had here.

Before you say it, yes I've thought about her helping me to focus, but she is getting on with her life and her career now that the kids don't need her so much. I could have gone back earlier but I don't think either of us would have been able to cope with it.

So fear is all that is stopping you now?

I'm not scared! I just don't want to...distract her.

It's been thirteen years and you keep telling me how you have changed a lot, and I can see how that is so, so why not see what you can salvage. What have you got to lose?

I don't want to talk about this anymore.

Ok, I won't push the issue. So what happened after you left MI17? What memories did you retain of your previous lives?

Surjeet Kapoor kept in contact for about a year after I left the facility. We would meet up unofficially and we would discuss some of the interviews I gave and he would ask me for extra information. I had taken to writing down some of my thoughts and memories so I shared these with him, along with the drawings I'd mocked up on my computer, they were so much better than the sketches they'd had their artist put together, his looked too cartoony; it was no wonder they'd pooh-poohed my ships as being too basic and unimaginative; they had made a big fuss about the rear engine funnels of the Apolly'on looking too much like a Menorah candlestick and that I'd taken inspiration for it from images I'd seen rather than it being a realist concept. They said that my design was impractical and didn't conform to the propulsion systems I'd previously described.

I got real frustrated with Kapoor over this. It was their lack of ingenuity and their insistence on making what I said fit into their established rules of science rather than accepting that an advanced civilisation can get around those rules.

Of course I knew he was still reporting back to Vost the whole time, that was until the department folded. Kapoor said they had no evidence for extraterrestrial life so they were earmarked to close prematurely despite previous assurances they'd been promised. Kapoor was being reassigned to another department as an analyst or something, I think he said Vost was taking a management job within the MOD.

You never saw Kapoor again?

Why do you always ask questions you already know the answers to? Tut tut Malachi, you're becoming too transparently obvious. Put those defensive hands down, you protest too much.

So, you are getting to know me too well. I hope that we are growing to be friends and that you are beginning to trust me after so long.

I've never trusted you. I'm not stupid, I know you sought me out rather than the other way round. You take on unique cases like mine. You're fascinated by the links between the human mind and the soul. That's the only reason that I agreed to these sessions with you. You're the only one who seems to want to find out more about our existence and the capabilities and links between our life and death.

That said, I never said I believe you.

But you want to. Even if it means you don't exceed in your chosen career, even if your peers hate you for it. In the eyes of the world you're wasting your talent, a gifted counsellor throwing it all away over personal interest.

A religious belief.

You want to know about your parents, and your sister. You want to know if there is more beyond this life.

I can see I have told you too much. I thought I was the counsellor.

But I thought you wanted us to be friends. Isn't that what friends do, tell each other their secrets?

You wanted to know what I remembered. Everything. Writing it down was a good way to ensure I didn't forget.

And you've told all this to Kapoor?

Mostly. I tried to clarify their errors and assumptions. They didn't understand me. They didn't get me at all - no one ever does.

3

Kapoor could see that I had changed. Over time I think he saw me as the great leader I was as I began to fully integrate my two characters.

We talked much but he never mentioned my physical change, which was fairly rapid, not to mention obvious.

How so?

I wasn't always this size. Obviously I've always been tall but I didn't bulk out till after late 2005 after a summer of kickback.

Kickback? You took your anger out in the gym, your anger at MI17?

Not just them, it was everyone I was angry with. I felt let down at every turn, but mostly I was angry with myself. If I'd done my job properly in the first place I wouldn't be in this situation now. I thought I was the dog's bollocks, but if I was that good I wouldn't have got a platoon of my guys killed and I'd still be flying around scouring the galaxy searching for resources for our people.

I got real depressed after I left that damn basement dungeon they'd been holding me in. I couldn't work, not because I was incapable but because my reputation was in tatters. I ended up having to survive off benefits until I could prove myself again, slowly getting back into graphic design as a freelancer, which in itself proved to be hit and miss. I made it all work eventually, but I kept to myself socially. I didn't mix with work colleagues. I didn't contact anyone from my old life, including Gemma and the kids, not to begin with anyway. I wanted to remain anonymous to the world and let the madness die. I moved out of the area and kept my head down.

I wasn't so naive to think that MI17 had forgotten all about me that easily. I suspected they had tabs on me, and it was pretty easy for a government department to find me as my address was listed for the benefits I was claiming.

I joined a gym and started exercising. You know I hated exercise before, but the routine they had me in under Dr Rosen had got me used to it and I found I missed it. I had little else to occupy my time so I spent a good number of hours each week pacing the treadmill and pumping iron. Within six months I had transformed my diet and my appearance. No longer was I the skinny lanky dweeb, I was now solid, my neck bulged, leaning out muscles that ran down my back to support my posture, my arms now the size of my old legs which were now tree trunks in comparison. I didn't need to learn how to bulk up, it was something I knew instinctively, it was something Abadd'on was used to. When I reached the size I felt comfortable with I slowed it down to maintain that size; I don't want to be Arnold Schwarzenegger and I don't want to stand out too much, I just wanted to be unnoticed. I'm good at blending into a crowd; I know how to stoop my body to appear smaller, drowning in oversized clothes and avoiding eye contact to appear more timid and unthreatening.

Before I parted company from Kapoor I would catch him staring at my bulk but he held back from commenting each time.

Those sessions with Kapoor often took place in coffee shops, but sometimes if the weather was good we'd meet in a park where we could talk without attracting the curious glances from people overhearing our conversation, besides I loved the open air; I've spent most of my life cooped up on a ship so being free of confined spaces was quite refreshing.

From what I could gather from Kapoor, Vost wanted me to clarify so much information: the differing wind pressures of the heliosphere, the intricacies of the tones of the V'hihyon language, the fine descriptions of various planetary landscapes, the complexities of our navigational systems and our means of analyzing habitable zones and planets of distant solar systems.

With some of these things it was easy to tell where they were going with it. As mad as I was deemed to be officially, they couldn't escape that I was an anomaly of scientific wonder and a deep source of information to tap into. You know, with things like identifying habitable zones in space, how valuable would that be to NASA? By searching the stars ahead of time my race survives without the need of interference or damage to any other ecosystem or way of life, but mostly conditions in space are not ripe for intelligent life to mature, but usually prominent ores or vapour supplies for food or smelting for construction can be found and mined and even planets that on the face of it seem barren can be colonised, if only for a short time, for the purpose of mining and survival. If NASA could figure out a way of identifying such zones they could direct future space flight so much more efficiently.

Navigating asteroid belts or investigating planets for their ore deposits is not something that would benefit Earth space travel, but knowing where to look, wow, just the potential ideas would be a funding winner in Congress.

Probing me over the same issues like deciding what planets to investigate were such a bore and I let Kapoor know it, but still he grilled me. 'Humour me', he'd say, and I'd repeat as though it was a mental recording on tape listing off the criteria that needed cross checking with each new planet: dense gravity, any signs of giant storms (some of the larger gas planets would have monster hurricanes the diameter of small planets that could rage for centuries), extreme temperatures, unstable land mass, breathable air (not such a problem due to terraforming although the strain of converting the chemical makeup of the air could sometimes have a detrimental long term effect on the ecosystem of the planet, so we needed to weigh up the short term benefits).

Kapoor would joke about the government taking my theories to some group called The Giga Collective, apparently they're a group of the world's brainiest people. They were apparently funded by some secret organisation or consortium of businesses that the government subscribed to. The whole designer babies is their concept as they're looking to create baby geniuses and halt the aging process at a prime age to be immortal.

And they criticised the scientific efforts and ethics of my people and say I'm crazy!

Some of our sessions were a bit like ours, not quite counselling in an office like this, but he was always wanting me to talk about my stories of Abadd'on and trying to convince me that I wasn't such a bad guy.

I would like to think that I ask you more than just about Abadd'on. My interest is in making you a whole and a well person.

Why did you think you were a bad person?

Kennedy had planted the idea I guess. For months it had been playing on my mind, brewing a murky cuppa I couldn't see through. I'd convinced myself I had abandoned my wife and family, ignored my parents and my friends, had sacrificed my own men and slaughtered tens of thousands of others over the years of space travel. It all fed my depression but I didn't want to accept that I was depressed, and of course I had no one to turn to to talk about it.

Kapoor tried to feed me stories about my life before, testimonies from Gemma and others about who I was before. Then he tried to draw out more positive stories about who I was as Abadd'on, but nothing he could say could convince me.

I'm sure there are many stories you can conjure up to reinforce this harsh image of Abadd'on, but surely you were able, even in your depression, to dredge up something positive about him? No one can be that inherently evil. Besides you have already told them of some positive stories when you were in detention. What did you say to convince him, and you, that this negative view wasn't true?

There was nothing I could think of. No don't look at me like that, I was down and could only think of the negative, like the story of what had happened to my predecessor, my old commander.

Ok, tell me about that.

4

Malachi Okeno listened intently with that in-depth reassuring and attentive stare that he gave all his patients. The problems and issues in the West were a far cry from the troubles of his homeland where the vacant stares of his patients were often followed by the wild screams and wailing of the tormented souls who were diagnosed with a plethora of psychological symptoms, mostly relating to alcohol or drug abuse in the men, and abuse, both physical and sexual in the women. There were many other social circumstances that brought a long line of casualties to his desk back at home: a raging and violent civil war in the north, malnutrition, HIV Aids, unemployment and the subsequent poverty - all were symptoms of the society and culture he grew up in, and it was an exhaustive list.

Here in the civilized West there were none of the same issues but that didn't mean the things he dealt with were any less complex or difficult to treat. At home many of those that never made it through the long line to his desk, or the desk of his colleagues, wound up at the hands of the witch doctors or the radical cultural church pastors who believed that any and all mental health problems were the result of demon possession. He had encountered many a patient who had been traumatised by the attempted exorcism practices alone: enthusiastic pastors laying on of hands and fervently praying for deliverance whilst plying on the guilt of the victim's sins as being the sole cause of their mental trauma. There too were the backstreet huts where the patient would be stripped naked by a witch doctor promising deliverance by slicing the throat of a chicken and pouring the fresh warm blood directly over the head of the kneeling sufferer. It was ignorant and primitive, yet all totally acceptable within the culture.

It was partly seeing this behaviour as a child and as a struggling teenager desperate to break free of the back trodden community he lived in that drew him to his profession. He became obsessed with understanding why people lived the way they did and what drove their behaviour. Despite his disadvantages socially he was determined to achieve an academic qualification in his schooling so that he could climb the ladder of society and earn himself a university degree. In the end he got two; he was a bright spark as it turned out and once he got his step up he applied himself with all the focus and dedication of a surgeon continuously applying the pressure to prevent a bleed out. He gained his foundation degree in Mental Health Psychology at the Gulu University Hospital before being sponsored for a place at the University of Johannesburg where he obtained his Master's degree allowing him to qualify as a Counselling Psychologist, which then allowed him to return to his home country to set up his own practice attached to Mulago Hospital in Kampala. His original intention had been to return to his home town of Gulu and practice there but he found himself drawn to the increasing number of intriguing cases coming across from Europe that he read about in the psychiatric articles and publications that winged their way to his practice; also the lure of a better pay day was always appealing. There was no doubt about it, life in Uganda, and in Africa as a whole, was hard, financially and professionally.

No matter how many patients he saw he always felt like he wasn't even scratching the surface. Every patient he felt he made headway with went back into the ocean to be absorbed once again by the society he was trying to rescue them from, leaving his queue of patients only to rejoin again at the back of the line. It was a hopeless task. He wanted to help people. He wanted to change his society, the way he had been taught in the orphanage by the Christian teachers who had rescued him from the horrors that had overcome his life which once upon a time had the potential to cripple him mentally and emotionally, but no matter how hard he tried he felt that he could do little to achieve his goal, so eventually he gave up and sought a better life for himself.

Maybe, he convinced himself, he could change things from afar, sending money back to help rehabilitate and rebuild the specific areas he thought needed the funds. So far he had kept to his plan, sending money to help fund the Psychology department at the University Hospital in Gulu where he had gained his first placement as a student, and also to the orphanage that had taken him and his sister under their wing when terror had struck. It was all very worthy and commendable but still it didn't feel enough, and he felt unsettled and itched to return home to his roots to do more.

"Satorie'on Apolly'on [he pronounced it Say'aart'oour'eey'un] was commander before me."

Malachi scribbled down the name on his pad and nodded affirmingly for him to go on.

"He had gone soft."

"How so?"

"He was a sympathiser."

Cade looked blankly at Malachi as though expecting him to know what he was talking about, eventually he recognised the confused look on the face of his counsellor.

"He had a soft spot for the mechas and the circuit boards. Rumour was he had a tin heart as he never let anyone other than the circuit boards attend his wounds in the medi units."

"Sorry, 'mechas'?"

"Cyborgs I guess would be the closest description, part human part robot. They were mostly disfigured in battle in the field without access to regen pods, their wounds beyond repair they were given Pa'as replacements, which turned some of these guys into freaks, hideous abominations."

"Were they all war wounded?"

"No, some were born disfigured. Some were refugees from fallen colonies, a mixture of races and creeds, not that you'd be able to tell with some, drug use and experiments left some of these mutants more robots than human. There were originally two main races on our home world, the differences in species I guess would be akin to Neanderthals and Homo sapiens and were often treated as such especially when it came to a class divide and a recognition of skills. It was judgemental and cruel and amounted to nothing less than racism, but the more dominant Car'oan breed, or clan, or however you'd like to classify them were, and always had been, too strong for the lower caste, the Ma'oui, to overthrow, out think, or ever have a shot at overpowering. It was generally the Ma'oui who were born with the most defects on the colonies as the gap in their DNA sequence wasn't repaired without the care of the circuit boards and specialist cloning equipment. It was another reason why cloning was the preferred method on breeding within the fleets; no one wanted to have to deal with disability in space; deformities were an unproductive waste of space."

Malachi thought back to home. How many times had he seen the abnormal birth defects of the malnourished and the addicts who lived a life with no hope of improvement? He knew first-hand the desperation of seeing a community who would do anything to improve their quality of life, including disfiguring their own children to improve the chances of an income from begging, but he couldn't reconcile in his mind the idea, nor the memory, of those who would discard an imperfect life.

"Satorie'on had the crew divided, but he was in the minority. Most of us were mistrustful of the mechas; their software could be manipulated by the circuit boards and it was often suspected that the two communicated to a common end of overrunning the ruling forces to create a new society, one they hoped would be better and more productive and more peaceful, but most of us were convinced they had more sinister motives that would have greater consequences to us normal humans.

"There was a rising tension on the ship. As you know I had no love for the machines but I was committed to my commander. I took my concerns about the dissent within the crew to him but he dismissed me out of hand. The atmosphere grew and again I challenged him about his inaction. This time he publicly rebuked me and called me a bunch of names I'd care not to repeat, but it was enough for many of the crew to question the judgement of our leader. I was his most trusted adviser and next in line for his chair but he treated me like a piece of dirt. It all added to the suspicion that he was under the control of the circuit boards and rumours spread further that he had an implant and was being manipulated by the tin cans."

"More and more you call them by earthly slurs, John Cade."

"I'm just adapting the speech. To call them by the names in my language your ears would not be able to differentiate the subtle tones I grew up in the practice of."

Malachi nodded his understanding. He knew the differences in the languages were sometimes hard to comprehend, his own language was Acholi, a tribal language of northern Uganda, yet those around where he lived were made up of differing tribes of differing tribal languages, some of whom had been abducted and dragged through the territories by the raging warlords of the LRA guerillas, boys tortured to conform as child soldiers, and girls and women mutilated and raped as brides of the soldiers, this was the real brutality of war torn Africa.

"I tried hard to learn the English language. Where I come from it is the national language of my people but few speak it in the villages outside of the cities. Even now I translate some words in English back to Acholi."

Cade seemed satisfied that Malachi understood, but he had no idea of the vent that was steaming from the African's chest at the real horrors he replayed in his mind from a perturbed childhood as he sat wondering how long he had to put up with Cade's unfathomable and underlying racist bigotry.

"I challenged him a third time," continued Cade, "this time we were alone in his quarters, and this time we got angry and physical. I was bigger and stronger than him, not by much, and he had the experience. We were well matched and I had the edge. I would say that I beat him, but in the end I could never win without killing him, and that was something I just wasn't prepared to do, he was too good a man to be slaughtered in such a manner. I was insubordinate and what I received was just. I was banished from the ship."

"This was your exile to, what was it...." Malachi flicked through his notes, "ah yes, K'avar?"

Cade nodded as though reliving his own memory of the event and quickly scanning over the years of abandonment by his commander.

"It must have been traumatic for you. How did you feel when he kicked you off the ship?"

Malachi could see Cade thinking about answering it honestly, the words were about to tip out like the trash from a wheelie bin into the mouth of the dumpster. At the last moment he seemed to come to his senses; he didn't want to talk about his feelings, that's not why he came to counselling, he just wanted to tell his story, over and over again - it gave him validation. The story was real so long as he could keep telling it.

"What was traumatic was the state that bastard had left the ship in. When they picked me up from K'avar the fleet was in tatters. A third of the Apolly'on's crew had abandoned ship after a gun battle that left a good score dead and a gaping hole in the hanger deck and another on the AI deck where all the circuit boards were housed.

"There had been a mutiny against the commander, the mechas, and the circuit boards. The circuit boards didn't take up arms, which was a good thing 'cause things could have turned out very differently if they had, instead they stayed neutral. Satorie'on ended up with his head caved in when the mechas had fled. It was my boys that did the damage to the ship, trying to prevent the mechas escape with our Arra-tets and destroying as many circuit boards just in case. Bearing in mind we all suspected they were behind the whole disunity to begin with. They never found any sort of chip on Satorie'on's corpse and all that they'd managed to achieve was to create a mini army of mechas out of some of our best and strongest fighters. The mechas had allies, every world has 'em and they'd fled to a nearby trading post for cover.

"Politically it was bad. My men were guilty of mutiny and of murdering the commander and were now flying about in an injured ship and a splintered fleet. Fortunately the law is vague when it comes to the replacement of admiralty and ships' flight command -

the weak don't deserve their position is the rule of thumb. The remaining crew knew their best hope was to reinstate me and for me to assume command. It would appease the authorities with regards to martial law and give them the figurehead they were lacking in their command. In truth this was what they wanted all along, they just knew I wouldn't be disloyal enough to take out the man who had raised me and mentored me for years onboard the Apolly'on.

"In the shelter of K'avar we carried out repairs and regrouped. Then we went out hunting."

"Was your wife with you during your exile?"

"No of course not!" he scoffed as though the question were a ludicrous one. He then seemed to switch personalities as he assessed the question from the perspective of Cade rather than Abadd'on. "To be exiled was to be exiled from all. Etera was the property of Apolly'on. She wasn't warrior class, although she was strong physically, and in her will, she was no pushover to any man, but her role was as service to her husband, that being me, and in my absence she became the subject of the commander once again."

"Did this make you jealous?"

"We don't get jealous over sex. In the colonies maybe, they are more possessive and exclusive in their relationships, but for the fleets, and amongst the soldiers in particular, sex is just that, sex."

"So why marry?"

"It is administrative. Some of my women are not so much a possession but a commodity who owe their allegiance to me."

"Your own onboard harem, so to speak."

"The concubines of kings."

"You see yourself as a king?"

He shrugged his broad shoulder mountains, gently lifting them in a tremor of an earthquake.

"Etera organised them according to my mood, knowing whom I would favour. She knew me the most but knew her place never to challenge me. She knew how to calm me and knew when to steer clear. The other women never had access to me in such a way, they were there primarily as physical tools for my release, and she, Etera, was like my PA in assessing who I would want and when and what they should expect me to do to them."

"But you allowed others to sleep with them?"

"Why not? Like I said, we didn't see sex the same way and

there was no sexual disease."

"But you must have had some feelings towards Etera? Surely you felt something knowing she had to be submissive to Satorie'on."

Once again the shoulders shook but no admission of emotion flew through the gap between his pursed lips.

Malachi sighed, he was getting nowhere in drawing his patient out of his shell. The character of Abadd'on was a rock on so many levels, but the hammer and chisel of his training was failing to crack it. Still he was determined to persevere.

"So when you returned to the ship was she there?"

"She was loyal, and she kept the others in line. Women who were known to have been defiled by mechas were slaughtered."

"What about the men?"

"We don't slaughter good men for taking advantage of weak women, no matter how deformed."

"Isn't that a bit hypocritical?"

"You say it as though double standards with women were a Furi'on invention. I never said our culture or society was perfect. I can appreciate an alternative viewpoint now, but back then that was all I knew."

"Or chose to know."

"I thought you were here to listen not judge!" Cade snapped.

Malachi held up a light tanned palm.

"You're right, I'm sorry. Please go on John Cade. You were about to tell me about hunting the mechas."

Cade diverted his gaze down to the table to recompile his thoughts, sucking in a deep breath as he did so as the memories conjured themselves in his mind's vision.

Malachi's mind also drifted back as the discussion of inequality and implied sexual abuse pulled him back to his childhood and being dragged from his village by soldiers who were setting fire to the straw of the round mud huts they called home. The women and young girls were being dragged screaming into one brick shed that was used as a meeting hall and school and were being repeatedly passed around the soldiers who were one by one coming out doing up their trousers. His father hadn't stood a chance, he had been shot immediately, along with most of the other men. Had Malachi been a few years older and able to defend himself he most likely would have joined his father with a bullet to his head. His mother tried to grasp the leg of a soldier who tore his sister from her breast and tossed her aside before turning back to his mother and striking her with the heel of his boot to the jaw to silence her, then bending down he grabbed her arm and pulled her towards the shed. Malachi broke free from his captives who were tying the boys to the trees. He crawled towards his helpless baby sister, knowing he could do nothing to help his mother, but his sister, if he could just reach her...

But he never did, the butt of a rifle to the back of his head turned the lights out and saved him the visual horrors of what happened next to his friends and cousins left tied to the trees.

"We had to resort to hunting them down using drones," took up Cade with a distant air as his mind drifted to another place and another time, whether he was making it up on the spot or whether he had conjured it beforehand it was impossible to tell. "We had initially sent Arra-tets out to scour the planets we suspected were harbouring their forces but they were all shot down before they could return any detailed information about the size of the enemy we faced. At least we had a strong indication of the sector they hid in, even if that did cost us in ships and men."

"Arra-tets, or Arra-tet Apolly'on to denote their origin. You've mentioned these fighter ships a number of times and described them as 'arrow head' or 'dart shaped' vessels, and said that Arra-tet is a slang term, so what is the proper name of them in your language?"

"Cuootarege-a-tet," his response was quick off the mark without having to think back to recall the information.

Malachi glanced down at his notes, transcripts provided by Kennedy, for the answer to the question he'd already had prepped to ask. Cade was bang on.

"We still needed intel so we resorted to the unmanned drones. We only had a few qualified fliers for these. The drones are set up on sensors connected to neural pathways, it's sort of a holographic booth where the pilots hook up to the interface of a drone and manoeuver it via the onboard cameras. It's complicated and requires a lot of concentration, the slightest lapse in thought could break the connection, as such it was fairly unreliable for regular use: your mind only had to wander for a fraction and that was it, we'd have lost the drone.

"Rarely did we use them in combat mode. Mostly we used

them for navigating through a dense electromagnetic field where our sensors sometimes got scrambled, or when we needed to transport cargo to an environmentally hostile site."

"If the electromagnetic field was so dense how did the pilots maintain contact?"

"With great difficulty, and the feedback could fry the pilot's cognitive function, but still it was safer than committing an entire ship or fleet into a belt of gastric fog.

"The drones worked. We got a fix on the mechas' forces before the drones got shot down. They knew we were coming for them of course, but at least we had an idea of what we faced.

"Their main leader was Twumbouha'el, an exile from Or'buk. He was mostly mecha, more machine than man, his face was mostly reconstructed with circuitry reaching far back into his brain, it was a delicate job and done on the black market before joining the crew of the Apolly'on. Satorie'on accepted him as a fine warrior, and granted to his credit he was, too fine it turned out.

"We fought him for too long, too hard, and lost too many."

"Was it just his face?"

"No, he was big and hollow in many places. He'd been burned in a blast in a rebellion on Or'buk, he had been a rebel commander who had tried to overthrow his government. The coup failed but many were loyal to him as they fled and sought refuge among the passing fleets."

"Satorie'on had no problem taking in a political refugee, and an enemy of the government?"

"It was a planetary government, not empiric of Furi'on. Besides we had no loyalties to Or'buk and were down on good fighting men when the infraction broke out."

"Why were you down on men?"

"The battle of Azeroth saw great losses on both sides, but we had been committed by the battle commanders of K'adar. We lost the moon of An'jou when they nuked the surface in spite of us."

"Tell me about Or'buk."

"Not much to tell. It's an overcrowded concrete slum half sunken beneath the flood waters of the tides of Mar. The poverty is intense. The crime immense. The living conditions appalling. Each sector has a toilet, you could smell the piss and shit before you hit the atmosphere."

"So where was Twumbouha'el hiding out when you went

hunting the mechas?"

"B'eirhe. It's a parched desert moon of Ka'des where the blistering heat has left the mutated inhabitants cowering in the perilous sands between underground trading posts. There were plenty of subterranean compounds for them to hide and the inhabitants were accommodating, most likely out of a sympathetic offer to improve their conditions with better tech."

"Another failed colony I take it?"

"We have littered the galaxy with them. We have never really found a planet to rival our natural home world.

"B'eirhe was perfect for the mechas, the gas giant it circled created enough cover for them to control the approach of any offensive fleet. We couldn't attack without committing all our forces, which was a gamble."

"And you had no support from K'adar in your campaign?"

"No, we were on our own."

"How did that make you feel?"

"We were outnumbered, outgunned, and they had the superior intelligence. But there was no way I was going to let that stop me from getting to that bastard Twumbouha'el."

"But you were left alone, abandoned by the military. How did that make you feel?"

Malachi was determined to force Cade to open up but he had once again fallen into a patter of storytelling where he failed to disclose his emotions.

"Stick an angry bull in a ring and he'll charge," was the only response he would give.

5

The metallic taste of blood had mixed with the dusty grit and saliva on his tongue and dried to cake the corner of his mouth and the side of his face, pale against the powdered ground where it had lain still and silent after the foray which had left him abandoned and unconscious.

He came around slowly, the wispy smell of smoke tickling his one free nostril. He opened a battered eye and strained to focus on his surroundings. He didn't recognise where he was, all was different, distressfully so. A mild growing panic seeped into his thoughts, before he had a chance to recognise it it had exploded into a silent scream within a tortured mind as he recalled the attack on his village and on his family.

He heard a faint distant cry of a baby which focused his thoughts back to the present. He lifted his head sharply but fell back, slumped to the ground, hit again by the butt of the gun. It was the same gun he'd been hit with before but no one stood over him this time yet the memory was so distinct the pain inflicted may as well have come from a fresh blow. He lifted a hand to his head and felt the wound. It didn't feel bad to the touch; internally it hurt like hell, the swelling feeling claustrophobic; externally the ridges of dried volcanic blood dressed the dark skin on that side of his face.

He blinked the tears away and gritted his teeth against the pain and then raised his head again. Slower. In front of him was the shell of a circular mud hut, the edges of the remains of its straw roof still smoldering. A foot lay sticking out from the doorway, it wasn't attached to the rest of the body, hewn off with a machete. He couldn't distinguish the features of the foot's owner who lay facing him within the shadow of the hut, beaten and cut. It was just as well. It wasn't his father; he knew where he had fallen.

He stood slowly and looked around. The village was all but destroyed. Tied to nearby trees were two people, one adult and one child. The child was three or four years older than him, he didn't recognise him at first behind the mask of swollen features that had been beaten into place with the bloodied stick that lay on the floor near his feet, it was only the clothes of his eight year old cousin, Samuel, that gave away the identity behind the cloud of flies that leapt on and off of his seeping carcass. The adult was female and her wounds were equally as gruesome. Her clothes had been torn off and her legs pulled wide to show that she had taken a beating to more than just her face and body. Five year old Malachi was too young to understand the trauma of a gang rape, but whatever had happened to this woman he feared had happened to his mother. He looked to the building he'd last seen his mother being dragged off towards, it still stood but its edges were charred and smoke still wafted from its doorway.

The baby cried again.

Meisha.

He followed the sound into the trees. It was calmer in the shade with his back turned to the horrors. He knew his age had saved him, his sister too, that and the fact that he had been knocked unconscious and would have been a burden to carry off. Others would have survived also, he hoped anyway. They would have run or hidden, or have been far enough away from the village to have escaped it completely. They'd all heard the stories of the guerrilla troops who had begun raiding the villages recruiting for their army. It was join up or die. The women were raped, the young girls carried off, the boys forced to tie their family members to trees and then beat them to death to dehumanise them ready for conditioning as a new breed of emotionless child soldier.

The crying got louder. It was a good sign. She was old enough to crawl away but not old enough to walk. He wanted to find her quickly before she stumbled upon a snake or her screams drew the attention of a dog or other wild animal. He assumed she'd been tossed aside in the chaos. How long ago that had been he didn't know, long enough for the soldiers to have fled but not long enough for any aid to have arrived from any neighbouring villages, but to be fair they were all probably in hiding themselves.

He saw her and ran forward a couple of steps, stopped to make sure it was safe then jogged forward again. His head hurt as he leaped over a log in his bare feet and slid to a stop behind her. She was on her belly trying to crawl forward but her fingers were bleeding from where she'd climbed over the log. From her perspective she wouldn't have had any idea which direction she was facing, in all directions were tall trees and bushes yet her survival instinct had kept her on the path towards the watering hole. Her small chubby face was streaked with tears where no doubt she had been screaming before exhaustion had dwindled her voice down to the few random whimpers she had left to give out.

"Meisha," Malachi said softly as he reached her and gently cradled her in his arms. A cry of relief bellowed from her tiny lungs as she gripped hold of her older brother. Malachi fell back onto his rear rocking his sister in his arms, tears streaming, washing the blood and dirt from his cheeks.

6

"There weren't many other life forms that we came across, not intelligent ones at any rate. You often had the leeches and worms that were common on most worlds, they tended to mainly be around water, that's where most life is always found, but the deserts and mountain ranges often had their own surprises."

"Like the ones that killed you?"

Cade ignored him and continued.

"You often got multi-limbed creatures where the terrain was tough to climb, not necessarily your cosy, soft padded woolly mountain goat or sheep; harsh terrains bred harsh beasts to battle, you'd do well to keep your wits about you when in unfamiliar territory.

"Deserts were no better. Fewer walking critters out on the sands but that didn't mean what resided there couldn't run you down before you had a chance to turn and find your feet. They didn't need a place to hide to jump out at you, the whole desert dune was apt for a grand game of hide and seek.

"B'erihe was like that. A thin atmosphere where the seas had dried up millions of years ago so that the only lakes and rivers existed underground, the giant caves surrounding them the only suitable habitat for cities to be built. Oxygen was plentiful underground, thriving from mutated plant life which had adapted to its cavernous environment. The only terraforming pads were ancient relics of the original settlers, platforms of half abandoned work stations and towns that had existed before the caves were stumbled upon. These towns weren't maintained, yet they had inhabitants none the less, and served as staging posts between the underground rail networks."

"So the people live underground and the monsters live up top?"

"Correct. The towns are fortified against the wildlife so there is a need for some heavy firepower on the surface which is also, obviously, in bulk storage underground."

"So if I get the picture correctly you faced an enemy hiding underground where you couldn't see them, harboured by heavily armed soldiers used to fighting with fast moving deadly creatures, under a thin atmosphere with little or no cloud cover so there would be no hiding your approach. No element of surprise."

"We were facing a long drawn out and difficult campaign."

"How did that make you feel?"

"Frustrated. Angry. Determined."

Malachi jotted down his answer, internally pleased that Cade had given him an immediate response. Was that progress? He didn't know.

"Just back track a second for me. You mentioned the different life-forms, did you ever come across anything intelligent?"

"On a par with humans you mean?"

Malachi nodded.

"No. We are the masters of the universe. We are the gods who rule."

"And you wished to be a god amongst gods?"

Cade scowled at his dark skinned counsellor. Malachi ignored it, even giving a slight smile to provoke irritation in his patient as he jotted down his emotional response.

"It is a big universe. I doubt even your race have even scratched the surface of our own galaxy."

Cade's shoulders now rose in his now characteristic fashion as he conceded the point: what else was out there in the depths of wide open space was still unknown.

"There's always someone bigger and better," Cade eventually replied after pondering the notion for himself.

"Something you've learnt from experience?"

"Something my father always taught me."

"Cade Senior?"

"I was always tall. He didn't want me relying on my size to be used to intimidate shorter friends. He knew the other kids would catch up in height, and I guess he knew I wasn't particular sporty or strong. To a lanky wimp there would always be somebody bigger and better."

"Looking at you now do you still feel that's the case?"

"I may have bulked out but I'm no idiot. It doesn't take much to kill a giant or a god, just another giant or another god."

"Who is claiming to be the god, John Cade or Abadd'on Apolly'on V'hihyon?"

Cade raised an eyebrow at Malachi's pronunciation, tilting his head in appreciation of the effort, but his smile declined to answer the question.

7

Cade didn't get to finish his story that day. He left the office building in the centre of town disillusioned and confused. Malachi Akeno was beginning to push his buttons; he could feel it: the probing and intrusive interrogating, attempting to prize open soldered over wounds with a crowbar expectant of an outpouring of emotion and a breaking down of a stolid personality. Malachi wanted the tower to fall, but Cade had no intention of giving him the satisfaction.

Yet still his mind was troubled as he stepped onto the pavement outside as his own motives circled above like vultures waiting for a place to land and feast on a tasty meal.

The sunlight burnt his eyes as he looked up to the day outside which peeped brush strokes of blue and white between the shadows cast by dirty grey, pollutant washed, old town high risers.

He looked down and around to the passing crowd milling about: shoppers donned in spring coats and dark shades lightly carrying bags, peering into windows as they slow walked passed the next parade opposite the office block; office administrators with company lanyards hung from their necks nipped to sandwich and coffee shops on a shortened break to return to consume their lunch at their desks; one such coffee shop was heavily laden with buggies parked up in the doorway as a regular mothers' meeting was underway. He looked to and fro slightly disorientated as he soaked in the ambience and detail, following every figure, listening to every murmur above the din of traffic - for a moment every face on a passing bus turned to stare at him, every pedestrian spun to glare back, drivers stopped and beeped their horns.

Someone shouldered him hard, he ignored the force of the impact; a smaller person would have flinched in pain and annoyance, but his mind was elsewhere, the bump just enough to pull him from his daze. He whisked round to see who had walked into him, an average Joe in a charcoal grey business suit wore a face of annoyance and cowardice as he looked up and back stepped from the collision. A muttered curse was all he dared flip in his direction as he redirected his course. It hadn't been his fault anyway, it had been Cade who had walked into him.

Cade rubbed his face and pulled his bulky frame back to the pavement slightly.

snap out of it!

He did. He pulled himself together. The sensation didn't leave him though. Someone was watching him.

The traffic that had stopped moved off from the lights, the car that had been tooted having stalled on the green. The bus moved off with its passengers absorbed in reading the paper or a book, or listening to headphones, some were sat but most were getting to their feet ready to get off at the next stop just passed the lights as they arrived at the High Street.

There was no one obvious, but his senses and training told him not to be fooled.

Maybe it was Malachi from the window. Maybe Kapoor or Vost were nearby keeping tabs on his appointments. Maybe Kennedy had assigned a special surveillance unit. He couldn't be sure of any of it. Maybe it was just the reliving of the past in counselling that set off the paranoia, MI17 a ghost of trauma he'd brought upon himself to shadow him in the gaunt and fickle memories he flitted between.

He glanced up at the windows behind him but saw nothing but the splinters of sun flickering off the glass.

His next appointment wasn't for another week, he would have to think hard about what he would have to say next time.

He fished his sunglasses from his jacket pocket and slipped them on, dipping his head to do so before joining the footfall.

8

Kennedy tapped on the adjoining door before stepping out from the shadows of the purposely unlit side of the office. Malachi looked up from his seated position behind his desk and nodded recognition of the imposing plain clothed figure that had entered. It was rare that he graced the office with his presence, usually he just left the observations to the grunts who sat next door with their recording equipment monitoring his sessions with Cade. He hadn't known that Kennedy himself was sat next door until he walked in, but he didn't allow any surprise to ride the ridges of his forehead that smoothed out to a wide smooth scalp of shaved hair.

"General Kennedy," he said rising to his feet and pronouncing every syllable with the natural preciseness of the English language that only Africans seemed to be able to master. "What brings you down here?"

"It's Major General. I was just in the area," he grunted. It was an obvious lie which both sides glossed over casually. "We need you to book in more sessions with him. We need particular information."

"I'm sure booking in the appointments won't be difficult as he likes to talk, however getting him to discuss specifics is often complicated. Take today for example: I tried to quiz him on life-forms as requested by your colleagues next door," he waved a hand at the adjoining office which had been rented out along with his for the sole purpose of observing John Cade. Cade wasn't the only client to visit his office, which he set up as a legitimate practice, but he was the main source of income and motivation for being here. "Swaying the conversation isn't always straight forward."

Kennedy snorted and half nodded, clearly not caring for excuses.

"Having had time to look into some of his previous claims we are now discovering much of what he said about alien life-forms to be accurate."

"Time? You have had years to look into his previous claims, has it really taken you so long? Is this why the renewed interest in this man?"

"Just ask the questions, Mr Okeno. You don't need to know the reasons why, nor what sort of threat we consider this man to be."

"So, he is a threat?"

"Not in the way you think. He has information we need to know and we need you to draw it out of him. I'm assigning someone else to take over the running of the investigation here while I deal with other more pressing security issues at the MOD. Due to the nature of the investigation we wanted to keep things within familiar territory and with a more hands-on approach, so you'll be overseen a bit more closely and intrusively. Expect the course of your meetings to be a bit more prescriptive from now on."

"That is not how I work, Major General Kennedy. I am a clinical professional not a spy for the government. I was employed to help counsel this man, and for all intents and purposes he believes this to be a genuine agreement. Sure he has an idea of the connection in which I was employed through MI17, but should he find out that I am being force fed questions to gain information I should not like to be on the receiving end of his reactions."

"You'll be alright, we always have men next door listening."

"I am more concerned for my patient, General. His mental position is of great importance to me."

"Never mind that," he said dismissively, "just do as we ask, that's all I came to tell you. It's unlikely you'll have any further direct contact from me. Your new boss will direct you accordingly and will report back to me."

"And who is this new boss?"

"We have drafted in someone out of retirement, someone who has been doing ad hoc consulting work for the government on and off for the last couple of years. I think you'll find him more amenable than me," he smiled a grimace that told he was proud of the mean demeanour of reputation he allowed to cloak his personality. "You'll know him from your interviews and our notes, his name is Louis Vost. I'm sure he'll be in touch with you soon."

With that the General turned casually and walked out of the room into the corridor outside, never to return.

9

Back at the his flat the remains of his breakfast cereal, the porridge bowl he'd lazily thrown into the sink in one of those *I'll do it later* moments, was still sitting in the sink where he'd left it this morning; he hadn't been quite in a rush but he did have a number of tasks on his list he wanted to check off before his counselling session. It was an off-work day, not quite skiving or throwing a sickie but rather arranged with consent of management so long as he made it up by covering an extra night shift now and then. Not that they could refuse his time off for counselling, he was still officially a mental health patient after all. He looked at the now dried and crusted bowl sitting in the sink with the spoon see-sawed in rest position over the edge, round end up. The porridge had set like glue to the curve of the ceramic, screaming an attitude of mock consternation that it might actually get washed up, but adding an aggressive web-like hold that yelled I'm not letting go or making it easy for you - *you shouldn't have left it till later, now I'm stuck on for good*. John seemed to read the thought as he looked into the sink and then looked away, walked off a step and then moved back and ran the hot tap into the basin. *Let it soak a little, I'll do it later.*

Gemma would never have let him get away with that, but Gemma was long gone.

He shook his head with sadness. What had Malachi stirred up?

He walked through to the living room of the third floor flat of the council block stashed away in the corner of nowhere in particular, just one estate among many of social deprivation crowded with people just existing, hoping for more, hoping this week's lottery ticket will buy them the escape to a Malibu apartment in the sun with a Ferrari in the drive and a pool with a sea view. The fantasy lived on in all of them but the realities of a win were unlikely to play out the dream; too many on the estates were entrenched in their way of life: their small town gossip, their regular contacts for their vices, their broken and dysfunctional family ties, and the friends that would never allow them to escape without taking their cut. Here he easily blended into the background of obscurity; no-one knew who he was, and more importantly, no-one cared.

He heard the dog padding around elsewhere in the flat and ignored it, the sound of it lapping at its water bowl in the kitchen followed by its sniffing the floor for crumbs was a familiar sound he tuned out.

A mascara brush lay on the shelf beneath the wall mirror that took up a large chunk of the plain pale wall behind it. The brush was partly pushed into the tube having been abandoned in a rush, a blusher brush and compact sat next to it.

Lucy had been asleep when he had left this morning. She was

a heavy sleeper and snored louder than he cared for. She was only a few years older than Mia, in her early twenties, a good looking checkout girl in the local supermarket. She was no brain of Britain, no university graduation photo hung on her parent's wall and probably never would. She was a product of a failing estate with few or no morals. Her parents weren't even divorced, her mother had never known her father's name and her mother's last boyfriend had beaten her and sexually abused her two daughters. Lucy was content in knowing that her mother was now happy in a lesbian relationship and her younger half-sister by four years was a single mum with two children of her own.

In some ways Lucy was doing better than expected, she wasn't on drugs (not the hard stuff anyway, the odd joint here and there didn't really count), she was careful with everyone she slept with, and she had a regular job and a busy social life. She saw no problem with sleeping with the likes of John Cade, a much older man with mental health issues and obsessions of his own. All she saw was a muscle bound beefcake with his own flat (although paid for with the aid of housing benefits) and a bed she could utilise when she wanted without him making demands on her other than sexual favours. It was a mutually agreeable relationship which neither side took too seriously.

He pushed the brush fully into its plastic container and wondered what else she'd left lying around in her rush to get to work, no doubt having left too late to get there on time again. He knew she was heading for a fall and she was unwittingly forcing the job to a premature end. He didn't want her dependency to be hanging round his neck when that happened, he'd never be able to unhook her then and he had no room for a needy female. One way or another she'd be gone soon.

He dropped down on the sofa, picked up the TV remote, picking off a long blonde hair from it as he did so, and pressed for the news channel. It blinked on, the volume too loud from where Lucy had no doubt had the music channel blaring. Tensions in Russia and the Middle East were ongoing, nothing new there, there were arguments in parliament over the deficit, again nothing new there either, no other headlines screamed out at him so he flicked it off. He would scour the internet later for the latest science and technology pages, maybe tonight, he didn't feel up to doing it now - *leave it till later.*

He thought about checking his emails for any design work that might have come in; the work had dried up considerably recently, partly a sign of the times as companies had less budget to play with coupled with the increase in younger and cheaper competition. There were more imaginative minds coming through the industry who could afford the lower pay as they tried to prove themselves. Of course things wouldn't look so bleak had he not lost his last two contracts due to shabby and late work. He'd got distracted with his mind flitting inwardly to other worlds and other priorities away from the life of John Cade, and as a result his work had paid the penalty, and by the time he refocused he'd missed the deadlines. It was just as well he wasn't reliant solely on the money from this line of work.

He had a few income streams: freelance graphic design was one, various long term social benefit payments were another, but his main source at the moment was working for the council cleaning and maintaining public property, in effect graffiti removal. It was a job that could be done day or night in a team of two or three depending on the severity of the problem. Often reports would come in from members of the public or from the police regarding areas that needed cleaning off or painting over. They prioritised offensive material first: racist, sexist, homophobic and crude language or drawings were often dealt with within 24 hours but there was so much out there that often it would take weeks to get around to some of the worst hit areas. He was part of a small crew working in rotation, sometimes, when it was quiet, they would just drive around looking for work, but that was rare and mostly only in the winter.

He got on well with his colleagues on a superficial level, never giving much away about himself, careful not to give any hint to anyone in his new life any idea as to his past dalliances with fame. To them, to his employers, to Lucy, he was John Cade, estranged from his family, suffering clinical depression and mild schizophrenia which no longer affected his day to day life as it was under the control of medication (something they all believed - he found that few dared to question too closely someone with a mental health issue, there was way too much of a stigma behind it that caused people to be fearful of probing too deeply, something he used to his advantage). To the world he lived in now few knew him for the name of his alter ego.

He thought maybe he should go into work and make up the hours he'd missed but then he thought, *no I'll leave it till later.*

Instead he got to his feet, autopilot driving him to grab his gym stuff ready for a workout to exorcise the demons and the haunting ghosts of John Cade that Malachi had instilled in his subconscious.

10

When he returned from the gym his attitude had changed. He was pumped, adrenalin flooding his system, his muscles swollen and tender from the exertion of having increased his training regime by twenty reps per muscle group and an extra ten minutes on the treadmill. He wasn't tired, far from it, on the contrary he felt energetic and ready to take on the world.

He tossed his sweat soaked shorts and vest in the washing basket and then swept up the make-up from the shelf into the bin he held up in his other hand to catch it. He ran the tap in the kitchen and squeezed in some washing up liquid and waited for it to froth up. He glanced over to the phone on the side, a red flashing light lit its base unit, he stepped over and pressed play.

"You have one new message," the automated recording read out before clicking off to be replaced with the missed call. "John, it is Malachi Okeno, it was good to see you today. I feel that we made some good progress today. I feel it would be beneficial to move our meetings to twice a week. How about Friday at 10am? Please let me know if that would be agreeable for you."

The message clicked off followed by the automated instruction guide kicking in: "To delete this message, press the delete button. To delete all messages press the delete button again."

He thought about the slow and precise tones of the counsellor, always trying hard to make himself understood, so self-aware of his strong accent. It was a calm friendly tone which said much of his gentle manner and warm personality. In truth John liked him a lot, despite the misgivings of mistrust that echoed from the Abadd'on quarter of his mind. He found the African endearing. He knew little about him except for what he had witnessed in their sessions, though he assumed much. Okeno wore no wedding ring. He looked to be of a similar age to himself, but he couldn't be sure as the darker skin was often deceptive and ageless. His eyes spoke of a wisdom that came more from experience than from merely education, leaving him to suspect his counsellor bore a burden of a past that would be unfathomable to a Western mind; he knew Africa had its own unique horrors and he thought Malachi had probably seen his fair share first hand, not that he had ever mentioned it or even hinted at it (although John had often teased out more than Malachi would care to admit to), but to put himself in the position of wanting to listen and help with the troubles of others earned him the respect of this patient at the very least.

Did he want to increase his sessions? He wasn't sure. Already the inflictions of Gemma and his feelings towards her and the kids were recessing on an outward tide. He still had his story to tell, he still wanted to finish his tale.

He knocked the tap off, the sink was full and foaming, much more so than he needed for the few items he had to wash up. He grabbed the scouring pad and attacked the porridge bowl, tossing a bright red lipstick marked mug into the sink as his mind pondered the sort of childhood Malachi may have experienced but certain that whatever he concocted it was sure to be far from the truth.

As was usual when he did the washing up, his mind wondered along the thin thread of tentative strands of thought and before he knew it he was replaying his own childhood memories.

"Sam, do you think there are aliens," he remembered asking his sister as they sat outside the tent of the French campsite where they'd spent two weeks of the summer holidays that year. What year was it? He struggled to remember but he thought he was 9 or 10 which would have put Samantha at 12 or 13. They were sat on the grass listening to the frogs and staring up at the stars in the crystal clear sky above, the sort of sky you only get when on holiday away from home and away from the city glow that obliterated the artistry of the nocturnal canvas.

"Are you waiting for ET to crawl out of the bushes holding a plant?"

"No, a frog."

"Dad says there are UFO's."

"What's that moving there?" He remembered pointing up to a slow moving star tracing the night sky drawing a line through the celestial map. She followed the angle of his arm and found the dim light at the end of his finger that blinked through a thin wisp of cloud. She waited for it to reappear clearly before confirming what it was.

"It's a satellite."

"Mum says aliens don't exist."

"Who knows. There's a lot of planets out there."

They both sat silent for a while hoping for a shooting star to fall into view. They had already tried drawing the shapes they knew were supposed to be hanging in view but neither of them managed to identify anything other than The Plough, or The Saucepan as they preferred to call it.

"If there are aliens," he had asked, silently fixating his imagination on another distant world drawn from too many science fiction films and re-runs of Star Trek, "do you think they are human, or like monsters with giant eyes and massive heads."

"Just big mouths to eat up annoying little brothers."

Another round of silence fell as they stared craning their necks. The tents behind shielded them from the slight breeze. Mum was having a shower over at the communal shower block and dad was at the bar socialising with the dad from the family two tents down. They didn't know it then but their paths would cross again over the next few years as their dad struck up a good friendship with them, a friendship that would end bitterly in an affair as dad got a little too close to his friend's wife. There had been plenty of arguments accusing him of having that intention all along, something he denied, but looking back now maybe his mum had been right, he could see the signs, or was that just his imagination filling in the blanks? Either way his dad had spent a lot of time with them and left his mum and the kids on their own much of the holiday. He tried to think of whether his dad had spent time on that holiday with the other mum on his own, he knew on subsequent holidays together they had done but he couldn't place it that far back. His mum had eventually given him an ultimatum and within weeks the affair was over and his parents were fighting to rebuild their relationship. They survived it, but it was a close call. And it had all started on that holiday in France.

They sat there alone. It was in the time when people were more trusting, before the days of paranoia at leaving the kids alone for a short period in case some perverted paedophile preyed upon them.

"Do you think aliens would try to invade us?"

"Why would they want to? Don't believe everything you see on TV."

He looked at the monitor, it was a newsreel of failed nuclear experiments on Dor'bak, experiments which had gone disastrously wrong and destroyed half the planet, killing millions. He flicked it over. An historic educational programme was playing about the history of V'hihyon majoring on the technology race which had led to its destruction. It was the sort of programme the circuit boards used to educate him and all the other children.

He didn't know how old he was, with the various birth cycles and the differing time zones no one marked the day of a child's birth. Birthdays weren't celebrated in space, on some of the colonies where births were still naturally occurring it was sometimes custom to do so, but generally no one cared for the practice.

He remembered sitting in the pod, he couldn't remember which one but he was alone, nor did he know why he was there, he just was, a little boy sitting there watching the entertainment feeds. Maybe he was hiding from the labour detail, maybe he was wanting downtime and hiding from the other kids, maybe he had been tasked to study - he couldn't remember. What he did remember were those newsfeeds playing across the screen as the circuit board dragged in Tiri'el.

Tiri'el was his friend. He was older but not by much, probably a similar age to John Cade on the night he had stared up at the stars from that camp site in France. Tiri'el was often a little slow of mind, his temple indented, caved in by a defective birthing chamber. His mother had died on one of the fleet ships, a diseased refugee whose body couldn't cope with the demanding and complicated pregnancy, as a result Tiri'el was transferred to a medi pod, still unborn within his mother's dead corpse, awaiting a surgical extraction before being placed into the birthing chamber to artificially continue the growth cycle. He was also missing three fingers on one hand which often made him clumsy, much to the annoyance of the crew whose feet he fell beneath as he scuttled about the ship trying to find his place in life - a place it turned out had been decided for him, the cards having dealt him a poor hand from the start as the deck was heavily stacked against him.

The circuit board, its emotionless metallic face appeared to grimace with hatred in his memory as its robotic arm dragged the boy into the room screaming, Tiri'el sliding across the floor trying to cling on to anything he could with his good hand to pull himself away from the android, but it was all to no avail, there was no way he could match it for strength.

"I didn't mean to!" he screamed. "It was an accident!"

The circuit board didn't react but was busy looking for something on the shelf in front of him.

Tiri'el spotted him sat there dumbstruck. "Tell him! Tell him Ab! Tell him I didn't mean to do it! Tell him it was an accident!"

But he couldn't. He didn't know what had happened, and even if he did he was too scared and stunned to react. He'd never seen a circuit board attack a human before. No doubt whatever had happened, knowing Tiri'el, it had been an accident, but still his voice wasn't forthcoming, it was trapped at the back of his throat refusing to rise any higher in case the circuit board turned his attention on himself.

When the circuit board did turn, still holding Tiri'el's forearm in its vice-like grip, it had a pneumatic drill, used for tightening its own body parts, in its free hand. It had attached a sharp drill bit and without hesitation turned it on and aimed it at Tiri'el's head.

The screams of pain echoed throughout that sector of the ship as slowly the robot pushed in and drew out the drill bit and then repeated time and time again until the screams and spasmodic flinching ceased. Blood splattered the deranged robot which then dropped the drill before leaving in the direction it had come.

Throughout he had sat still, unmoving, unbelieving. Men came running, but they were too late to be of any help to Tiri'el. A cold shock engulfed him and froze him in place. He would later be told the machine, an early model, was defective and had been destroyed, but it was enough to muddy his view of how this emerging life-form viewed the humans that created them and lived among them.

Yes, the John Cade of today had unresolved issues. Did he need extra sessions with a counsellor? Yes, most likely. He was sure he had only just scratched the surface of two lifetimes of issues. If only his emotional conflict over Gemma was the only turbulence in his spirit.

He zoned back into the room and shook his head, taking his

wrinkled hands out of the now lukewarm water - don't go there - *leave it till later.*

11

Tell me about the life-forms on B'eirhe, how did they differ, I don't know, say to the moon you were killed on?

I assume you're not talking about the rock creatures but the sea creatures in comparison to B'eirhe's desert creatures.

Precisely.

I have told much of this to Kapoor back when they had me in detention. Sea life was often the same on each planet: creatures that swam in a similar manner and adapted to the differing lighting conditions in size and colour. Sea life was always full of surprises due to the depths that life could thrive. We as a race are particularly, and willingly, ignorant of most aquatic life-forms.

You fear the sea?

We fear nothing. We are simply not equipped to delve into dark waters where we can't see or identify subaquatic giants.

So you were scared of the seas.

I didn't say that. Did I say that? No. Don't write that down!

Most alien life is found in water, both big and small, and most of what we've encountered is toxic to humans in some way. We breed our own fish in purpose made lakes where some colonies trade with the other drier planets, such as B'eirhe. We also farmed a small amount of live fish within the fleet along with other livestock. The replicators could create sustenance for our needs but sometimes there can be no substitute for the real thing. Whenever we fought well I would treat the men to a live meal, it was tradition; it was what Satorie'on did, and I honoured him by doing the same.

A small natural lake, even the most toxic in its chemical makeup, was most likely teeming with life, and usually various types, some that would interact, some that wouldn't, but would co-exist alongside each other in an ecosystem that was replicated across the galaxy.

Life on a planet's surface was always more varied, mainly because we could see it more obviously. Plant life varied little but animals developed due to the bitter climes of the planetary conditions: radiation, climate, food supply, terrain, the planet's place in the habitable zone, all had an effect on the development of what we encountered.

On B'eirhe the worms, spiders, and lizards developed in the sand but the place where I died.... aarh, I can't really remember.

Why not? Why can't you remember? What do you picture when you think of that place?

Sometimes I can see it all so clearly, but as time goes by much is just a blurred memory eclipsed by terror and pain. I keep seeing those Pa'as beasts rising out of the ground like the walking dead: an army of impervious zombies slowly coming to life, but once they woke there was no stopping them.

Try to see past it.

Some sea life is bright, luminescent, a chemical found in deep water is activated in many fish when they are threatened causing them to glow defensively to ward off prey. None of that was present there. It was all grey and deathly.

Were the waters not red?

Yes, but the image, the impression if you like, in my mind is one that is grey and threatening.

The colour of guilt? Regret?

Maybe.

The chemical you spoke of, in the deep water, do you know what is was?

No, I don't recall what we called it. It wasn't something I needed to know.

I feel we are getting a little repetitive and this does little to help me understand you. Let's move on now to your campaign to track down and capture Twumbouha'el, what was your plan of action to flush him out?

I had no plan to track him down and capture him, I intended to flush him out and kill him in clear sight of all who followed him.

12

Louis Vost looked down at the script on the table in front of him. So far he was impressed with the Ugandan, he was doing a good job at getting the relevant questions in.

It was his first day back in the saddle, with the exception of the briefing he'd been called in for at the Ministry of Defence offices in Westminster. Seeing the newly made up Major General Kennedy brought back all the memories of the years he'd spent in that basement office struggling to keep his department afloat. He had welcomed retirement, but in the end, with his children grown up and his wife constantly busy with voluntary work at the local church (something he had no interest in) he found his life empty and lacking. He kept up the consultancy for various government departments but on the whole his involvement in MI17 had fallen into a distant memory.

Sitting in the adjacent office now with a Surjeet Kapoor replacement called McCaan staring at the monitor with a set of cans on his head, he suddenly felt a sense of deja vu.

He adjusted his own set of headphones and pulled at the cable draped across his notes. He hadn't had much time to refresh his memory of the case so had brought a laptop with a digitised record of the entire file pre-loaded onto it: video audio, transcripts, and assessments, were all loaded on and easily referenced at the touch of a button, yet with all that in mind he still preferred to jot things down on paper. His face lit in the glow of the laptop reflecting off the thin grey hair touching his ears as he punched in what Cade had said about sea life in his previous interviews.

The questions with which he'd primed Malachi were written down in front of him and if he'd had time he would have looked up the relevant answers before now, but he'd barely had time to meet and brief the counsellor and get up to speed with their recent conversations let alone study up on what Kennedy was wanting answers to. He missed Kapoor. He would know the answers off pat without having to look them up, he had been keenly reliable like that. Maybe his new companion next to him could fill that void, he looked at him trying to figure out his character: he was young and technically capable but had a gormless expression which didn't fill him with confidence. He wondered whether there was any chance of getting Kapoor reassigned.

Why the renewed interest in Project Furion he didn't know, not fully. All Kenndy would say was that time had gone by and some of John Cade's revelations were being borne out in some way or other. Secrets, that was all Kennedy was concerned about; who knew his dirty little secrets, who was leaking what and why. He didn't care so much for the truth so much as he cared for protecting the walls of his compound.

Louis Vost wasn't all too sure what he cared about at this venture. He was glad to be doing something, and doing something with responsibility, putting on the old glove and sinking back into the old pattern of listening in on John Cade in the other room. The set up wasn't as sophisticated but it was adequate. He was sure he would get into the swing of the investigation soon enough, but did he care about the outcome? At this point he couldn't give a definitive yes but was just pleased to be valued for his experience.

He typed in the recent technical research notes Kennedy's department had provided to cross reference Cade's stories. Some of the questions he had he was sure he could Google if he needed to but Kennedy's notes seemed pretty in-depth. Without looking at the screen he knew for himself that much of what he'd heard Cade say was fairly accurate. Vost had heard him say it all before, years ago, but now he also remembered seeing much of it on more recent nature programmes on TV, with David Attenborough's narrative explaining the bio-complexities of life. How many times had he reflected on so many things in life over the past decade or so, reflecting back on the words of John Cade? Too many. Cade it seemed had rarely been far from his mind.

The computer screen displayed a number of colourful pictures of luminous jellyfish and squid with footnote descriptions and complicated scientific names. A column of description, no doubt taken from a scientific journal, told the story of various jellyfish dissolving their silhouettes by having silvery sides, the silver functioning as a mirror allowing the varying aquatic creatures to blend in by reflecting the water around them. He thought of sardines and suddenly found his mind transformed to the rocky moon where rocks fed off camouflaged fish in the nearby rivers.

He read on, there was a section on anglerfish, one of the most voracious predators of the deep sea, luring in their prey by dangling an orb of light before them to draw in an unsuspecting meal thinking it to be food, the light it produced being luminous bacteria. He skim read the passage, one ear to what Cade was saying but knowing he could replay the digital recording if he missed anything. To make light, the article claimed, three ingredients were needed: oxygen, a luciferin, and a luciferase. A luciferase being the spark that allowed the luciferin molecule to react with the oxygen to emit a flash of light energy as a photon. He thought of the Latin for Lucifer meaning 'bringer of light' and then coupled it with its common usage as the name of Satan; with so much of John Cade's case there was, and always had been, a double edged meaning to all the sharp words he spoke, and like the devil himself he hid lies within truth so that even through the years deciphering the intent and purpose under his devious tongue was still a conundrum.

Science clearly was supporting Cade's story with examples in our own ecosystem and the biodiversity of the oceans. The question was how much of that had he researched beforehand, how much of it was intuitive, how much of it was coincidence or lucky guess, and how much, if any, was truth?

The article went on to tell more of the natural availability of luciferins in deep sea water and expanded on the various compounds and variety of life-forms. He didn't need to read on, he got the picture. It all substantiated what Cade had been saying. No doubt his topside land-forms would bear out in a similar manner if he conducted a quick study of the evolution of various creatures depending on their environment on Earth.

He glanced back again at the monitor and the bulked up image of John Cade who seemed to have put on about eight stone of pure muscle since he'd last seen him. He repositioned the cans again and tuned back into Cade's voice and picked up his story mid-flow.

13

We shuttled in troops under cover of darkness. There were natural platforms of rock protruding from the desert, windswept remains of mountaintops scoured away by the grating sand that buried them, crumbling monoliths whose scalps barely touched the surface. Most were unsuitable for landing on, with sharp jagged peaks, a few others were flat enough in places but the sand had bored deep tunnels which led far down into the nefarious caverns where we decided the risks were too great to venture. One plateau we identified as suitable for dropping a platoon in small groups at a time. It was a long night of flying back and forth securing the men and then bedding them down on the plateau so that they couldn't be seen by aerial scouts. They were close enough to the tunnel system to be able to climb inside the underground rail link after a day's hike across the sand.

Considering what you've said about the desert creatures wasn't that a bit risky?

Of course, but war is risky. We had no choice, it was the only way to cross the desert without being detected. The men crossed in groups of twenty, so they had enough firepower each to fend off a short attack by the wildlife - not all made it across the desert. Once within the tunnels they could regroup and hide out of sight in the maintenance corridors and then make their way through towards the cities, picking off rebels along the way.

The objective was to cut the power underground and disrupt the communication network. We could then fly in and attack the overground turrets. With surface superiority all we needed to do was seal off the vents, poison the air, and wait it out; we could pick them off one by one as they reared their heads above ground, swatting them like flies.

An underground world as big as you have described surely would be able to seal of upper contaminated areas. You have described it as self-sufficient. Surely an established facility and community, a colony as you have described would have contingencies in place for such an event?

Oh I agree. We had thought of that. We didn't think the war would be won so swiftly. That was just phase one: confuse and disrupt. Phase two was to increase the panic by bombing the crap out of every hidey hole we could find. We bought a grid plan of the entire planet and targeted all but a handful of targets ready to unleash hell from above.

We didn't expect the casualties to be great but we thought it would be enough to turn a large number of the colonists against the mechas. All we needed was to force them out of hiding so we could fight them in the open. The colonists would be too

concerned with plugging the holes to keep the bugs out to give alliance to the mechas.
Did it work?
Eventually. It took a long time.

In the room next door Louis Vost was shaking his head and exchanging glances with McCann. Cade's responses sounded forced and spurious as though he were reacting and thinking on his feet. He was burning to ask his own questions and missed the facility to email Malachi as he had done with Kapoor in days gone by. He ripped the cans off his head and paced the room frustrated, stopping to listen at the adjoining room to the voices muffled behind the wood.

Surjeet Kapoor was at that moment at his desk in Whitehall, sat pretending to look busy. It was a difficult task justifying his role collating statistics for the cabinet minister he was assigned to, but in reality information gathering was far easier than it used to be as most figures could be obtained at the touch of a button, the hard part was trying to distinguish which figures were reliable, what with budget constraints and set targets, too many departments in public service were under pressure to provide figures that would satisfy rather than upset the status quo and risk their jobs in the process. As a result Kapoor spent much of his time reading between the lines to identify those reports which had their figures massaged so that he could provide two reports to the minister: one was the official account where the document's author could roll the crap downhill to those providing the figures, should it get smashed about in Parliament, and the other was the unofficial verbal summary he would personally brief the minister with so that he was prepared should a red face moment present itself, especially in front of the press.

He kept half an eye on the door, always careful not to be caught out twiddling his thumbs. He was too efficient for his own good and felt completely wasted in the role, but a job was a job and in the age of austerity cuts, much of which was hitting civil servants, no one wanted to rock the boat. It was a situation he'd been in before, and one that seemed to be perpetual.

He scrolled down the screen which in his downtimes, of which there were many, he flittered away the minutes perusing his own research. If anyone checked his internet searches from his work terminal he'd have a lot of questions to answer to.

John Cade was now a hobby, an obsession. He kept a close eye on the latest scientific research and any military projects that could be linked in anyway. He watched closely the strange and the bizarre collections of UFO and unexplained accounts that got reported through the official channels and maintained his contacts at NASA. It was fair to say that on all things Project Furion related, Surjeet Kapoor was an authority, a resident expert: MI17 without the infrastructure of a department. He used his privileged position with access to various departments to gather all the intelligence he needed, careful to position his computer screen away from prying eyes who suspected nothing (so he hoped) of his pet hobby. He knew of Major General Kennedy's renewed interest in the case and he knew of the Bansteads and their direction by Sentinel to stare at Lyra, not that he thought they'd be looking there for much longer. He also knew of Malachi Okeno's counselling sessions, and he even knew his old boss Louis Vost had been drafted in. That was good, he'd look beyond the blind vision and ambition of Kennedy.

If there was a way of reuniting Abadd'on to his people he wanted to find it. All the displaced souls needed to be returned to their rightful place. He knew there had to be a way of uniting the lost civilisations to our own, making the first official contact with our cousins whom he suspected we were born from in the first place. Forget this Adam and Eve stuff, or that we evolved from monkeys, so far as Surjeet Kapoor was concerned, and in this he was convinced, we were descended from the early travellers from Abadd'on's home world.

He scrolled through the screen, there was nothing new to report that he didn't know already. It was time to request a transfer. He pulled out his mobile phone and dialed a number.

"Hi Louis, it's Surjeet."

14

In his dream the soldiers were coming. There were few trees around the settlement and those he could see had giant sandworms slithering around the bases of their trunks, and in places on the path dark indents of shadow would appear as unseen creatures popped space above their heads as they scurried beneath the surface.

The women were wailing a high pitched warning, licking their tongues around their mouths to resonate a distinctive tone that he had only ever heard used on joyous occasions or when the women worshipped God in praise at church on Sunday, but now that tone held an oppressive and fearful edge as panic was driven from one hut to another.

His mother already had hold of his sister and was making for the door. His father was still trying to coax his tearful son from the far wall away from the entrance.

His legs were frozen. He couldn't move.

His father stepped across to lift him and carry him out away from the danger; there was no safety to be had in staying in the huts: they would be pillaged and burnt. They crashed out into the blinding light of the desert that should have been the sheltered shadows of the jungle that surrounded his home, his mother nowhere to be seen among the fleeing villagers. His father was looking for her but the delay in getting his son out had meant she had run off ahead assuming they were following close behind.

Gun fire whistled passed their ears. His father dropped him to the ground and at that moment he thought he caught a glimpse of his mother running for shelter among the other women, no doubt trying to locate her sister and her family before fleeing into the woods - *where the snakes will eat you! Stay off the sand!*

He turned to reach up for his father's arms to be carried away to safety but his father was facing the other way, a gargantuan figure in silhouette in front of him blocking out the sun. And then his father's head exploded.

Blood splattered his boyish frame as the hole in the back of his father's head showered him in tiny fragments of bone and brain. The lifeless figure of the man he absolutely adored fell back towards him. He crawled aside just before the body landed on him, the face, now wearing a newly fashioned gunshot wound beneath the right eye, falling almost flush to his own.

He didn't scream, not at first, not until he looked up at the giant that had shot his father as the rebel warrior stepped forward, his pale smirk bearing down on him, John Cade turning the butt of the rifle ready to strike him.

15

You look like you had a rough night.
I'm alright John Cade.
Not sleeping too good?
Let us finish your story shall we. We seem to run out of time in every session. I am keen to hear how you captured your prey.
Nightmares? About your family?
You are not here to counsel me, John Cade.
I know that, Malachi Okeno, I'm just joking with you.
So, you are in a jovial mood today. That is good! What is it that makes you happy today, John Cade? And no shrugging your shoulders.
Nothing in particular. The sun is shining. The birds are singing. I had good kinky sex this morning when I got in from work. And it looks like I might have some design working coming in.
Yes, the weather is indeed good, and the birds are singing. I am pleased to hear you have some more work coming in, is this the local school project you were telling me about?
Yep.
And the sex? Lucy?
Oooh yes.
I thought you were wanting to move on from Lucy?
You don't wish to answer that question, that's ok, we'll go back to it. What made the sex kinky?
Now that would be telling.
I see. Was it violent?
You don't have to answer if you don't want to, it's just that I'm curious as to the redness of your knuckles and the scratch on your

neck.

Surely you're not trying to ruin my good mood Mal?

Maybe, with your permission, we can go back to it at another point, maybe our next session?

We'll see.

Do you want me to finish my story or not? Or do you have something else to ask me?

Very well then.

Twumbouha'el was no fool. He planned to stay underground for as long as possible. Maybe he even thought he could tunnel his way out and escape in a ship somewhere. He sent the circuit boards out first but by the time they got topside we were gone.

I wanted to know the strength of their forces, I figured he'd sacrifice thirty percent of the androids in the first skirmish and I knew the amount of capable and willing mecha fighters was far less. We brought our ships into orbit and fired down on anything that glimmered in the sun.

We had already blasted the landing platforms and the main ports from orbit and the rag tag band of ships they still possessed came under fire and fled once we'd located them. A few pleaded mercy with us as they surrendered.

Did you show any?

I sent word out to my allies, those who were faithful to me in the past; even though I hadn't been the commander of the fleet I still had a reputation and had gained many friends among the colonies and independent ships that travelled the regular trade routes. Any of the escaping ships were unlikely to encounter many trustworthy friends once word was out that Abadd'on Apolly'on was besieging B'eirhe in a war against rebel mechas.

Picking them off was easy. The hard part was always going to be getting to Twumbouha'el and his core group themselves.

Hiding on B'eirhe may have seemed like a good hiding place to begin with but the pitfall of his plan was that once found he had nowhere to run. Sure he could hide, but he couldn't escape, and I can be a patient man when the cause is great.

So you waited him out.

Yeah, danced a real tango for a couple of months. No power underground would have been grim. I've been in flight a few times when we've had system failure and time really drags and everyone gets agitated and uncomfortable, morale drops and then the cabin fever and infighting starts up.

Sure they had some generators but they had nothing underground that could produce the harness power of the solar collectors that ran in fields from the staging posts. We blasted those early on. No power, no communication.

No supplies?

They would have had enough in stores to last years but the fear of not knowing whether we would tunnel down to get them would have made the whole colony jittery. They would have to be on the lookout for the bugs and us, not to mention that any loyalty that remained with their allied residents would have been sorely eroded leaving them open to attack on all fronts.

It would have driven them mad; they would have been itching to get topside to engage us.

Unofficially a few renegades based out from K'avar helped us with our supply runs so we didn't need to let up on our siege forces. They would have joined in the fighting if they were allowed but they couldn't officially been seen in government marked ships aiding what in their eyes was a vendetta. Saying that, various mecha strongholds were targeted along the shipping lanes by unknown forces bearing the resemblance to military vessels. Mistrust and violent angst was building among the outer planets as the people turned slowly against the mechas in a similar way they had the circuit boards years before. Not that it would last, the mechas were after all cyborgs, partly human, so would always have a large contingency of human sympathisers.

For sport we sent regular skirmish patrols to the surface of B'eirhe to battle the indigenous life-forms, drawing them topside with pulse thumpers so that we could hone our skills and learn their weak spots so that we didn't get caught out by the worms and arachnids topside when battling with the mechas and preventing their escape.

Was there no chance for their winning the battle in your eyes?

There is always a chance in battle. No battle is won until the last soldier falls, or surrenders. No matter how much blood drips from the blade it only takes one strike to turn the tide.

Was I confident? Yes. But it was a confidence of pride and anger.

I took every precaution to ensure the odds were in our favour.

What was he like, this Twumbouha'el?

He was a good fighter but a poor tactician.

I meant as a person. Did you ever get to know him as a person?

His head was too full of sentimentalities. He was too sympathetic to the underdog; his wounds had softened his heart and the metal cage he wore couldn't hide it.

So you didn't try to get to know him?

He was a mecha.

So you were prejudiced against him from the start? You don't need to answer that, I get it, you were mistrustful of all things robotic. Tell me, is John Cade racist?

I'm sitting here with you aren't I?

So you would say you were not? Can John Cade not see then that the actions of Abadd'on would appear as racist?

You're trying to say that Abadd'on was the bad guy, that he was racist and set about on a personal campaign of ethnic cleansing.

Your words, not mine, but as you have used them I assume you have given this some thought and that the perception of the actions have not been far from your mind. So do you doubt the sincerity of Abadd'on? Do you regret, now as John Cade, the persecution of a minority race?

John Cade may view things differently from an Earthly perspective but Abaddon was correct in his pursuit.

Which one of you speaks?

There is only one here.

Do you recall what he looks like?

Twumbouha'el?

Of course. Abadd'on you see every day in the mirror. But do you recall the innocent?

I never stated he was innocent. And yes I recall his snivelling features: the scars across his burnt skin, burnt and melded into metal casts that were as much a part of him as his internal organs.

But his eyes, did you not look deep into his eyes?

Only when he died.

Why was that?

He said something as we stood upon the dunes, it confused me, so I looked him in the eye and then stabbed him in the stomach.

Just like that! Was that not a bit callous?

Not really, my blade broke on his armour. It pierced him but not deep.

You look confused.

I have missed out some chunks from my story.

There were many areas of the planet, or the habitable continent at any rate, where the mechas could seep out from. They dribbled out slowly at first, testing our reactions and hoping not to be monitored. We were ready for them. We allowed them to escape in enough numbers to lull them into a false sense of security, withdrawing visibly so that word reached the depths that we had left orbit.

Then we descended.

They were sitting ducks. Many welcomed the end. Our forces welcomed the battle. There was a bloodlust as we painted the sand crimson.

I waited aboard the ship. The men had orders not to harm their leader - he was for me. As soon as he was sighted I took an Arratet and swooped down. He stood there waiting for me. He knew the battle was lost to him but he stood willing to die with honour.

You speak as though you admire him.

He was my enemy, but he was still a man, and for the most part a good one. We had fought together side by side but he challenged my command and knew he would never be trusted aboard the ship again.

We fought hand to hand on the unsure footing of the dunes. It was a good fight and he died well.

What was it he said, when you looked into his eyes?

He was playing the politician, justifying his cause. I think he expected his death, and the loss of the other mechas of that sector, to send a ripple of sympathy across space. He wanted his words recorded I'm sure, for me to repeat them, but I never uttered them to a soul, and never will.

16

Blood red was the moon above shadowing the desert gloom and the seas of sand. Fireflies buzzing, darting from ear to ear from monstrous ships descended from the skies with gaping mouths to swallow the earth and burrow down to hidden caverns, metallic worms seeking life and meal underground.

Blackened charred remains of malfunctioning mechas twitching and sparking a spasmodic dance amongst laser fire, molten flesh singeing the pungent air.

His eyes blared fierce flame, one a diametric discord of mechanical muscle and algorithm, the other a single welling tear of pride and anger, stern and unswerving with conviction of purpose and a moral high ground that rose his stature upon the dune.

In Abadd'on's hand no longer did he hold a short blade but a spear with which to reach his foe. Strange evaporating waves of moisture blurred the mirage of the dream waving the muddied flesh and burnished Pa'as of Twumbouha'el's frame, his face half obscured behind his fused mask that reflected no emotion to his pointed threat.

Thunder echoed in the distance as lightning flashed an electrical storm across the desert plain.

"Do what you do, you cannot kill my spirit," mouthed the leader of the mecha rebellion.

Abadd'on lurched forward and pushed through the armour, drawing his sword and screaming with utter hatred.

Twumbouha'el made no reaction: no flinch of pain, no cry of regret, and his eyes fixed open as his head was wrenched from his body by the sharpest of blades skillfully swung.

The head rolled with a life of its own but no blood spilled from the cauterized wound from the torch he reholstered.

Silence reigned. No battle cries flung by the wind. The thunder abated and the lightning drew to the planet's core and held there. No breath was heard as the giant worm rose up under the shuddering sand engulfing the metallic walls of the dune that was Apolly'on and the two warriors that stood upon its sandy landing deck in a cell of dreamy change.

The body fell and the head rolled towards his feet where he stood braced ready for his opponent's spirit to attack. The eyes remained fixed but the lips moved and the sound carried to echo in his mind in the melodic tones of a faraway language: *It is a far better thing that I do, than I have ever done...*

Abadd'on echoed the final words himself as he finished the sentence, the words still whispering from his dry mouth as he lifted his head in the dream, his own voice bringing him to and trying to tear his guilty conscience from the cursed work of his hand, his waking mind lifting from the pillow in a jolt.

"Malachi, what poison have you worked into my mind to cause me to doubt?" he muttered to himself with disdain.

17

Vost played back yesterday's recordings, listening intently to the same phrase repeated over and over. The words, coaxed reluctantly from the lips of Cade after much persuasion, were bugging him. He recognised them, and they were taunting him.

He began writing down the words and then stopped and began typing them instead into the Google search bar. Within moments a list of references filled his screen confirming what he had harboured in the back of his mind but was unable to recall.

"Damn it! We've got him!"

Kapoor and McCaan looked up from the adjacent desk, looks of curiosity wrinkling their brows.

"We've got him!" Vost repeated. "He's finally slipped up."

18

Is this a comedy of errors, a twin tale, the same body in both lives?

I don't understand.

Are you a fan of literature, Mr Cade?

Not particularly, why?

Never read any of the historic greats?

Such as?

Dickens for example? Hemingway? Dumas? No? How about Shakespeare? How about the Holy Bible, the book of Revelation in particular?

I've never been much of a reader.

Really, I would beg to differ. I would like to pick up on this later John Cade. For now I would like to know more about your activities after you left the facility thirteen years ago. Where did you go? Who did you speak to?

What's with the books?
Later, John Cade, later.

"You've got to hand it to Okeno, that's a damn clever move, get him unsettled and then ask him about something else; he'll be on edge the whole hour session."

Kapoor and Vost both nodded their agreement at McCann's observation but both had opposing objectives in mind.

Vost was keen for Malachi to trip Cade up even further and for the whole story to unravel for what it really was, a story.

Kapoor was hoping for Cade to rebuke the accusations with a plausible explanation. After all these years of believing he wasn't prepared for his faith to be shattered. Besides, he knew it to be true - it had to be!

I drifted for a bit, hitchhiked, bummed around the country. I never truly disappeared off the map but I sunk to some low places. I'd lie under the stars at night pining for the old life I could never reach, that place I could never go back to.

So out of the two lives you preferred the one of a space warrior?

I guess. Why not? It was more exciting. This life is just full of ties and complications. The system is constrictive. On board the Apolly'on I was free to do as I willed.

I eventually meandered my way back down towards Somerset and fell in with my folks. I didn't want to be a burden on them, they had enough to deal with, what with Sam's issues. I stayed for the best part of a year.

They looked after you.

They didn't pressure me with questions but they gently tried to encourage me back to London to be near Gemma and the kids. So yes, they looked after me. They fed me and helped me out financially, but mainly they gave me the mental breathing space I needed. Plus I got to spend time with Sam and her family so that was a bonus. She was doing much better by then and we had some good times together.

It was good to run in the countryside; I probably could have taken up marathon running with the amount of land I covered. I didn't really use a gym at that point but kept my fitness and strength on the increase as I tried to attain my former stamina level.

You mean Abadd'on's.

Yes, of course.

Your connection with your parents, how did that make you feel towards your own children?

I missed them more I guess, especially being able to talk to dad, not about anything serious but just about the everyday, you know, and also with Sam, reconnecting with her made me think a lot about Mia and Toby. I guess moving back to London was a positive decision to reclaim that part of John Cade I'd lost: get my own place, get back to my old line of work, try to be more of a father, try to rebuild the relationship with Gemma.

But things didn't go to plan.

Oh they did, at first anyway. I got my flat and lined myself up with some work, and kept tabs on the kids, but...

But you couldn't bring yourself to reconnect with Gemma?

Abadd'on wouldn't let me. He just wouldn't let me get too close.

His mother never smiled anymore. She couldn't bear to have him nor his sister nearby. Meisha was too young to know any better and, though she cried to begin with at the separation from her mother, she soon forgot the bond she once had. As for Malachi, he acted as carer for his mother and parent to his sister. For three years he ran the home whilst his mother sat in an almost vegetative state.

It wasn't the trauma of the brutal gang rape by the soldiers that weakened her, nor was it her husband having his face blown away leaving her a widow and unable to fend for herself or her family. Her spirit and her resolve soon after the attack were of determination and of a faith that she had to be strong for her children, that God would not leave them like this but that he would provide for them. Then her body began to weaken and her mind grew desperate, and eventually, frustrated by the horrors of her life, she inwardly crumbled.

It was HIV Aids that got her in the end. Who knew how many of the soldiers she'd been raped by had carried the virus, but their actions that day left more victims in their wake than those that they buried. Her death was slow and agonising and Malachi had been there with her through it all, nursing her, feeding her and changing her soiled clothes, and in the end digging her grave.

He took Meisha on the streets after she died. Unlike John Cade he had no parents to flee to and no family to comfort him. Meisha was withdrawn and skinny, they both were. Malachi was too serious for a boy his age. He spent his days sat on the roadside begging for scraps, having lost any faith in the God of his mother and wishing he could die.

In some ways he could relate to how John Cade had felt. He had longed for his old life when both his parents were still alive, before the war struck their village. If it wasn't for his sense of responsibility in caring for Meisha, who couldn't yet care for herself, then he would have thrown himself in front of one of the many army trucks that often thundered down the Acholi Road into Gulu. He found small comfort that he wasn't alone: there was a growing community of displaced children filling the curbside careful only to be noticed by those who might help, for there was still a menace on the streets, a cold reaching hand that would grab at the kids old enough to carry a gun, and Malachi was nearing that age.

So Abadd'on was a dominating force. Was it his fear of you having responsibility for others that held you back from being a father and a husband?

Abadd'on was not scared of responsibility. He was a commander. The dog's bollocks.

You like that phrase.
In the same way you like shrugging your shoulders.
Whose responses are they, yours, or his?

They are all mine, I have told you, we are one.

"McCaan, is there a way we can get a two way communication

with Okeno that's not obvious?"

"You mean like the laptop we used to use?"

Vost nodded. He was getting frustrated with the direction Malachi was taking the conversation. He understood that Malachi was a counsellor and wanted to probe the depths of his patient's psyche and get him to acknowledge Abadd'on for the figment of his imagination that he was so that he could bring healing and restorative treatment, and he too wanted a similar outcome, only he also had other agendas which included a rapid conclusion to show what they all knew, or suspected, so that they could move in over Malachi and take it over as an official judicial investigation. All Vost needed now was the admission and then they could begin questioning where he got his information. He suspected Kennedy would try to take back control at that point, but honestly he didn't care for the long term outcome once it was handed over; his onetime intrigue and desire to seek the truth of a life beyond was destined to die with Cade's story.

Kapoor's mobile phone vibrated a brief burst announcing a text message had come in.

"I can probably get hold of a small two way earpiece," replied MaCaan, "the problem is they're silver and Malachi doesn't have any hair to cover it. Major General Kennedy would probably be able to requisition something better but I'm not in the position to beg."

"Ok, I get the hint. Email me the specs for what we need and I'll send it to Kennedy.

"Surj, anything of interest?" Vost nodded down to the mobile phone his colleague was staring down at and studying wide eyed.

"No, it's personal," Kapoor replied turning the screen off on the message from the Bansteads and hiding the phone from view.

It wasn't an easy fight. I know I've probably painted it that way but you have to remember we are primarily a terraforming fleet, not a military militia. Sure we are armed and trained, and probably the most renowned fighting force outside of the official army, but our role was to identify, secure, and colonise new planets.

We lost a lot of good men fighting the mechas, and some good women too.

We lost Kyte; she was my favourite.

Your lover?
My sparring partner.
She was a true warrior. She bore the blood of an Amazonian, so to speak. She feared no man. We don't have many female fighters among us, not good ones anyway, so she was a rarity.
We found her on a planet where the colonists had turned rabid, attacking each other with a madness brought on by a virus which had contaminated their water supply. She had been beaten and raped over and over and tossed aside as a toy. She could only have been about eight when we found her but by then she had already learned how to fend for herself; she killed two of my men by luring them close with her innocence and then tore at their throats with sharpened nails and gnashing teeth.
You look uncomfortable Malachi.
I am ok, John Cade, but our time is drawing to an end.
Did I hit a nerve?
Don't play games John Cade.
Of course, I apologise.
My point was that I liked Kyte. I know you think of me as heartless but I could have had that child killed. I saw potential in her, and I pitied her. I took her in and had her raised onboard the ship. Sure she had emotional baggage, we all did, we are a broken race after all, but she rose to the challenge and flourished. She was loyal to me and I favoured her.
Were you sad when she died?
I mourned her passing by funneling my anger onto the remaining mechas. She would have wanted it no other way.

19

"You didn't ask him the questions!"
Vost was fuming. He wanted answers but now he had to wait.
"It wasn't appropriate. I have to look after the mental welfare of my patient."
"You seemed to be looking after your own interests. He seems to be getting into your head a bit and pushing your buttons. Maybe you've been treating him too long."

"No, no, Mr Vost," Malachi protested by holding up his lightened palms in defence. His fingers were thick and stubby and told of a hidden strength behind the gentle persona of patience and slow time reactions that came from the Ugandan.

"Do I need to replace you?" Vost was serious, or at least his tone was, but it was a threat he hoped not to have to carry out.

"Mr Vost, please. John Cade is suffering a severe case of paramnesia, his memory is a confused distortion of fact and fantasy, even if he is aware that one of his personalities is a fabrication to just blurt it out would only be met with angry, possibly violent, denial. What I have done is plant the seed of doubt, given him a hint of where he may have built his fantasy so that he can challenge it himself so that when I confront him on it I won't be striking such a hard wall."

Louis Vost pondered this. It was the most he had heard the councellor say in one breath. He sat back down in his chair from where he had risen to challenge Okeno when he had entered the room through the dividing door.

"Is he still on medication?" asked Kapoor who sat pawing through notes on a laptop seemingly searching for anything he didn't yet know.

"He has a regular prescription of Zyprexa tablets which he has admitted to not taking. They make him too drowsy to concentrate, he claims. He did have a course of Olanzapine injections at one point (that's the active ingredient of the tablets) but he refused to continue with those, in fact his medical report shows that they made little difference anyhow. Even with the lack of medication I do not believe him to be totally non compos mentis."

"Do you think he could be violent?" asked Kapoor.

"I have not seen any signs of this in any of our sessions together, but obviously he is a very strong man so I would take all precautions not to provoke such a reaction from him.

"Mr Kapoor, you have a much deeper connection and history with John Cade, do you think he would manifest the violent character of Abadd'on?"

Kapoor stopped what he was doing and thought for a moment. His mind drifted back to the basement interview room all those years ago when he had seen the grimace of Abadd'on staring through the eyes of John Cade. He knew the alien within wasn't far from breaking through the surface.

"John Cade is too much of a calming influence. No, I don't believe he would be violent, not without reason."

"Helpful Surj," Vost quipped.

"Forgive me for saying so, Mr Kapoor, but you sound as if you believe his story."

Again Kapoor gave it thought before answering the mild mannered African.

"I admire his imagination and the character, and I believe John Cade to be a genuine person with many troubles."

"That's all well and good gentlemen but our objective here is to discover just how much of that character and imagination is his own creation and how much of it is leaked government secrets." Vost was not in the best of moods and the echoes of Kennedy's voice emanating from his own mouth was disquieting. He thought revisiting this case would be exciting but now he was here he found it frustrating as he rode the same merry-go-round that Kapoor had never let go of.

20

Lucy was ranting in the kitchen. He picked up on the odd word but cared little for the procrastinating foul mouthed, four lettered tirade that pummelled the air between the rooms.

Frustrated at being ignored she came out into the living room where he sat on the floor with his eyes closed meditating, or trying to.

She flicked on the TV as she plonked herself down on the sofa with her freshly made cup of tea. She hadn't even bothered to offer to make him one.

She echoed her own words, more for her benefit than for his; the whole one sided conversation was to satisfy her own disgruntlement. Something about a woman at work, a slag, a box breaking and a shelf collapsing, an argument, the slag and what she did in the storerooms on a night shift. He tried to block it out but she wasn't making it easy.

He was really regretting having let her keep the front door key.

He figured he'd give it about 30 seconds before she started on at him sitting on the floor ignoring her.

The dog padded round him seeking solace from the barking banshee on the couch; at least she wasn't kicking him today. He nuzzled his nose under his master's armpit until he had raised the arm high enough to slide under and flop onto his lap with a comforting arm drooping to a cuddle on his back.

The dog was a golden Labrador named Charlie. Toby had named him. He tried his best to find reason to keep his son engaged on the odd occasion when he came round, those rare appointed moments Gemma disapproved of but knew she'd be foolish to interfere with; she wanted Toby and John to get on but would prefer it be under her supervision rather than in a degraded council flat she'd never graced the door of. In the end it was the dog that drew him in and gave him cause to want to come round.

Charlie was five years old and John had had him for four of those years. He was a good companion, but he was no Dyson. Dyson had been calm, fun, and quiet. Charlie barked too much and jumped on the sofa and the bed. Often he would come in from work to find the dog sitting where it knew it wasn't allowed with a guilty upward turned eye and a high pitched whine. Dyson reminded him of the good times. Charlie reminded him of what he had lost.

The music channel flicked on grating with the silence of his mind but a welcome change from the sound of her voice. He didn't open his eyes but knew the song and the accompanying video, only due to her insistence on playing the same channel whenever she was round. The video was set in space, a black rapping crew aboard a ship flying between the stars seeking out a love affair with scantily clad alien vixens that looked more fitting in a porno than a pop video.

Then the unthinkable happened. Without prompting Lucy asked a question borne out of intelligent curiosity. He was so dumbstruck he opened his eyes.

"Say again," he asked.

"If space is as big as they say how come all the aliens only come from our galaxy? I mean, why do the aliens never come from other galaxies, there's loads of 'em i'nt there?"

"Have you not seen Star Wars?"

She looked at him blankly.

"'In a galaxy far far away...'!"

"Oh yeah. So they aint all from our galaxy then? So all the aliens are from other places, yeah? So does that mean we is the only ones in our galaxy, or solar system, or whatever it's called?"

"Lucy, humans have little imagination beyond the immediate. The universe is vast and we are but a tiny pin prick on the head of a tiny pin head. We are one life-form among many in our galaxy, and there are a multitude of galaxies in the universe with dense empty space in-between. Who knows whether there is other intelligent life in this one or any other. What I do know is that there is intelligent life in my world, and you're not it. Now shut up before I shut you up!"

His tone had been calm and level for the duration but the end comment had enough bite in it to draw tears down her cheeks and to choke her voice. With that he closed his eyes and focused his mind elsewhere.

21

How are you sleeping?
The disturbed violent dreams you only get on a blustery night.
Tell me about your dreams.

Everyone dies. I run across a sandy, gravelly landscape, there's a low hill in the distance. My men are running beside me. We are all barefoot but I don't feel the uneven ground that should be digging painfully into my flesh. We breach the hill and stop to assess the new terrain. There is a village, small and primitive, we are on the outskirts of it where a few farm houses are nestled peacefully minding their own business. We scamper up, ducking behind the hedgerows. Cages of chickens flap and rattle. Dogs sit up sleepily in the sun uncertain. I creep around to the cage and peer through at an aging woman milling about. My attention is disturbed by movement behind me: native wanderers returning, oblivious of our intrusion. They are dealt with swiftly and silently, their deaths signalling our assault. We all run forward seeking a victim, I find mine, an old man caught unawares coming out of a shelter, and he looks at me with a confused innocence. Hesitantly I stab him in the stomach. He falls back, my blade falling with him as I release my grip and stand there staring in shock that I have just killed someone in cold blood.

In another, I and a faceless colleague race up a dirt hill, a steep climb where we scramble with all our strength and speed. At the top there is a dusty road curved through a grassy bank, where a box cart sits waiting for us to jump in. We do so and begin our descent on the far side of the hill but the bend is too sharp and my passenger is propelled out and over the edge of the bank. I stop with my heart in my throat listening to his fall over the steep cliff and the eventual thump of his head striking solid ground below. I get out to view a vast empty plain where he lays a lonely still figure.

Can you associate these dreams, these situations, with things that Abadd'on has done?

In a way. Not so callous. Attacking villages that have harboured enemies. Losing flight partners in a firefight in our Arra-tets.

Your dreams are conflicted by your personalities. Abadd'on is a man with little conscience but a solid determination to complete a task. He has his own morals and standards which do not conjoin with those of John Cade. Your dreams are a blend. You, John Cade, are the conscience. Abadd'on is the warrior. In your dreams he knows what needs to be done but you are the one questioning whether it should be, questioning the end result: the loss of the innocent, the loss of a colleague. Abadd'on has those feelings too but he buries them. John Cade has a desire to be more than he is, so he creates it and lives it through Abadd'on. You two are one person but you have separated the two sides of your personality. Do you see this, John Cade? Do you understand?

You are wrong. I haven't created Abadd'on.

You said you never read Shakespeare, do you remember that?

Yes.

Yet you have quoted it.

What's Shakespeare got to do with anything?

Everything. 'Because the unconquered soul of Cade is fled.'

You look confused.

That's because I am.

John Cade was beheaded for treason. The quote was from

Henry VI part 2. You have mentioned various planets in the past, both to me and to Surjeet Kapoor, one of those you have named is Anjou, the land in France lost to the king in the play.

So what are you saying, that I've made up my whole personality based off of a Shakespeare play I've never read?

If you have truly never read it. There is enough coincidence to suggest you have: the soul's flight of the character which shares your name and the use of the name of a fallen land, and then there is the comment from Twumbouha'el.

What comment?

You quoted Twumbouha'el's last words as, and you stated it as a loose translation from your language: "It is a far better thing that I do, than I have ever done; it is a far, far better rest that I go to than I have ever known." Does that sound accurate?

You're reading it, you tell me. Is that what I said?

Is that what you said, John Cade?

You know it is.

Those are Twumbouha'el's last words to you?

Yes, but why do I feel like I'm about to be caught in entrapment.

This is not entrapment. I just want to confirm that I am not putting words in your mouth and that you hear yourself saying those words, the words of Shakespeare.

Rubbish! Pure coincidence! You're talking absolute...

Calm down John, please. I want you to listen to this line from Shakespeare, you can look it up for yourself afterwards if you don't trust what I'm telling you. It is from A Tale of Two Cities and it is the last sentence of the play: 'It is a far, far better thing that I do, than I have ever done; it is a far, far better rest that I go to than I have ever known.'

What, John Cade, have you nothing to say?

He said it as an accusation. He wanted to show that I knew nothing of humanity. He wanted to demonstrate that the mechas and the circuit boards knew more of humanity than the rest of the human race.

That, or John Cade/Twumbouha'el was confronting John Cade/Abadd'on with the failings of his own broken life.

You're saying I've imagined it all, that the different characters are just individual fragments of my own mind?

You tell me. If that were true, how would it make you feel?

What would you want to do about your life in light of it? Would this make you want to reconcile with your family?

But I don't remember reading those books.

Maybe you didn't, you may have heard the quotes within popular culture: Shakespeare is often quoted. The blow to your head during the Christmas Day incident may well have dislodged those memories, replacing them with new ones as your mind created an alternative reality for you. Who knows? The brain is a complex organ and we don't fully know what it is capable of. Some people have a blow to their head and wake up speaking a language they've never learned, or talk with an accent they've never heard. You wouldn't be the first casualty of selective amnesia, nor would you be the first to think you were someone else.

But... but... I felt the memories of Abadd'on before I hit my head.

22

The rendezvous was subtle. The redheaded female and the office geek passed instruction and information with the sleight of hand of master magicians.

The handover could have been done electronically without either party ever meeting, but to do so would leave a trail of sorts that could be traced back, and it would serve neither party for their link to be exposed to interested parties.

Theirs was a brief encounter, silent and public and in broad daylight where the natural passing of strangers, no matter how familiar to each other, could be explained away as coincidental. No sooner had they met than they had separated.

To the onlooker nothing was amiss. To the initiated and those familiar with the subjects maybe there would have been a hint of suspicion, but neither party needed to fear for no one was watching, and no one cared.

23

Malachi smiled to himself, his task was almost complete. He put down the phone and searched through his desk for Vost's number to update him on the latest development.

It was almost a week since he had confronted John Cade with the Shakespeare text, almost a week since the seeds of doubt had been planted and the coil in his head had begun to unwind.

He tapped out the number and waited for the ring on the other end. As he waited he found himself once again sat on the dusty curbside with Meisha huddled under his arm, the church truck pulling up with its multicoloured 'JESUS SAVES' banner slapped to the top of the windscreen. The smiling man in crisp clean clothes and gleaming teeth, an African with a calming and trusting expression strewn across his face, stepping out and crouching down in front of them. Meisha squeezed him tight, but that was ok, he didn't feel frightened of this man: he wasn't like the others, he could tell the difference. This was one of the good ones he'd heard rumour of.

"Are you from the IDP camp?" the man asked in English.

Malachi had picked up enough English on the streets of Gulu to know what he was referring to: the government set up displacement camps where all those fleeing the civil conflict had sought shelter. Malachi shook his head.

"You live here?" indicating to the street.

Malachi nodded.

"Mother? Father?"

Malachi shook a tearless head.

The man sighed then shook his head, then to Malachi's delight he smiled the most welcoming and friendly smile he ever thought possible on a human being.

"Would you like to go to school and sleep in a bed in a home with other children?"

Malachi nodded eagerly, his sister emerging slowly from under his armpit as she sensed her brother's body language begin to loosen up.

The man held out his hand and Malachi tentatively reached out to take it. All three of them stood as the man led them to the back of the truck.

It could all have ended up so differently: the wrong truck, the wrong destination, the wrong welcoming hand, but no, even at a young age Malachi had learned to be a good judge of character, he had learned to read deeper into the heart of man. Had he got it wrong that day he and Meisha could have ended up as child soldiers or sexual toys for some perverted group of low life in a land where the law couldn't trace them, slaves to some lost land hidden deep within the jungle never to resurface to the wakeful world where the plight of the abandoned children is rarely noticed. The decision to climb into that truck that day had hit the reset button on his life, for the both of them.

"Louis Vost," murmured the voice on the other end of the phone.

"Hello, Mr Vost, it is Malachi Okeno. I have some very good news."

"Malachi, great. What is it?"

"I have just come off the phone to John Cade and he is in a very positive frame of mind with regards to accepting his situation. He has said that he has spoken at length with his wife and she has confirmed that he used to read Shakespeare, in fact she still has his books at home, quite a selection she tells me; he was well into his classics: ancient philosophy and religion, mythology and historical warfare - he was a well-read individual as it turns out, he even took classes in classical studies and Latin for a short period. She described him as being a frustrated intellectual who liked to quote stuff to make himself appear more superior than he actually was."

"Ah, that is a turn around. Why did we not think to look into this before?" He said it to himself as much as to Malachi and neither felt the need to answer the question; they both knew the investigation had always been too focused on the alien rather than the man. "It sounds like he's always had an issue with his identity."

"My thoughts exactly."

"So where does that leave us?"

"We must give him time to adjust to this new reality. It will be hard for him, he has dedicated almost a decade and a half of his life, which has destroyed his family, to something that he has made up. He will be suffering an enormous amount of guilt and will need the acceptance of his wife and children in order to adapt. Only then will you be able to ask your questions."

"Are you saying we need to put him on suicide watch?"

"I don't know that we need to be that concerned, I hope at least, but it would be prudent to ensure I continue to meet him and guide him through this transition."

"Good. Keep on top of it and keep me informed. If we need to add in any more sessions then we will do. I'll let Kennedy know."

Vost hung up the phone and Malachi put his end down slowly, pleased that he was able to make a difference in John Cade's life.

24

The doorbell went and Toby was quick to answer it thinking it was one of his friends. The door swung open and he stood there with mouth hung open for a moment before closing it and nodding a silent but awkward greeting.

"Mum!" he shouted back into the house, unmoving with the door hung wide and gaping.

Gemma came to the door wiping her hands in the darkness of the hallway as she emerged from the kitchen where the smell of chilli wafted through to the rest of the house. The last two steps were slowed as she caught sight of the visitor stood on the doorstep.

Toby ducked under his mother's arm as she gripped hold of the open door and he escaped back into the house to avoid a potential confrontation at the unannounced visit.

"John," she said confused but not at all upset by his presence, "you should have called first."

"I know, I'm sorry. Gemma, I..." John choked, a tear streaming down his face, "I'm so sorry."

She stepped forward and drew his head down to her shoulder into a hug. Within moments he was sobbing, his arms slowly reaching around behind her to hug her back.

Part Three

The Dawn Of Things To Come

Id quod circumiret, circumveniat
(What goes around comes around)

1

A ghostly half moon hung shrouded in yellow, the man peering out of its empty dark pits circling coyly, mouthing 'boo' across the sky at the ants that scuttled about down below in the blue. The cold of the night had seeped in a chill through the open bedroom window and had awakened his bladder to his own body weight laying upon it, leaving him to stir uncomfortably. He changed position so that he no longer lay on his stomach, tossing and turning trying to slip back into that restful place where his mind would drift off again, his body curling into the warm patch of the bed and avoiding the cold edges where his frame hadn't lain. It was no good, he knew he wouldn't be able to get back to sleep until he'd dealt with the problem; too often this was happening now, whether it was age or too much caffeine in the day he wasn't sure, but he was getting wearisome of waking night after night with the burning need to pee. Getting up to deal with it wasn't his main concern, that was just inconvenient. It was the dreams he awoke from that plagued him.

Regularly now he awoke from dreams that were forcing his mind awake rather than the cold and the desire to urinate. The dreams, the images, the buried memories were taking on a life of their own as they screamed out defiantly not to be forgotten.

Even now, with a blurry cloud hanging over one eye as he walked through the dark of the apartment, his feet drunkenly stumbled the path of his hallway on automatic as his mind echoed the last images before waking. The clouded eye was barely managing to stay open as it fought the wakefulness of light penetrating from the bathroom allowing the other to see and adjust to the contours of the room and the obstacles within as he, in a weighty stupor akin to the fogginess of intoxication, fumbled his way across to the toilet.

He hung his head and allowed the fluid to flow from his body, keeping half an eye on the direction of travel as his mind searched for the rapidly fading memory.

It had been a month since he had reconnected with Gemma and Toby, although Toby was still suspicious and Mia, now away at university, was reluctant to engage with him for similar reasons, as she rightly sought to protect herself from what she saw as inevitable disappointment. Gemma was warming to him, and he to her, but they were far from a happy couple. They were still married, and even though estranged for so long, it was clear that she had still held a torch for him all these years, but they had a long way to go before he would be in a position to move back in.

His mind was too unsettled. Abadd'on still haunted him. It didn't matter that he was coming to terms with his...

"Insanity," he said aloud cutting off his own thoughts, purposely blocking out the intrusive thoughts of the alien within. He fought hard to keep the image of his alien wife from his mind, that alien woman who was more an administrator of his concubines than an emotional crutch to his command. He felt his chin rest on the body armour of the Pa'as outer suit as he sat in the loading shuttle awaiting a transport drop to the planet surface.

He snapped his eyes open to realise he was still peeing with his head drooped and his chin resting on his chest. He shook his head and his manhood as he finished off.

He washed his hands and splashed his face and stared into the mirror to see Abadd'on staring back at him grimacing. He tore himself away and walked back to the bedroom, all the while feeling as though someone was walking behind him, hovering over his shoulder. He wandered into the bedroom and clambered under the duvet to the sound of a high pitched groan.

Lucy pulled the cover up over her shoulder with her back to him.

Damn, he thought to himself, *she's still here. Why the hell have I let her stay again?*

2

"All I can tell is what they've reported."

The General sat in his office leaning back in his chair with one hand on his forehead in a thinking pose and his other hand holding the phone to his ear whilst Lauren Kenny at Sentinel's HQ sat patiently waiting for him to digest the news. She was the project liaison with the government for Sentinel but Kennedy was often frustrated by her lack of fine details as she always tried to give him the minimal information. He got it, it was a control issue: Sentinel, although appreciative of the extra government funding, quite naturally wanted to keep the bulk of their observations and discoveries to themselves.

Kennedy flung his seat forward to the desk and picked up a pen.

"Ok, give me their number."

"What? Er, you mean for the observatory? In Hawaii?"

"No, in Timbuktu! I want all of the information, Miss Kenny, and if you don't have it then I want to speak to the people that do, so give me the number, and I don't want some obscure office that doesn't get answered, give me their direct mobile numbers."

There was a moment of hesitant flapping on the other end as the flustered Miss Kenny searched for the direct number. She read it out and Kennedy jotted it down and then hung up arrogantly and without any pleasantries.

He dialed the new number immediately, it was a long mobile number with an international dialing code.

"Marcus Banstead," said the English voice on the other end.

"Dr Banstead, this is Major General Kennedy calling from the Ministry of Defence in London. I've been passed a report from your employers, Sentinel. As you're probably aware we have a controlling interest in the area of space you are looking at."

"Ah, General Kennedy, yes." There was an annoyed hesitation on the other end. "I wondered how long it would be before someone got in contact. To be honest with you I thought it might be the Americans who would call first."

"You may be on American soil but this is a British project. You were supposed to be looking at a specific area in the Lyra constellation were you not?"

"Yes, that's right, and we are. But I don't know whether you are aware but we were originally set up to look at the Cygnus constellation. We calculated that we could focus on Lyra and continue to train one of the smaller telescopes on Cygnus. After some arguments with Sentinel we eventually came to an agreement on this."

"So you've had no sign of what we've requested you to look for?"

"Well to be frank General..."

"It's Major General."

"Sorry, Major General. We weren't given enough information of what we were searching for. Looking for a gravitational distortion that typifies a planet out of alignment isn't as easy as it sounds. The light we see from that distance is from stars, such as Deneb, not planets and we can only see the time in space that distance allows. Besides that there are a number of nebulas in the system that make long term searching quite difficult, for example the Veil Nebula, which as you can imagine from its name casts a shadow over much of the space we wish to observe."

"Very well, so what have you seen?"

"Well, nothing. Not in Lyra, nor in Cygnus."

"Get to the point Banstead!"

"Sorry, yes, of course. Our telescope obviously sees everything in the path of where it is looking but is focused on a distant point. If we are looking at a bright star, say Vega or Deneb for example, then we are unlikely to have anything obscuring its view, anything passing in between will be quite obvious. Momentarily something blocked our view, we don't know how long for because we didn't notice the distortion for quite a while as our main focus has been on Lyra as requested. There was something on the edge of our solar system in direct line of sight of Cygnus, something that hadn't been there before."

Kennedy leant forward further on his desk.

"What was it?"

"Well we don't know. It just shows up as a blur slightly obscuring Deneb, and reads as an anomaly in our data, which indicates it is relatively close. Nor do we know how long it had been there. But it is gone now. We can't find it - it just vanished."

"Another planet?"

"No, it was too small and too fragmented. It wasn't a solid mass. If it hadn't been so close and blocking out Deneb's light we probably wouldn't have noticed it at all."

"Was it moving?" Kennedy gulped audibly, he couldn't believe he was asking the question.

"Moving?" Marcus Banstead seemed confused by the question as though it had never occurred to him. "No, I don't think so. I mean yes, everything in space is moving, but no, no more so than everything else I suppose, but I don't know for sure, I would have to go back and analyse all the data, but no I don't think so."

"But it's gone so it must have moved?"

"Well, yes," Marcus hesitated, "from that perspective you would be correct, but from our perspective we track the movement of planets and stars, we're not equipped to track anomalies that just appear and disappear. We can record them and theorise around them but we can't give a definitive."

"I thought your initial project directive was to search for alien life?"

"Yes, of course, but only within the parameters and restrictions that our equipment permits."

Kennedy took a breath of patience as he tried to accept that he was dealing with a flaky scientist. "And where do you think it went?"

"There is no way of telling. All we can do is keep looking."

"You do that. I'll be sending you a liaison officer to monitor your progress. I want to know as soon as you see anything more."

"Yes, of course." Kennedy could hear the unspoken objection in the scientist's voice but ignored it. He wasn't interested in his personal opinions or objectives. They worked for him now.

He hung up the phone. He had other calls to make.

3

As dinner parties go this one could have been better. Philip Whitehouse was sat at the corner placement of the table with his wife sat opposite, two spaces across. It was an unfortunate placement for he usually relied upon his wife considerably should he be placed on the outskirts of conversation, or conversations, as was the case with multiple lines of flow titillating his ear as he struggled to catch the odd word snatched from each as they cut lines across each other. His wife, Carol, gave him an occasional sympathetic glance, lingering long enough with a questioning care to check he was holding up. Each time he would nod appreciatively in a lie; he wanted nothing more than to leave.

The formalities of being a guest at such dinner parties were something he always struggled with and could not, no matter how hard he tried, conform to. It had been the host's decision to separate the partners, both business and marital, in order to break from the subtle mix of shop and pillow talk which tended to filter in as private conversations, the knowing words and gestures that were made to those sat next to each other; that was all well and good but it created an environment where conversation was louder than usual as those very same people who had been separated just talked all the louder to be heard by those they had been purposely separated from. For Philip Whitehouse, who struggled on any occasion to distinguish focused sounds in amongst any background noise, this scenario was a nightmare, leaving him unable to tune into any one conversation long enough to join in; those with the loudest voices that naturally carried through the candlelit atmosphere of the room stealing his attention no matter where along the twelve place settings they were sat. He smiled and nodded in reaction, along with everyone else, but on the whole kept quiet hoping no one would ask him a direct question where his absence from the conversation would be unveiled. Now and again his name would be mentioned and his mind would automatically try to tune in in that narcissistic way we all perk up when we think we're being talked about.

Healy, a nerdy looking fellow who worked for a private enterprise but somehow always seemed to turn up at governmental functions, was sat to his right and was in deep conversation across the table with the husband of the chairman of the Bank of England. They were animated, reminiscing about a corporate fishing trip in Canada they had apparently both attended some years ago. Whitehouse smiled at a private joke he didn't understand or hear properly. He marvelled at the ease in which Healy seemed to engage with different members around the table; having only spoken general pleasantries to him briefly at the beginning of the meal Whitehouse had found him aloof and mysterious and felt insignificant in the sense that Healy was there with an agenda of his own and he wasn't part of it. Whitehouse had brushed it off without offence, that was politics after all, and besides, he couldn't be sure that it wasn't just a reaction to his own lack of focus in the conversation.

A vibration in his pocket distracted him. Ordinarily he wouldn't answer his mobile phone on such an occasion but he welcomed the intrusion, besides he was on call. He took the phone out of his pocket and held it above the table cloth so that those around him could see it was ringing silently. He pressed the call button. "Whitehouse," he said with an air of upper class command. Something of importance was said on the other end, not that it mattered to his actions for they would have been the same had it been a random sales call or a wrong number.

He asked the speaker to hold for a moment then made his excuses at the table, placed his napkin on his plate and slipped sideways from the table, for once glad of his place setting at not having to squeeze passed anyone. Carol gave him a concerned look and he returned one of his own that only a long term married couple could pass with total reading and understanding: it said 'we have to go'. She nodded back and went about preparing to end her conversation with excuses that Philip was being called away to the office. They would all understand, that was the nature of his job as Defence Secretary.

Whitehouse stepped out of the room into the hallway and closed the door behind him, knowing that, whether the call was important or not, when he reentered the dining room it would be to give his apologies and to fetch his wife.

He put the phone to his ear knowing the person on the other end would be waiting patiently for him.

"Major General Kennedy, I trust this is important for you to be calling me directly and at this hour...I see...I'm on my way, be ready to brief me fully when I get there."

He hung up the phone with a worried expression riding the ripples of his face that hadn't been there before he took on a cabinet role. This was new. This was something he'd never had to deal with before. This was a call he was pretty sure his predecessors had never received, or if they had it wasn't recorded in any files he had access to. A sense of excitement and fear shook the phone still held in his hand. This was big.

4

Fiona Roberts stood observing from the far side of the viewing platform overlooking the bleached enamel dish. The wind was blowing and her long maple locks were waving back at the giant dormant eyes behind her on the mountain top.

The Bansteads were below in the car park arguing, their voices raised but not enough to cut across through the wind to reach out to her. She didn't need to hear anyway, she knew what they were arguing about: this time little Timmy was the problem, again. If it wasn't childcare (being so passionate about their work, it left them with a constant battle over who was doing the home schooling and the babysitting) then it was the intrusion of 'the government spy' in their midst and the hijacking of their project. She understood both arguments, even sympathised with both, despite she being 'the government spy', but she had the benefit of being outside of the situation and was able to see the huge bonuses to living the life they had. Very few could claim to live in a paradise with exclusive access to a mountain top observatory, with constant government funding (albeit by proxy through Sentinel) far longer than their originally pitched project life-term and parameters, in a job that was their life dream, spending each day together (which for some might be a strain but for the Bansteads, who clearly adored each other, it was a joy), and with a fit, healthy and handsome six year old son who hung on their every word. Yet even with a life like that the troubles and turmoil that teettered on the edge of every marriage bubbled over into conflict, and ever more, so it would appear, since she had arrived on the scene.

She was envious of their life, and why not, she was a lonely spinster in her late thirties. It wasn't that she was bad looking; she attracted enough attention in the bars and boardwalks down by the bay. She had a good job travelling around picking up various confidential jobs for the Foreign Office and the MOD, and spoke no less than five languages fluently and held a wealth of knowledge on various subjects due to the study needed to undertake the wide range of contracts she was presented with. Yet with all her intelligence, beauty, and self-sufficiency, she was lonely. Had she flirted with Marcus Banstead in the few days since her arrival? Sure she had, but only professionally to keep him on side for friendly information should it dry up and become frosty at some point in the future. Did she want to take him to bed? She wouldn't say no, but she was no home wrecker and she wasn't that desperate to be fool enough to get stuck in that sort of trap; she knew too well the implications both personally and professionally.

Julie didn't like her and for that matter she couldn't blame her. For years she'd had the undivided attention of her husband but now he shared the observatory with a mysterious good looking redhead whilst she was at home playing housewife and mother. The fight to switch roles more often was becoming fierce. If they and their work had to be observed and the data verified by an external examiner then Julie preferred she were the one stuck in the office and not him.

All that aside she was here to do a job and the latest results, coupled with what she knew to be happening with Kepler, were fascinating, if not a little frightening.

5

Surjeet Kapoor sat over the bureau desk in his study writing in his journal, his glasses fixed firmly to his nose as he peered through them. His eyesight had always been a little vague but now age was deteriorating his vision, especially in one eye, almost as though he'd suffered a traumatic blow to blur the optic nerves. He'd had no such trauma; his life wasn't so dramatic.

He put his pen down and sat back in the chair thinking. He had no worry of distraction from his thoughts; he lived alone with no wife or kids to rattle the fabric of the cave he had created. He kept the lights dim, the glow from the computer the only permanence as it monitored the information he collated in his obsession about the world of V'hihyon.

Things were happening now. He could see the pieces of the puzzle coming together. There was an imminence to the train that was coming into the station and he was lined up on the platform ready to greet it. With all the information he was able to tap into he knew Cade would have been able to do the same with the right contacts, but he wasn't fooled. He didn't share Vost's views, though he was happy to use him to remain on the inside.

At the beginning, all those years ago, he would never have thought he would have these views or live this life, but things had changed and his eyes had been opened to the truth. If Vost knew the extent of his obsession and lack of impartiality to the role he would never have invited him back in; this was his secret, his guilty wonder.

He lent forward again and picked up his pen once more and began to write: *Something big, an event, we either look forward to it or dread it, yet it's an event in our inevitable future nonetheless. There's a sensation that accompanies it, a butterfly flapping its wings gently in the pit of our stomach, waiting patiently for the wind to beat harder against the current of time as the event approaches. Then it's there before us and that well of bitter sweet saliva builds beneath the tongue to then dry up to parched desert lands as the heart races and the blood pumps and the skin shrinks pale at the pinnacle of time, which stands still, momentarily waiting at the head of the downward dip as the lead car pulls along gravity's arc beyond the point of no return, no brakes, no turning back, the ride is in motion, the starting pistol fired, the time, the event, the unavoidable is here, just as we knew it would be but never thought or truly imagined we'd get to live through or experience. We just sat back and watched others go through it, it always happened to someone else, their story intersecting with ours as though we're observers not participants. Yet we know that day will come, but we never prepare for it. It's always a day far off in the future, as though it will never come. Yet it does. Death, if not something else.*

On the other side of the event we blink back as though to a dream, it happened, it was experienced, it was felt, and it will be shared, at least by me.

When they come, oh what a glorious day it will be.

He closed the journal and locked it away. His secret thoughts were nothing more than gibberish he felt compelled to write down, but it was information, and he knew information could be dangerous; information was his work and his life, he knew better than to leave it just laying about. He thought about the day he anticipated, the day he dreamt about, the day he had fantasised about for years: it was coming, the signs were there, and he could barely contain his excitement.

6

Philip Whitehouse had a pile of paperwork on his desk that needed his attention but would have to wait, the box file that rested beneath his hands in the middle of the desk was more important, not that he understood it all, despite the hours he'd already devoted to meetings trying to grapple with the fine details. There was all too much information too fast and his mind was struggling to take it in. It wasn't that it all went over his head, it was more that it was unexpected, a revelation he wasn't prepared for, and so hadn't quite digested it enough to configure a justifiable plan of action.

He told his secretary to hold all calls for the next hour, especially if it was the Prime Minister, and that, unless it was vitally important, he wasn't to be disturbed. He didn't know how much the Prime Minister was in the loop but he wasn't ready to explain or debrief him in any detail just yet. He wanted time to read through the reports and wrap his mind around the situation Kennedy had presented him with.

He opened the file and pulled out a few of the loose documents on top, then thumbed through a bound report before shuffling the pack and delving in again. He settled on one detailed glossy report in one hand and Kennedy's abbreviated summary in the other. The glossy text with its highlighted and diagrammed notes was clearly well financed and appeared to be co-authored by NASA, Sentinel, the NSA and MI6. He flicked through a few pages until he found something to cross reference with Kennedy's summary.

NASA's Kepler Space Telescope had been launched in 2009 and was specifically charged with the task of finding Earth-like worlds orbiting distant stars in the Constellation Lyra. It had turned up only a handful of planets that could possibly support life within an habitable zone, but it had produced some magnificent images that had wowed the scientific community and captured the hearts of many a would-be astronomer. But why focus on Lyra? The answer to that was clear, as Kennedy explained in his notes:

Kepler had been primed to look elsewhere originally but information a few years before its launch resulted in a collusion of authorities to redirect it in search of a specific object. On a couple of occasions Kepler had identified an object with a light signature which could have resembled what they were looking for, but space is a vast area, and without a definitive set of coordinates none of the distant discoveries could be verified as ident to what was being searched for. And so the search continued whilst the boffins studied the data and scrutinised the images.

This Whitehouse understood. What confused him was the Mauna Kea Observatories and where they fitted in. He read on, pulling a stapled document from deeper in the box file.

Fiona Roberts stood alone in the office with Marcus sat before her. She had emailed the detailed findings of the report over to Kennedy's office after summarising the latest over the phone. The Bansteads were frayed, the threads of their paradise tapestry beginning to unravel. Sentinel was breathing down their necks amid concerns about how much the government interference was now eclipsing the control of their projects, directing the pressure downhill at the Bansteads in frustration at their being battered down from the high reinforced walls manned by the heavy artillery of the MOD's office archers.

They seemed to be getting it from all angles. The cam belt on their Chrysler Jeep broke half way up the hill leaving Julie stranded for hours waiting for recovery, all the while her thoughts split between worrying how she was going to collect Timmy from school at the end of the day (not really a school but a playgroup for lonely home educated kids to integrate and socialise with other children their own age) and about what her husband was doing all alone at the observatory with the hussy spy - gone were the days when a trip up the mountain was filled with the expectation of what was on the scope. Then there was the credit card, it had maxed out somehow causing the overpayments from the bank to go out before the mortgage on the beach villa they had overstretched on four years ago, subsequently leaving them temporarily in default. On closer scrutiny it seemed the card had been cloned, but it became apparent quite quickly that it wasn't the only one and that they were the victims of identity theft.

Unfortunately the bank was still claiming they were liable until it had been investigated properly - how they had come to that conclusion they couldn't fathom but it caused a big financial black hole and a tornado resting upon their wind battered abode. Even the weather seemed against them as the natives battered down the hatches for the incoming hurricane that was a day out on the pacific. To top it all, little Timmy wasn't sleeping which meant they weren't sleeping, the boy was reacting to the discord in the family home and the arguments that were getting more and more common place.

Fiona had seen it enough times to know that only so much of the Bansteads misfortune was coincidence, and the rest was contrived. How much finances and security and reliability they would be able to cling on to once their reputation was discredited and torn to shreds was anyone's guess. It wasn't all a lost cause for them, not yet anyway, depending on how it all played out.

She looked down at the new data coming in that Marcus sat over scrutinizing as he concentrated hard on identifying the blurred printouts of multicoloured blotches and comparing them to the fresh input coming in on the computer screen direct from the twins.

She brushed her long auburn locks, which were darkened by the dim light, back passed her ear and lent forward with feigned interest, her cleavage hanging forward and slightly exposed more than usual as she bent down to his shoulder. He purposely tried not to notice, keeping his hands busy by shuffling the printouts to draw his eyes down away from her distraction. She reached forward to reach for one of the papers.

"Is that the same as that?" she asked pointing from the paper to the computer screen.

He withdrew his hand sharply as she brushed over it as she tapped the printout. Clearing his throat nervously he replied in the positive without making eye contact. She smiled to herself; the damage was done.

David McCaan had the room set up as usual. It was a standard routine now. He ensured the boss was happy that all was set up: microphones and cameras all working and no glitches on the computers, mobiles on silent, that sort of thing. His role was basic in the grand scheme of things: he was generally the tech guy who was privy to a bizarre set of circumstances and information which on the surface sounded ludicrous were it not for the interest from up high and the further dissemination of classified information coming back down to them. Louis Vost wasn't fazed by any of it at all, at least he appeared not to be, but then he'd played this game before.

Vost was always in on time and fully briefed and in the loop but he was increasingly showing signs of getting frustrated with the lack of pace that things were progressing at as he dropped hints of regretting taking on the job and of wanting to get back to his comfy retirement, well as comfy as it gets on a civil service pension.

Surjeet Kapoor was the one he was finding irritating. For some reason Kapoor kept parading in just on the cusp, never truly late but cutting it fine all the same, and always on edge and jittery. He knew Vost had picked up on it, he'd seen him watching Kapoor out of the corner of his eye curiously. He knew the two had worked together before but from what he had observed of Vost's reactions Kapoor hadn't always been this flakey. It had to be said though, that Kapoor was a deep cavern of information, you had no need of the computer files when Kapoor was around, he'd swallowed the encyclopedia and then written a few extra chapters of his own when it came to anything related to their subject matter of John Cade.

For all its mystery and fascination, and despite all he'd heard and witnessed whilst sat in the room as part of the team, to David McCaan the job was just that, a job. He had no real interest in delving in deeper, nor did he care much for the outcome. It was a better job than most which kept him free of the bureaucracy of some of the political situations he was usually ordered to monitor, at least this one so far seemed unlikely to involve any big scandal.

His favourite part of any of the consultation days without doubt was the early mornings when he would come in to set up and find Malachi sat in his office with the adjoining door open waiting for them. He would wander in to pass pleasantries over a morning coffee and the two would laugh and joke about the different ways of the world and put things to rights in their own minds. They would have good conversation and he felt they both started off the days well enjoying each other's company.

Of all those involved in this whole project he liked Malachi the most. It was just a shame that things were soon to come to an end and that one way or another John Cade would have judgement passed upon him.

"We've got Kepler, we've got Hubble, James Webb and Spitzer up in the heavens as well as having Arizona's LBT and Hawaii's Keck Observatory on the ground, and you're telling me we don't have enough data! Identify it and get back to me!"

With that Kennedy slammed down the phone. Fiona Roberts had told him pretty much the same thing but there was no way he would dare talk to her in the same manner, she was too valuable a source and he trusted her to relay the relevant intel when it became available, besides they'd had that brief thing between them which he hoped one day to revisit.

His anger was vented at Derek Beauchamp, the fuddling CEO of Sentinel who was supposed to be collating the various strands of data from the collection of space telescopes which the numerous Western governments and space agencies had a stake in; ordinarily it would be Lauren Kenny that he dealt with but it appeared the liaison had decided she no longer wished to speak with Kennedy directly. Between the various agencies something significant had been identified as moving on the outskirts of our solar system with the potential of cruising through the system towards us, but Beauchamp wasn't competent enough to name it for what it was, and without a verified authentic label by an official authority he couldn't take it to the Permanent Secretary. Even the Defence Secretary was hesitating, the hot air flapping silently, whispering down the corridors of Whitehall as Philip Whitehouse froze over what he'd been presented with. He would have to call him again. So far they'd managed to keep the Americans in the dark as to what they were sitting on; they could see the same data but they didn't have access to Cade so had nothing to join the dots, but now they were requesting explanations, no, demanding them. NASA had put Kepler up to search for planets back in 2009 but it was the UK's request through Sentinel which dictated where it pointed.

He shook his head frustrated.

"The bloody idiots have no idea how serious this is," he grumbled to himself, then reached for the phone to make another call.

Philip Whitehouse was on the defensive. How Kennedy had him on the back foot he didn't know but his lack of understanding and his uncertainty of how to proceed left him in a state of confusion that he could only answer with a politician's bluff of avoidance.

"We need to take action," Kennedy insisted angrily on the other end of the phone.

"Of course, I agree, but we must seek verification of the facts before we take this further."

"How much verification do you need? Why do you think we've been watching out for this?"

"Of course, you have had your priorities and these have been set by my predecessor as part of a different government, so I apologise if I am still a little vague of the origins of all this. Now as far as I am concerned we are looking at the appropriation of stolen intelligence from an unknown source..."

"The source is not unknown, nor are the origins of the matter, but all that is irrelevant now. To be frank I couldn't care less about the source."

"Please Major General, it is important I have a full understanding if you wish me to brief the Cabinet."

"I don't want you to just brief the Cabinet, I want you to call a bloody Cobra meeting!"

"Major General, please calm down. Remember who it is you're speaking to! As I'm sure you can appreciate I cannot call a Cobra meeting on the information you have provided as the threat has yet to be fully assessed. You only have one source and that is sketchy at best, and it does come across to me as very much a sole agenda - your agenda. I don't think I need to remind you of your rank and position, and that you are in no position to make such a demand of the government, such a request needs to come from your superiors."

"Need I remind you, Mr Whitehouse, though I be only a Major General, I have been placed in command of a special task force answerable directly to the Defence Secretary, which puts you immediately in my firing line."

Whitehouse took a breath in response to the calm statement Kennedy had just delivered with a tone of malice, warning he was prepared to rock the boat if necessary. This wasn't going his way.

He needed to deflect to buy himself some more breathing space.

"This John Cade character, where do we stand with him?"

"He's irrelevant."

"How so?"

"He's insane. We haven't managed to discover how he came by his information but he's verifiably a loon. Granted he is the reason we had the telescopes redirected, out of curiosity and as a precaution, but what we have now has no bearing on him."

"Why are you so dismissive of him, not so long ago he was integral to your investigations?"

"Of finding a leak in our intelligence, yes. What we have now is not an internal intelligence matter. This is pure coincidence that we've spotted something."

Whitehouse recapped quickly the files he'd read. "So, all those telescopes haven't seen anything to confirm this man's story but by chance have seen something else?"

"Precisely."

Whitehouse looked at the box file he'd had sprawled out on the desk and wondered why Kennedy's written summary report hadn't said just that, maybe it did, maybe he was just flustered by the background noise.

"The intel regarding this object, is it contained?"

"For the moment, but that's only because it's no longer there and we've been quick to analyse and control the flow of data, but it won't be long before it's picked up by our counterparts."

"How long?"

"Don't think you've got days to sit on this. You need to move now." The urgency was returning to Kennedy's voice.

"Crap," he said aloud without thinking. "When you say it's not there anymore...?"

"We can't see it. It was there briefly, just long enough for us to spot it, but we don't know where it is now."

"Double crap."

"Precisely, make the call," demanded Kennedy again before putting down the phone at his end.

Whitehouse looked at his receiver. Despite Kennedy's insistence he knew what the response was likely to be from the Cabinet; there just wasn't enough information and what was being presented was inconclusive, and he for one wasn't prepared to make himself look a prat in front of the Prime Minister, not based on the ramblings of a soldier with an attitude problem and an apparent blinkered view of his objective, and certainly not when there were whispers of a Cabinet reshuffle in the offing.

You look distraught today, John Cade.
Tired is all. Quit with the curious puppy dog look, you don't need me to spell it all out, you've got it all sussed anyway. Tell me I'm wrong.
Naturally I have ideas on what is going on in your troubled mind, John Cade, but I don't always assume I am right, nor do I sit in judgement. Please, enlighten me as to what is troubling you. Maybe I can help. Maybe just talking about it will lift the burden from your weighted shoulders.
Malachi, I don't know what I'm doing. With Gemma I mean.
Well why don't you tell me how you feel about her, and the kids.
I'm not a bad person, really I'm not
But...
But I've kinda got this Jekyll and Hyde thing going on.
I love my wife, at least I think I do. No, I'm sure I do. The kids too. And I'm trying hard to be the man I used to be: the husband I once was and the father I should have been. And yes, I get that things will never be perfect 'cause there's a lot of baggage and hurt and I simply wasn't there for any of them. At least Gemma understands: she knew me before all this, but for the kids all they've ever known is this crazy old man who should have been there for them but instead screwed up their lives. Damn, it's amazing they've turned out as good as they have, and that's all due to Gemma. So I'm trying hard to make things right, to rebuild our relationship, to cast out the demons.
Is that how you see him now?
No, not quite, but I do see him as a destructive influence in my life. Even if my mind screams that he is real and his life and history is real, he still has no place here, and it's still unfair that he has wrecked my life.
Even though you are one being, one soul?
Even then. I had a life here, and it was a happy one. Then something switched inside my head, rightly or wrongly, but either way I think it's fair to say that I've not been happy ever since.
I am pleased you have come to this on your own, John Cade,

but what is it that's holding you back?

There are two sides to me now. This foreign invader which had taken over, or was trying to - even that isn't really true - I wanted him to take over, but he couldn't exist without me, just like I can't exist now without him.

There is a dagger of self-destruction in my hand and I don't know how to let it go. Gemma sees it, so do the kids. You even see it. It's making me do bad things. Well, not bad I guess, more out of character - for me.

Vost, Kapoor and McCaan were listening intently in the next room. Not a murmur passed between them as they strained to hear every word.

Vost was eager for Malachi to sway the conversation around to where Cade had got all his information from so that he could appease Kennedy so that he could turn in his report so that he could slope back into his retirement; he was ignorant of the developments and new leads Kennedy was now focusing on, tales subconsciously driven by paranoia having lent his ear too much to the burning war cries of Cade.

Kapoor was on the edge of his seat listening for any hint of information he didn't yet know of life amongst the colonies and the movements of the fleets and the direction of their searches through the uncharted sectors of space. They would be here soon he hoped. His focused mind sat in denial of the admission of Cade's delusions.

McCaan was listening to the crackles and hiss and wondering how he could improve the lighting on the camera hidden about the room. His mind flitted between this and the cute blonde with the light jeans he'd squeezed up against on the tube. He'd seen her before, more than enough times for him to know her routine: where she got on, where she got off, which carriage she was likely to be on, what music she liked to listen to as he peered over her shoulder to glimpse the tunes as she shuffled the tracks on her phone as he breathed in close to her ear and the white cables hooked into her ears. He'd brushed his hand against hers a number of times as they both gripped the hand rail, and he had managed to rub his leg up against hers in the crush a number of times, but today was an exceptional achievement as he managed to thrust his crotch against her rear in the squeeze of rush hour passengers. He thought she liked it. She had smiled at him once, at least he thought it was a smile, not a grimace of annoyance. She hadn't moved away, not that she could have done anyway. Had she felt his excitement? He wasn't sure. She didn't wear a ring. He thought she was Polish, she looked it, and he thought he'd heard her say 'excuse me' to someone once and had picked up on a slight Eastern European accent. He kept his left hand hidden whenever he saw her.

Cade said something of note, his tone lowering in admission of something causing McCaan to tweak the audio, pulling his mind away from his illicit fantasy.

All three of them sat forward in their seats, each driven by their own unspoken purposes, each dreaming of a different place away from their own reality.

7

He felt better for having lifted the lid off his burdens and admitting to his own failings and struggles to Malachi. Malachi's office had become his confessional booth and the African counsellor his priest. He didn't offer absolution and gave him no prayers of penance with which to kneel outside the room with rosary beads threaded through his fingers like the slow lowering of the bucket into the depths of a well, if anything he was sent away with a promise to repent and turn back to his old self, to cast off the alien self and regain control of the old, to no longer become the new creation he had spent the last decade and a half changing into, adapting to, and clothing himself with. It wasn't quite the evangelical approach to a new life but he was prepared to put his faith in this African pastor who seemed to genuinely care about restoring his life and making him whole.

He had spilled his heart out about the dark side, the cloud that brooded over him and thundered his mood and poured torrential rain down on any potential happiness flooding the already damaged ruins of his family home. He told Malachi of his misuse and abuse of Lucy and his struggles to free her from his bed: she was a sex object, a toy, a commodity he picked up and used mainly when the cloud drifted over. He'd begun to push her about, not so much knock her about (except in the bedroom which she seemed happy to tolerate), but it was getting close to it. She didn't like his aggressive side but he knew she was the type to put up with it. He was getting addicted to her, a bad drug whose smell of sex got him fired up for a short burst of excitement which he then discarded as he sank quickly to a low point of guilt and shame and self-loathing. She brought her drugs with her, and that was becoming more frequent as she got used to using his place as hers. The drugs hadn't been there to begin with but she had made new friends in the block who were pushing, and she was buying, reluctantly at first but now readily as she slipped into the downward draw of the whirlpool that would keep her forever part of estate life.

Malachi had been firm with him about Lucy: she had to go, he had to break free before she became a crutch he couldn't live without. She was stopping him from embedding his relationship with Gemma, and Lucy's growing dependence on him was destructive to her also. John knew all this, he had spoken similar words in the privacy of his own thoughts, but it was refreshing to have Malachi echo it in his own firm malleable manner.

Lucy wasn't the only thing he had confessed to.

It was six months ago, he'd finished the night shift early - that in itself wasn't uncommon; if things were quiet they often knocked off in the early hours knowing no one was really checking up on them. If a supervisor did happen to be on duty then they would park up and keep their heads low and wait for a job to be assigned. They could, and sometimes did, hide away in an office back at the depot but cameras monitored the entrance so if management wanted they could always check how long they were sitting around on their arses for. The night shifts were usually reserved for the weekend or for when the local nightclubs or pubs had special weekday events on. Unsurprisingly the vast amount of street damage, graffiti, and general bin tipping happened late evening around kicking out time. Usually by 2am most of the damage was done, with much being reported on the 24 hour hotline in the days following, but the worst and most obvious was usually found by them by 3am allowing them to clear up the bulk of it by 4am and then disappear off home. On the really quiet nights the clock ticked slower and they (there always being at least two of them) dreamt of the end of the shift as they covered the time in meaningless trivial chatter.

On this particular night it had been fairly quiet for the most part. Some little scrote had spray painted a handful of lamp posts with an identifiable but ineligible scrawl of a tag. John and Hardeep had spent about a half hour driving round finding the path the unknown youth had tread on his way home and quickly cleaned off as much of the paint that they could in the dark. The trail led them to a bus stop where the youth had clearly been sat waiting for his ride out of the area. The youth was long gone but three drunken lads in their late teens or early twenties stood bullishly waiting for a night bus. As their council marked van pulled up to clean off the graffiti the three puffed out their chests and sought to make fun of the two council cleaners. This was nothing new, they were used to it. They shrugged it off, or at least Hardeep did.

"Come on, we'll do it later," he remembered Hardeep suggesting before moving back to the van. He was right of course, they would only have to wait twenty minutes or so and the bus would have taxied the problem away and they could get on with the job in hand without any of the hassle. But they weren't the only ones who could puff out their chests, and John had a considerable amount of muscular chest to parade in front of him. There was also the issue of who was among the group of three: Joey, he didn't know his full name or even whether that was his real name, but he lived on his estate and was an ex-shag of Lucy's. He cared little for Lucy's ex-lovers, or even for her present ones, it wasn't as though he cared whether she slept with half the block so long as it didn't affect him in any way, but he did care about the reputation this Joey had for bullying the kids and pushing his skunk upon them and getting them to run for him. The guy was a thug who needed putting in his place.

Joey rose to the challenge. Of course he would, he had two buddies with him and fancied his odds with three to one. His two friends sidled up, one on each shoulder, sniggering and glaring daringly.

"John, come on, leave it." Hardeep repeated his plea a few times before getting back out of the van and physically grabbing John by the arm so that the two, who by this point were stood head to head breathing in each other's testosterone, were pulled apart.

John bowed to Hardeep's cowardice, or was it wisdom, and

climbed back into the van amid the cajoling taunts of the three drunken louts.

It should have ended there but it didn't.

Twenty minutes later and the graffiti was cleaned off. Half hour after that and they called it a night. John went home. Had he gone straight home he would have climbed into bed, maybe woken Lucy up if she was there and demanded sex, but he didn't go straight back, instead he took a detour just on the off chance.

Joey lived on the far side of the estate away from John's block. There was a green, a large grassed courtyard separating the named blocks with their haphazard numbers. As John stepped along the alleyway between two of the blocks, his footsteps tapping hollowly in the still air under the dim light of a rubbish strewn, piss stinking stairway, he could hear the low muted voices of a couple of young men talking. He had no doubt who it was. No longer three; now only two. He hung back out of sight of the green and tried to gauge exactly where they were. He waited only a few seconds before it became clear the two were about to part. He stepped back further into the walkway and then checked his surroundings: Joey would come this way. His instincts told him the other of the two would go in the opposite direction but that Joey was fated to fall straight into his lap; that made things simpler and cleared his mind of the uncertainty of what he felt he needed to do. He stepped forward again so that he stood on the edge on the cusp of darkness - he didn't want the bully to find his legs at the first sight of a one-on-one challenge.

Joey didn't disappoint. He turned the corner and walked straight into a gut punch. He didn't stand a chance. He went down winded but had no time to take a breath before he was pulled up and clocked square in the face.

If those two strikes were the only two that he inflicted he wouldn't have felt so bad. He had toyed with Joey, had pushed him back and allowed him to compose himself, allowed him a fair0 ight, but he was no match for the skill and experience of the warrior that was tearing out from John Cade.

There would be no comeback, no retaliation, no complaint made to the police. This was street justice and street code. Joey the ousted alpha male was beaten by the usurper who wanted no claim on his territory but just wanted the respect of his position.

In the months that had passed since that night Joey had kept a low profile. He still dealt his gear and had a huddle around him, but on the few occasions when their paths crossed he would give John a respectful nod and then quickly look away. John was sure he never confessed to a soul who had beaten him, and was sure he never would.

8

Surjeet Kapoor sat in the Edinburgh lecture hall watching the array of disinterested students who in their distracted youth missed the importance and relevance of the teaching they were forced to sit through as part of their academic studies. Some took notes as they listened intently, staring across to the platform below them. Others allowed their soporific and alcohol laden eyelids to hang heavy as they set their ipads to record the session. Others still appeared to be working on different subjects all together as they played catch up whilst claiming their credits for attending the lecture. There were a couple of older students in the room who were there by choice, having a genuine interest in the subject matter, but none he suspected were there with the same professional incentive he had.

Kapoor looked around at the thirty or so students and surmised that he was probably the oldest person in the room, save for the lecturer himself that was. The aging, and slightly pompous English tones of Professor John Hipkiss washed in monotone over his Scottish audience. By the patter of the way Hipkiss cruised through his dialogue it was obvious that he had given this same talk on numerous occasions and was as bored of it as they were, as he was clearly just going through the motions.

Hipkiss was expounding on the future of the universe, expanding on the idea that the Milky Way's peaceful place in the universe was about to come to an end as it flowed through our inflationary universe on a collision course with our nearest neighbour Andromeda, the two similarly sized galaxies blending in a potentially violent merge of planets - fortunately for us, he added, this wasn't due to take place for another four billion years, which he explained was no time at all in the longevity of space.

As he sat waiting for the lecture to finish Kapoor thought back to what had brought him to this place. It wasn't just that Vost had ordered him to catch the train up and nail down the Professor and grill him for information, it was deeper than that. It was what had drawn him into the folds of MI17 in the first place.

Even as a child he had this vision that he was born for something greater than the mere existence he lived, never feeling quite complete. He had sat up in his bedroom staring out of the window of his home in Southall praying to the god of the night sky, Varuna, for the clouds to clear so that he could gaze upon the stars, and pray to Aha and Soma and the other gods that denoted the various orbs that hovered above. Even in his youth he held lightly to the faith of his parents: it made no sense to him to believe in mystical creatures; if there was life outside of what we could observe then he had an inner sense that it was tangible and intelligent, rather than distant and unreachable. It became an obsession which he hid from his parents until, for his fifteenth birthday, he asked for a telescope so that he could look closer from his room. All his school options were tailored for a career in science or computing, but his real skill was in research and analysing data: he could cross reference subjects and link topics easily and show his field of reference even if his performance in the exams themselves was flawed.

When Surjeet was 17 he saw what he thought was a satellite tracing the night sky, he watched it closely for about a minute as it slowly crossed a line through the other static stars above his head, but then inexplicably it changed direction and then suddenly vanished. He tried every rationale he could to argue it wasn't something of alien origin, determined to implement a scientific approach to what he had observed, but no, it hadn't been a registered satellite that he could trace, nor was it a weather balloon, or an airplane, it could have been some sort of unconventional military test flight but there was no way he could verify the idea; to all intents and purposes he was forced to label it as a genuine UFO. And so his obsession with the phenomena grew from there until he'd managed to merge his skills and his dreams with a job that would fit, eventually ending up in the secretive basement of the MI17 offices in London.

He never forgot that night as a teenager staring confused at the night sky begging the observed to observe him, hoping that they would see him and beam him away from his life in Southall back up to the stars where he knew he belonged. That feeling had never left him; he knew he had another life to live.

"Professor Hipkiss." The students were filing out, leaving the lecturer to pack away his things at the front of the auditorium. Kapoor had made his way down the few steps away from the chattering crowd exiting through the back doors. "Surjeet Kapoor, I work for the Defence Department."

Hipkiss looked at him blankly as if it meant nothing to him and even if it did what did that have to do with him.

"I'm on secondment to a project involving John Cade."

That did the trick. The expression on Hipkiss' face suddenly changed to one of indignation and dismissal.

"Honestly, Mr Kapoor, I am sorry you have made the journey but I really have nothing to say on the matter."

"You did have the initial contact with John Cade?"

"If you are who you say you are then you know I did, in fact I vaguely recognise your face as one of those who questioned me at the time. It was a long while ago now and I had hoped that the fiasco that was John Cade and the embarrassment it caused to the scientific community had long been forgotten."

"Indeed it was. John Cade was adequately discredited as a paranoid schizophrenic, and I believe we did our part in exonerating yourself in being duped innocently as you quite rightly examined scientific proposals in a routine manner."

Hipkiss tipped his head in acknowledgment and gratitude.

"So what is this about?"

"Recent scientific developments, both in mainstream technology and in military advancements over the passing years, have borne out as accurate to what Cade had proposed in his theories."

"Yes, I must admit that hasn't been lost on me over the years, and I have often wondered where his ideas came from."

"That's the problem, Professor. You see we have had cause to interview him again recently for that specific purpose, desiring the origins of his detailed knowledge of highly classified projects."

"And?"

"And, he has eluded that much of what he learned was gathered information which the two of you colluded on."

"Preposterous!"

"You deny it then?"

"Absolutely! I evidenced it at the time of my initial contact with Cade and all the information shared between us and my colleagues was laid bare to your department. I held nothing back. Now I don't know what he has been saying to you but it is a bare faced lie, and honestly I am insulted that you should waste your time coming up here to interrogate me on it."

Kapoor ignored the vehemence of his outburst. "So to confirm, you had no access to any of the ideas Cade purported to prior to meeting with him."

"Of course I did. That was why we were drawn to him in the first place. He was expanding on ideas and projects which were already in the minds, if not in the works, of many a scientist. Many of my colleagues, as I'm sure you know, are contracted to various government and military departments. It was as much a mystery and a concern to us, as it was to you, as to how he had come to his conclusions. We withdrew our interest as soon as the press got wind of it, for we all knew where that circus would end up and we had no desire to be part of it."

"Quite rightly, of course. Do you know of anyone of your colleagues who could have leaked any of this information to him?"

"No, of course not. The idea is ridiculous."

Kapoor nodded his head and outstretched his hand as if to conclude their meeting.

Confused Hipkiss reached out his to loosely shake.

"Is that it? If you don't mind me saying, you don't seem all that convinced of the need for your visit."

"I'm not. I think I know where Cade got his ideas. Thank you for your time Professor, sorry to have bothered you."

9

To say Julie didn't trust the redheaded harlot that had been thrust upon them was an understatement. Marcus was becoming more and more distant with her around and they were arguing more, that she could cope with; she knew her husband's weaknesses and his strengths and knew that no matter how tempted he was his conscience would win over and he would bear all to her and crumble at her feet rather than betray what they had built up together. Julie prided herself on being good at reading people and saw beyond the tilted head and flick of the hair and the ever so obvious brushes against her husband. The lingering looks were all so orchestrated and manipulative. There was no doubt in Julie's mind that Fiona was working to an agenda and that part of it was keeping them distracted by division so that they didn't see what she was up to.

Marcus was out adjusting Keck II's mirrors. Fiona had taken the helicopter from the port over to Honolulu to the Pearl Harbour-Hickam military base where she was meeting with another Sentinel contractor attached to the MOD; not that she had said as much but Julie had pieced it together from snippets of overheard phone calls and lingering glances at her online diary. It was a shame she hadn't taken the boat off their remote and isolated island, for the journey would have taken her that much longer, if she was lucky she would hear her return as she flew back in.

Fiona was careful to take most of her important documents with her and what she didn't carry she locked away in a cabinet she had requested when she first arrived. Julie had lied about how many keys were available, making a claim that they needed to lock up very little on the island as the population was so small that they knew the intimate details of everyone in their immediate vicinity, and to escape in the event of a crime was a futile and laborious task as boats leaving the island were easily traced as the islanders took pride in their surroundings and kept a keen but welcoming eye on tourists. The observatory itself was so secluded from anything else on Hawaii Island that visitors were rare and easily spotted on approach, and main access to the facility was fairly secure anyway.

There was a key safe on the wall in the main office where all the monitors for the observatory were housed. The key safe itself wasn't locked but instead hung open with all the facility's keys on display. The bunch of keys she held in her hand as she knelt at the cabinet allocated to their visitor was the large unlabelled bunch she kept at their coastal house in Hilo.

She opened up the cabinet, there wasn't much in it, as she had expected. She hadn't honestly thought that Fiona would be stupid enough to leave anything incriminating behind. She shuffled through the few papers that were there: some copies of stellar charts and calculations and spectral readouts, but nothing out of the ordinary, these were all things they had openly been looking at. She sat on the floor double checking the data to make sure she wasn't missing anything obvious. A handwritten note on one page read: 're-sent nothing received', it was dated two days after she had arrived on the island.

What had she sent?

She stood up and put the files on the top of the cabinet and walked over to the main computer. She glanced at the camera monitors and could see Marcus still doing his external checks on the telescope having aligned it to his satisfaction. He would come in soon so she would have to be quick, he would side with her no matter what, but to catch her snooping around in an apparent jealous witch hunt would only lead to an argument she would rather avoid.

She punched in the date on the file and searched outgoing transmissions. All transmissions from the observatory to the mainland, be they to Sentinel, NASA or emails home, were all logged on one system. There was little activity that day, all run of the mill stuff: a routine update to Sentinel, she had emailed home a dessert recipe she had found whilst searching online in a down moment (of which there were many), Marcus had phoned the garage a couple of times getting advice from the mechanic about a knocking sound on the jeep, the bank had called about their loan repayments, and there had been a call from a photographer wanting to visit to get some shots of the facility (this was quite common as the views from the observatory were spectacular and many a keen photographer, both amateur and professional were prepared to make the trek up the mountain). There was nothing else of note to grab her attention.

She noted Marcus climb in the 4x4 as he moved away from Keck to head back in towards the office. She closed the link on the machine and put the files back in the cabinet wondering what it was she was missing.

10

The blonde was there at the far edge of the carriage, he was sure she had been looking at him when he snapped his head round. She now seemed to be looking at the reflections in the windows of the darkened tunnel. This wasn't her usual route; he hadn't expected to see her here, not at this time, on this route. A happy coincidence.

McCaan wondered how he could manoeuver his way to the other end of the carriage to get close to her, meandering through the crowd, brushing shoulders with the other passengers he cared little for. He rehearsed a line or two in his head: 'Hi, fancy seeing you here.' - too cheesy; 'Hi, are you not working today? Fancy grabbing a coffee?' - too forward; 'Hi, where are you off to today?' - he might get away with that if she recognised him and was attracted to him enough. Of course she would recognise him but her reaction would tell him just how welcome or unwelcome all his advances had been. Had he overstepped the mark all those mornings on the way into the office? He would know soon enough.

The train slowed towards the next station allowing him to make a move as if he were about to get off. The slot puzzle of people shifted as he worked his position around the picture as bodies shuffled towards the doors. The train stopped. People got off. People got on. McCaan casually sauntered over to where she stood against the glass of the single exit door.

He wasn't close enough to touch her without making it obvious and he suddenly became conscious of his words being overheard and scrutinized by the other passengers, strangers who couldn't care less, but being under the spotlight of a guilty crime held him back.

She turned and gave him a blank stare, then turned away again but the curve of the reflection betrayed a slight smile. She lifted her hand and drew back a lock of hair from her cheek to behind her ear. He thought she was blushing.

Then he saw her hand. She was sporting a new ring. It sparkled on her left hand.

He shrank back, guiltily stroking his own ring finger in his pocket as he did so.

Changes in her life had probably brought about her shift of routine. She had a future life to plan and a cheap sexual fling with a stranger was unlikely to be part of her thinking. Flattering, he was sure, but not realistic.

Suddenly he was embarrassed of his actions and the imagined smile on her face became a frustrated grimace of annoyance at his presence. He turned away to face the opposite door, planning to get off at the next stop and not look back.

"McCaan, thank you for coming at such short notice"

"General, I'm not sure Mr Vost would approve of me meeting you without him."

Kennedy gave a light roll of his eyes at the misuse of his title but didn't comment as though McCaan wasn't worthy of correcting.

"Of course he wouldn't, but then if he were here I couldn't very well ask you to make sure he doesn't withhold any information from me."

"Sir?"

"Relax, McCaan, I'm not asking you to do anything untoward. I just want to ensure Mr Vost doesn't keep back anything. Remember, you work for me at the end of the day."

"Yes sir, of course."

Kennedy opened a file on his desk and passed over the top paper so that McCaan could read it.

"This is the transcript of the last interview with Cade, can you just verify its accuracy."

McCaan looked over the printed words, nodding occasionally as he slowly soaked it in.

"You could have just cross referenced the audio file."

"And miss the opportunity of having your ear, not likely. If there are any offhand chats not recorded between yourselves or with the counsellor then I would like to know."

McCaan gave a curious look which Kennedy read simplistically.

"What I want to know is what the transcripts don't say. I want to know attitudes. I want to know opinions. I want to know moods. I want to know if I have to worry about anyone involved in this investigation. Do you understand?"

"This is because he has admitted to being in receipt of leaked information?"

"This is because I don't believe he's telling the truth about where the information is coming from. Kapoor has already confirmed as much. Any conjecture about Cade discussed amongst the team I want to know about it."

"Yes sir."

"That's all."

McCaan turned to leave then stopped half way towards the door and turned back.

"Sir," he asked, curious to know the General's thoughts, "is John Cade dangerous?"

"Are you good at hiding in plain sight, hiding the truth of who you are from your family and those around you?"

McCaan shrugged, then thought of the girl on the tube and nodded.

"We all are, McCaan, but I'm more concerned about that which is worn on the sleeves out in the open. What concerns me is who Cade really is."

11

Whitehouse couldn't stand the distractions: voices echoing and shattering his otherwise serene command of the ministerial debate. For the most part the arguments put across were respectable and intelligent, but occasionally someone would make a quip certain to anger the opposition which would be met with a cacophony of cat calls and groans and other such childish banter which belonged in the playground of their children and grandchildren. He was often ashamed by the behaviour of those of his colleagues who prided themselves on being a cut above the rest as leaders of the country, and he would often shake his head in dissent, adding in his own cries of dismay and anger at the comments passed. In reality he was no better than those he criticised.

It was those distractions though, the outside chimes of bells and high pitched tinnitus tones held through the air on an invisible vibrating string linked to his ear, along with the whispers and papers passing between MPs and the speaker's gavel bashing out against the raucous tribes in an attempt to silence the dissent, that blanked his mind from the job at hand and made him feel nauseous.

Not that he was likely to be sick, far from it. He could control what he needed to control and command those whom he needed to command, but get those sounds out of his head and focus on just one person speaking took all his concentration. He imagined a bombardment of explosions on a distant desert planet as his fleeing mind fought to tune into it across the cosmos as he raced away from the battle.

He shook his head and tipped the thought from his mind. It wasn't helpful; that too was a distraction, and one he would have to deal with soon enough. He had made an appointment with the PM to brief him after the parliamentary session was over and had held off calling for a Cobra meeting as Kennedy had demanded. He was vindicated in his decision as it turned out as no new information was forthcoming and therefore no urgency could be reported as pressing. He was fast coming to the conclusion that Kennedy had lost sight of his directive and was obsessing over the issue with a personal agenda; it was almost enough to have him replaced by someone more amenable.

It was a shame really, having come to terms in his head with a potential extraterrestrial threat, he was now growing quite curious as to who this alien race were, and whether they were one of many, and what had we done to attract their attention. He found his mind drifting away from the parliamentary debates and wondering, despite Kennedy's lack of evidence, who had found them and what they looked like, and which members of this new gargantuan alien empire were going to coming knocking at their door.

12

According to Kennedy she wasn't the only one sniffing for information. There were agents circling in the shadows tiptoeing around for any snippet offered or to fall from the table of the tapestry being weaved by the various groups dotted about the globe observing things they didn't understand, or were ignorant of the unjoined links between them.

As well as the officials investigating there were also the kooks with their conspiracy theories linking the various online clues but failing to draw the dots to make a complete picture. Surjeet Kapoor was having an unhealthy interest in the case and his behaviour indicated he had no idea he was being monitored. Kennedy ran a tight ship and everyone involved was under the microscope, even her own feelers that she put out would have been tracked, not that she had anything to hide so far as Kennedy was concerned, as all she did was under his instruction anyway.

Her phone call with him earlier had been unsettling. He was nervous about the lack of action but she couldn't tell whether it was out of fear of a potential threat or out of being ignored by the Defence Secretary and therefore undermining the power he believed he should command within the government. He could of course take it to his own military superiors, but that would mean admitting defeat and giving up his power and authority - no, he would stick it out and hope Whitehouse and the Prime Minister came to their senses, preferably by begging on their knees.

According to what Kennedy told her the Prime Minister actually laughed Whitehouse out of Downing Street. No credible evidence, he claimed. And wasn't that the problem all along? Wasn't that why he'd brought her on board?

Now she had the problem of getting Keck I looking in a new direction, which wasn't going to be easy now that the Banstead woman was rifling through her things: moving her files wasn't going to go unnoticed, not with her eye for detail. Fiona wasn't stupid enough to keep anything discriminating in reach of the enemy.

She thought she still had some leverage with Marcus to manipulate him, but she would most likely only have one shot at it before she was forced to explain herself and all faith with him was lost; by then they would have addressed their differences and reconciled her role in their disunity, then the gloves would be off and the curtain lifted and a generous boot would be placed to her backside. She planned to be gone by then anyway.

Kennedy's think tank had been busy and had assessed a potential travel vector based on the stories told by Cade and the last visual sighted through the telescope, along with a potential second sighting by the Calar Alto Observatory in Almeria, Spain.

Throw in an imagined theory of space travel technology from a mad man and you had a course plotted and a potential new area of space to stare at.

She didn't think Kennedy was afraid of looking a fool, but she wanted to make sure her name wasn't attached to the investigation when the eggs smeared down the glass of his office window and broke to smack him in the face. If nothing showed up on the scope then, fickle to her alliances as she was, she had every intention of jumping ship.

13

The four of them were gathered in the office next to Malachi's. John Cade wasn't due to arrive for another hour or so. This was their usual pre-meet scrum down where Vost gave them the direction of where he wanted the session to go, and where Kapoor interjected with his own angle and take on things, which on occasion had a positive sway to the course on Vost's thinking. It was also the briefing where Malachi sat intently nodding and agreeing with whatever he was instructed to do, even taking notes, only to then ignore it all as he followed his own course once the session started - of all of those present he was the only one who actually cared about the outcome for John Cade. McCaan, as usual, sat silently observing: he would give an opinion, but only if asked, and only if he felt he had anything worthwhile to say and could be bothered enough to say it.

Vost thought back to those days of years gone by when he had gone head to head with Kennedy over the future of MI17 and the importance of who ran the Cade investigation. It all seemed so unimportant now. They hadn't really gained any new information in this recent round of interrogations; a different approach maybe, but the goal was the same. Cade wasn't about to give up anybody new as a source of his secrets and Malachi, though pleased at having reintroduced his patient into a life with his family, was first to admit that the feigned figure of Abadd'on was far from distant in Cade's mind.

Malachi wanted to medicate Cade, a decision which had been taken out of his hands as Vost required him lucid for the sessions, not that Cade would take the tablets anyway, he had admitted so early on. Now, however, Vost was beginning to think that maybe medication wasn't such a bad idea. Cade was a danger to himself, and his new physical stature was a danger to others should his psychosis get out of hand. Vost no longer saw him as a national threat but merely an unfortunate soul with an overactive imagination and a chemical imbalance in the brain. Whether or not Cade had been privy to secret information he couldn't tell, nor cared less; he thought that maybe at some point in the distant past he probably had received information he shouldn't have from someone missed in their investigation - it could have been anyone, a random set of tales told one night in the pub by a stranger, an overheard conversation on the Tube, a series of 'what if' debates by peer students at school or college, maybe one of them had a father who worked in Defence - who knew? The conclusion Vost was drawing to was that they would never find out, and most probably even the lucid mind of Cade had built a wall around the truth of the matter. Better to dose him up and cloud his mind and protect him and his family from any more heartbreak and disruption.

"Unless Mr Cade reveals anything sensational this morning," Vost addressed the room, "I'm recommending to Kennedy that our involvement ends here."

The three other faces in the room dropped. Each had their own agendas for being there and wanting the project to continue.

"Obviously Malachi I understand you may, for professional reasons in the interest of your patient, wish to continue your sessions with Mr Cade. Should you do so, your original disclaimer will still apply and any information pertaining to this investigation you would be obliged to hand over, and we may request your files on the matter at any point."

Relieved Malachi nodded his compliance, "Of course, Mr Vost. I feel it would be a shame to leave John Cade at this point when he has made so much progress on his road to recovery. I would very much like to continue the sessions with him."

"Very well. Dave, you don't look too happy."

"Sorry boss, I was just getting used to this place. It's a bit of a cushy number for me, if you know what I mean."

"Louis, are you sure about this? We have so much more to

learn from Cade."

Vost took in a deep breath, let it out in a sigh and then turned to Kapoor before addressing the other two.

"Malachi, Dave, do you mind giving me and Surj a few minutes."

An uneasy shift in the atmosphere rippled through the room as the two men stood and walked towards the adjoining door. Once through it Vost turned again to answer Kapoor's question.

"Surj, what's happened to you? You've become obsessed with Cade. You think I'm not aware of all the extra digging you've been doing? It's got to stop. You're one of the reasons I feel this investigation has exhausted all it's going to turn up. If there was anything else out there you would have found it by now. You're a good researcher Surj, but you need to go back to your day job."

Kapoor sat dejected. Part of him wanted to cry. Part of him was speeding down the highway searching for an alternative route. Eventually he lowered his head in acceptance.

"What about you, Louis?"

"Me?" asked Vost chirpily, "I'm going back to my retirement and going to put my feet up, for a while at least. I'm sure they'll call me up to consult on something else pretty soon. There's already something else on the horizon they'll want my expertise on."

"You seem pretty confident."

"Oh I am, I'm not without sources of my own."

"You're not going to invite me in next time, are you?"

"No Surj, not this time."

Kapoor nodded, resigned to his fate to all appearances.

"Surj, let this one go, for your own sake, let it go."

Kapoor nodded, but his mouth betrayed him.

"I can't."

They had been talking generally, picking up their usual banter from earlier, neither of them trying to hear the conversation on the other side of the door. McCaan lowered his tone and wormed his way over to Malachi's desk and pulled a cable beneath the lamp.

"I hit the mute button next door but just in case they knock it on, you know."

He gave Malachi a cautious look which was returned with a

nod and a knowing look to the adjoining door.

"If you keep seeing Cade," McCaan warned, "don't think they won't be recording you. I don't think Kennedy will abandon observing Cade even if Vost calls it a day. Odds are they'll call me back in to record it all."

"They are persecuting an innocent man, a sick man."

"I know, but Kennedy is like a pit-bull who's had the taste of blood. Even if there's nothing there he's not ready to let it go yet."

He plugged the cable back in. Malachi nodded his understanding and they returned to the banter.

The interlocking door opened and Vost stepped through alone, Kapoor was nowhere in sight.

Vost checked his watch as if to say 'positions, he'll be here soon'.

14

So, is there anything else you would like to disclose?

Disclose? A rather formal usage is it not?

You seem concerned with the door.

No, not overly, I just thought I heard a sound coming from there. Another office I presume?

It is let out to a private firm I believe and not always occupied by its staff, it is likely they are in today. Please, John, don't let that distract you.

When we spoke last you said that you thought much of the information you built your character around was gained by a combination of internet searches and scientific magazines and journals and television programmes coupled with contact which you had from Professor Hipkiss. Was that helpful in remembering such facts, gaining more insight into the character you had developed?

Yes, I have been able to match various threads of Abadd'on's story to certain areas of science fiction. Part of it has been quite liberating, but to be honest much has been disturbing.

I understand. The complexities of the human brain can be

quite fearful when we acknowledge its potential to distort our reality. Accepting these false truths that we tell ourselves subconsciously goes a long way to detaching us from those we love. Breaking those links, or mentally building a wall around the falsehoods to contain them can set us on the road to recovery and reconciliation with who we really are.

Tell me John, have you thought of any other sources for your troubles, or things that have contributed to the character you have created? The more you can add to this the less power and hold that character has over you. The more your wakeful mind see's Abadd'on as false the easier it will be for you, John Cade, to regain control.

I have racked my brain but cannot think of other sources. I remember dreaming as a kid about being an alien, you know, daydreams based on Star Trek or Battlestar Gallactica - that sort of thing. Probably every kid at that stage of life fantasises over similar things, I don't know.

That is perfectly normal. Every child dreams of an attachment to a life apart from the one they are living. It is a healthy way of finding our way in life and examining who we are. To be creative with a distant personality or setting is how we learn what to aspire to. As a child I dreamt of being a policeman arresting rebel leaders in my country. As I grew up and became aware of things in the West I imagined I was an ambassador for my people and winning over justice for my nation.

My fantasies were never that noble.

No, but then you didn't live my life. Surrounded by Western television and the creativity of your social setting it was quite natural to dream of being a movie star or an astronaut, or even an alien. Now whether your fantasies took on life on that Christmas Day or not is irrelevant, the fact is the lines in your mind got blurred. You were running parallel train tracks: one real life, the other imagined, but at some point one of those trains derailed, jumped track onto the other side so that both trains ground along the same track, neither being able to go any faster than the other, both slowed and unable to flourish. To get one back on the other track you need to acknowledge that it shouldn't be there in the first place.

Deny it, to force it to jump track.

Precisely!

I think I'm getting there. I've thrown Lucy out for good. I think Gemma and me are going to be ok, not perfect, but we'll get there. I can feel Abadd'on slipping away. He hasn't derailed yet, but he's slowing down. The faces, the images, they're blurring and becoming more distant. I can still picture the ship but the fleet has gone. I can still sense the battles but I can't see the faces of those I fought or those who fought beside me.

This is good. John, I am so pleased. The rest will go eventually, when it does don't kick yourself for being fooled by it. You have been ill and you are not to blame for things that you were unable to control. The illness has brought about some good things in you, it has brought out the strength of character and physicality that the old John was most likely too shy to let loose. Focus on the good things and abandon the bad. Become the John you were always meant to be without the constrictions of a fantasy life. Show your wife and all those about you who you really are. Promise me that.

I will. I promise.

15

Gemma stood outside the flat, hands cupped up against the window trying to peer in. There was movement but it wasn't John she could see inside. A flash of blonde hair and a sharp snap of reaction as the feminine figure shot across the living room floor towards the front door. The door pulled open with an angry swing as the young girl stepped out to challenge her.

"What's your problem?" yelled the girl, and she was a girl; now that Gemma could see her close up in the flesh she could see just how young she was - barely out of her teens. She suspected John had been seeing someone, at least now she knew who. In some ways she was relieved. She doubted there was any strong emotional attachment to her; this was all about sex and fulfilling a physical need. She didn't like it but she understood it well enough. She missed the company of a man in her bed, she just hadn't acted on it.

"Do you live here?" Gemma asked cautiously taking a step back. It was the first time she had been to the flat. John had been over to the house on many an occasion recently but had been reticent about discussing anything regarding where he lived or how. Toby had been of course, but she had never been invited, nor had she pushed to come.

"What business is it of yours?" She kicked back at the dog that was nudging her leg from behind the door. Charlie trotted off back to the living room, clearly used to the neglectful rebukes of the girl.

"I'm just looking for John." It was a lie. She knew he had a counselling session this morning. She wanted to check out his place without him being around just to see what he was hiding.

"So you're the bitch reason he's trying to kick me out!" She took a step forward forcing Gemma to shuffle back against the balcony railing.

"So you do live here?"

"Occasionally," she admitted. "Where did he pick you up from? You're a bit old for him, aren't ya? Can't believe he's dumping me for some old milf!"

Inwardly Gemma smiled. He was dumping her. He was cutting ties with this life. Her old John was coming back, slowly and gradually, but that was ok, she was prepared to wait for him; she had waited all this time, she could cope with a little longer.

"Well?"

Gemma snapped out of her thoughts, suddenly realising she hadn't answered the girl's question. The girl's face was flushed with anger, and something else. Her eyes were welling up and Gemma could see dried streaks on her cheeks where her mascara had run and been wiped away earlier. Had they had an argument this morning? Had he only just told her this morning to leave?

"What's your name?" Gemma decided to go on the offensive. The girl was young and impressionable and had no doubt fallen for the dominating man with his own flat, and no matter how rough around the edges she maybe with her common slapper tongue and low cleavage top, Gemma knew she had the trump card.

"Why the hell should I tell you my name? How dare you turn up here making demands! Who the hell do you think you are?"

"I'm his wife," Gemma said flatly, to which she got the desired reaction.

The girl's face dropped and she stumbled back a step and the spring burst forth from her eyes unchecked.

"I take it he didn't tell you he was married then? I guess he also forgot to mention he has two kids and has been spending most of his time recently with us."

"I... I kinda knew he had..." She let the words trail off, unable to find the strength the finish the sentence. Gemma finished it for her.

"You knew he had a family but didn't care less. So long as it didn't intrude on what you got out of the relationship why should you care that you're keeping him away from his family. Well now you know. So do yourself a favour you little home wrecking whore and stay away from my husband. Is that understood?"

Gemma was shaking with adrenalin, her neck and cheeks swollen scarlet with a rush of fury that was out of character and totally unexpected. She stepped forward and held back a smile as the young blonde hussy shrank away into the shadows of the doorway.

She wanted to say more. She wanted to threaten her further. She wanted to push her inside and give her a slap, collect up her things and throw her out of the flat, but deep inside she knew it wasn't her place. She was no fighter and suspected the younger girl was more likely to have scrapped her way around the estate growing up. If she made too much of it she risked pushing John away further. No, what she had done was enough. It was enough to get her point across that she was prepared to fight for what was hers and that it was time John drew the line under this life and moved on.

16

"You went over my head!" Whitehouse was furious. Spittle flew across the desk as he stood over it with his knuckles digging into the leather bound covering beneath the neatly compiled paperwork.

For once Kennedy remained silent. He knew he'd overstepped

the mark, and contacting the Prime Minister directly was beyond his reach of authority; Whitehouse could make real trouble for him over this if he wanted to.

"What the hell do you take me for? Am I, or am I not the Defence Secretary? No, don't answer that. Just tell me, despite your insolence, do you still think there is a threat?"

"You know I do."

"Well the Prime Minister disagrees. In fact he laughed it off, just as I had, and he was annoyed at being confronted with it for a second time in as many days. You have no evidence. All you have is circumstantial and gut instinct."

Kennedy hung his head in shame. He'd been given plenty of rope in having the authority running the revamped and rebranded MI17 department, but in his zeal to impress and get results he had to admit that he gave the appearance of incompetence through his keenness, willing to abandon solid evidence in place of whimsical fantasy, and not just that, he had allowed himself to be taken in by Cade himself, pulled into the whirlpool of his imagination.

"I know you have history with this particular case but you are just one of many concerns that I have to deal with right now. There are wars raging in the Middle East, and we have an increasing growing global threat of terrorism which affects our national and international interests. When I deem something of importance enough to alert the Cabinet then I will do so. I will not be bullied into premature action by an impetuous military commander. Is that clear?"

"Yes, sir."

Whitehouse sat down. The fury flushing through his ears in waves was subsiding and the pressure of the weight he had felt was lifting, making him feel slightly lightheaded.

In truth he had no reason to be as angry as he was: no harm had come of Kennedy's actions, in fact it may have worked in his favour, not that he would tell Kennedy that. The Prime Minister was now aware that it wasn't he pushing the issue, and that he was right in raising it as a concern without the need to elevate it as pressing, taking on board his advice that for the time being the issue should be monitored and a dialogue opened up with the Americans regarding the matter, something Kennedy was reluctant to do as he selfishly tried to hold the reins himself - a potential new threat to assess meant that he could divert more public funds to bolster the Defence budget. Any new challenge from Kennedy would firmly be countered with the full backing of the PM who now had a rightfully sullied opinion of the man.

"Sit down."

Kennedy did as bidden. He was on damage limitation now; he could easily be removed from his post and so far didn't know whether his superiors in the army had been appraised of his gaffe.

"There are secrets within secrets, Major General."

Kennedy looked at him curiously.

"You and I are not the top tier. We don't hold all the cards. Politicians and generals are just puppets for those who control the real power: businesses and conglomerates with the finances to buy countries and topple governments, they're the ones with the real power, and the bigger secrets."

Kennedy wisely stayed silent.

"A few days ago I would have dismissed this as a random and wild conspiracy theory, and were I not in this position in government, where I am able to communicate with my counterparts around the world, I would not believe a word of it.

"Do you remember Reagan's Star Wars program?"

"Of course."

"That wasn't driven by a cold war arms race with the Soviets. Those missiles were never supposed to point down at the planet, they were designed to point out. Secrets, Major General Kennedy, there are secrets kept from even us. I don't know to what extent we have had contact with other life outside of this planet, but I don't think this is the first threat we have faced.

"If this is real I need someone I can trust, someone who is going to do as I say, and someone who is not going to be a wild card and run off doing his own thing. There is a bigger picture you, and most likely I, am not privy to."

Kennedy nodded. He read the unsaid dialogue clearly and acknowledged that he was being given a second chance, unworthy as he was, but on the basis that all information came to Whitehouse only, he was playing chess like a true politician should. Whatever Whitehouse had been enlightened to he clearly wanted to be in on the action and wanted leverage to open up the further secrets hidden from him. Kennedy understood the draw, more than that, he was attracted to it also. Was he prepared to be Whitehouse's bitch? - hell yes.

"Those missiles, are they still there?"

"Not only are they there, they have been fired at least once. STS-48, STS-114."

Kennedy thought for a moment. The reference was familiar, from files he'd read.

"NASA missions."

"Shuttle footage. It's in the public domain without the audio commentary."

"You've heard it?"

"It was played for me. STS-48 goes back to 1991. We're not the only ones looking at this."

Kennedy suddenly felt small and insignificant. He was leading a department that was being taken for a fool. He thought that what he was investigating and researching was big and important, and classified, but now he was being told that somewhere in the world there was a dedicated team dealing with the real thing - and he wanted to be part of that team.

"Do you understand?"

Kennedy nodded.

"Good, then we never had this conversation."

17

John hit her with a backhand. She went sprawling across the living room. How dare she confront him in such a way? This was his domain. She was nothing. He owed her nothing.

Lucy's head hit the edge of the sideboard before falling heavily to the floor. She was out cold, maybe even dead, not that he cared. She had no right talking to him that way.

Charlie, who had cowered whining in the corner of the room, padded forward slowly and sniffed at the cheek of the fallen figure on the floor.

So Gemma had graced his doorstep, it was only a matter of time before she grew brave enough to come over. It was just a shame Lucy was still loitering about when she got here; an hour later and she probably would have been gone. Now he was left with this mess.

He thought for a moment, his mood wasn't endearing to mollycoddling a pathetic wimp of a female who demanded his attention. Dealing with either of the women in his life right now was furthest from his mind.

He was angry, and not just because of the four letter tirade Lucy had presented him with about his wife when he had arrived home. He had been angry before he got here, silently simmering as he calmly conducted his journey, having sailed through the calm winds of the counselling session, all the while rushing violent currents swept beneath the hull.

It was Kapoor's doing. Kapoor who had always been faithful to him, who always believed in him; Kapoor who wanted the true Abadd'on to be revealed for who he was.

Kapoor had lain in wait for him on the High Street and had pulled him aside as he stepped off the bus and filled him in on the listening room next door. Malachi wanted to help Cade only. Kennedy only wanted information. Vost wanted to help no one but himself. Only Kapoor wanted to continue with Cade *and* Abadd'on, all the rest were deceitful enemies of Abadd'on.

John Cade was nobody's fool, he knew that Kapoor, despite his faith in him, was in no position to help him. He couldn't get to Vost or Kennedy, but he could get to Malachi.

He snarled at the limp form lying on the floor. There was a trickle of blood seeping from behind her head. He ignored it. He wondered whether Gemma would react when confronted with who her husband had become. Malachi wanted him to show her who he really was, and so he would.

18

Julie had been scrutinising the logs. She had taken them home and spent the last couple of nights running through them without fear of Fiona looking over her shoulder. Marcus was finally on board; there had been one intimate caress too much and, as she predicted, Marcus was too faithful to his family to allow the guilt of his attraction to her to tear him away from those he loved, as a result he had confessed all to her: that Fiona had been flirting openly with him and that he was growing increasingly uncomfortable with it. It was just the admission she needed. It allowed them to speak openly for the first time about what they thought Fiona and Sentinel were up to. Their careers and reputations were at stake, possibly more, but together they would work it out and face it united as they had done their entire married life.

They concluded that whatever signal had been sent had probably been sent from the array to a point at a relatively short distance. They expected it to be within the solar system purely on the basis that Fiona was awaiting a response; any long distance transmission was unlikely to return a signal. They had come a long way in understanding the rate of transfer of radio waves since the early days of sending messages into space via satellites. Signals sent to our own satellites, including radio transmissions, television broadcasts and radio programmes, were all splashed out into the outer atmosphere, firing rays of live signals into the empty darkness of space. Fifty light years away, should intelligent life with the technology to receive those signals exist, it would be tuning into the junk and misdirection that had educated generations as a form of entertainment. That said, in all that time not one signal had been received back. Not that the Bansteads were aware of any. Certainly no confirmed signal had ever been published in the science journals.

The oldest signal to be sent from the Keck Observatory was when they had first started at the site, pulsed out in the direction of the telescopes: a simple message paraphrased as 'we are here, contact us'. The static of space was all that responded. Even the monitoring of the static had changed over the years, no longer did someone have to sit deciphering the different graphs of information on the computer screen, now the computer did it all, saving the ears, eyes and minds of everyday folk who could easily miss the patterns echoed through space.

Julie scanned through the lines of information looking for anything Fiona may have sent in the short time she had been there.

Coffee cups lay empty and her eyes hung heavy when she finally found what she was looking for, but it wasn't what she expected. A coded set of numbers she identified as a cypher of some sort. Who in space would understand a coded message sent from Earth, and why send it expecting a reply when nothing lay in its path?

19

"So is he schizophrenic or is he an alien? That is the question we have been examining through all of this. If alien, what impact does that have on how we as a society, as a health care system, as a government view and deal with schizophrenics?"

Louis Vost sat in the recently renovated office deep in the Cabinet War Rooms building close to the entrance of Whitehall. He had walked the length of white stone buildings with the concrete balustrades in front shielding them from the road as he tread the heavily worn, yet cold, paving from Trafalgar Square for what he hoped to be the last time.

The remnants of paint fumes had the potential to give him a headache - another reason why he didn't want to hang around. If he stopped to think about it he could probably come up with half a dozen reasons why he didn't want to be there, but it was a necessary evil: they needed the debrief and for the file to be closed, this time permanently. He'd thought hard about the consulting work he'd been offered, but really he felt he had served his time as a civil servant and lackey for the various departments within government who had shafted him from pillar to post throughout his career. In the end he trusted his employers little. He knew enough to realise they had secrets and hidden agendas and that little of what he was instructed to do was handed him with the full facts, and that despite his position of authority he was still a pawn.

There were four of them in the room: Kennedy, Malachi, himself, and Daniel Healy. Healy was a new face he'd never seen before; he'd been introduced as an observer who was assessing the future of the department. Vost didn't believe it. Healy had piercing eyes which out slashed the sharp suit and expensive watch and trim figure that hid beneath. There was an alertness in those eyes that spoke of a caution and aloofness above the pay grade he was parading before them.

"So, Mr Okeno," directed Kennedy seeking an answer to Vost's question, "Telling the truth or just mad?"

Malachi was slow in thought.

"You must understand my position. I came into this with the intention of helping a sick man, and from my perspective he is still sick. There is nothing he has said to convince me that he is otherwise. I understand the concerns that have brought us to this point and which drew your attention to him in the first place all those years ago, but I believe it can all be explained away by the imaginations of a creative mind. Coincidence, possibly insider knowledge, all may have contributed to his psychosis, but I see nothing to warrant further involvement from any external security forces. I do not believe he needs further observation. Counselling and medication, yes, but not observation."

Vost spied the other two men out of the corner of his eye and caught the exchange of esoteric knowledge pass between their glances. He long suspected Kennedy was holding back on him. Clearly there was a bigger reason why he had re-ignited the burnt embers of a case he thought he himself had torched and blown away the ashes to the wind of a decade past. He didn't try to hazard a guess as to what Kennedy and this Healy fellow were hiding, he didn't care, he didn't want to know; whatever was hidden from him would rumble on whether he was involved in it or not.

"So, is the general consensus that schizophrenics the world over are not possessed by little green men from a distant planet?"

"I think it would be fair to say, Mr Vost," replied Malachi with a chuckle, "that the mental health issues of our population are complicated enough without muddying the waters with fantasy."

"Can you say that with certainty?"

"General, I can understand your need for certainty, but our world is full of enough horrors of its own to drive us insane. I myself have witnessed enough personally and professionally to know that the pressures on the human mind are so intense that it takes very little to splinter the realities that we all hold so dear. We all wish an escape, we all dream our fantasy, and for some we just cannot keep a firm hold on what is real, for which there are many reasons."

Kennedy closed the file on his desk as a mark of symbolism that the case of the mysterious alien possession of John Cade was concluded. At least so far as the official documented investigation went.

Vost was keen to rise to his feet. He could feel a headache brewing from the fumes and the new bright fluorescent lights bouncing off the white walls of the old building weren't helping. Malachi stood too, followed by Kennedy who raised a hand to conclude their working agreement. Healy remained seated and made no gesture but instead watched all intently.

Vost escorted Malachi through to the security at the rear of the building so they could sign out at the first checkpoint into the open air, before reaching the exterior pathway to the final security gate where they would surrender their visitors' passes.

Once in the open air Vost turned to Malachi and looked up into his eyes, which he had observed previously seemed older and wiser than his years. "You said we all have our fantasies and desires of escapism. I know mine. What's yours Malachi?"

The tall African looked down to him and smiled, wagged a finger and chuckled.

"In another lifetime, Mr Vost. In another lifetime."

20

Fiona stepped off the plane to grey clouds and cold damp rain trickling to dirty the soles of her high heels which clamped around her swollen feet, it had felt so good to be free of them for the duration of the journey and now she regretted not just wearing comfy flats to get her home.

The climate was certainly a change from the Pacific but it was a welcome one. As paradisiacal as the Hawaiian Islands were she had grown claustrophobic cooped up in the observation rooms on top of the mountain. The call home was a relief - her job there complete.

She planned to go straight home, have a hot bath, make the necessary calls to check in and then make her way to Whitehall to file her report. Predictably her well laid plans were destined not to be. She spied Healy loitering with scanning eyes by the crowd control bars that guided debarking passengers and separated them from the waiting relatives and friends, and in her case her employer. She thought about giving him the slip; she didn't think he'd seen her yet, but then why put off the inevitable. A couple more steps and she wouldn't be able to avoid him anyway.

He saw her, gave a cautious subtle nod and waited until she walked past him before falling in line behind her towards the lift that led to the taxi rank outside.

She waited for an empty lift and he followed her in then blocked the way of a family trying to enter in behind. The father tried to complain but Healy gave a scowl not to be messed with; despite his slight appearance and office geekish look there was a menace of calm and calculated aggression behind his eyes. The family held their ground outside the lift and the doors closed to leave the couple alone for the duration of the journey.

When the doors opened again Healy was first out and turned left towards the car park. Fiona didn't follow him but instead resumed her initial plan to head for home via a taxi. It would be a brief stop. The new information was delicate. Things had escalated beyond Kennedy's pay grade, beyond Whitehouse and Parliament. They would be informed when it was appropriate, but for now she had the job of keeping Kennedy from the truth.

A few hours later and Kennedy was sat in his office, Fiona across the desk from him wearing her usual poker face. She was always a hard nut to crack: she never gave anything away, and if she had a tell he was yet to discover it. That said, she was holding something back. There was nothing in her words or in her expression, it was her eyes, a distant light hiding a dim beacon to another ship in the night. She had changed allegiances and whatever she was holding back was going to them.

He didn't feel betrayed, though he should have. Nor did he feel jealous, not that he ever claimed any ownership over her; she was, as always, a free agent. What he felt was satisfaction: for once he saw it coming, for once he knew he was being played. Whatever Fiona had to say he knew to take with a pinch of salt and read between the lines, knowing there was a bigger picture. He didn't know who she'd sold out to but he could guess: there weren't many places higher up the ladder she could crawl to, not regarding this anyway, not in government or any official capacity, unless she sold herself to private interests which she was in the frequent habit of doing. He tried to guess which nation: the Americans were the most likely, or the Chinese, but most probably that corporate giant of sophisticated conglomerates that hid in the shadows of broad daylight manipulating the reflections of the glass towers of the city financial centres around the world. He didn't know their name, he just knew they existed.

The Bansteads were beginning to question Sentinel's motives, she reported, so the timing was right for her to leave. There had been no incoming signals to Keck, and no other global listening posts, be they ground based or in orbit, had recorded anything untoward. There had been no new discoveries regarding any planetary systems that could corroborate Cade's version of events, nor was there any further sightings of the mysterious shapes that had previously appeared in view on the edge of our solar system. She questioned whether her role in this was completed, in essence asking permission to take her leave. Kennedy gave her his blessing with every intention of having her tailed.

She stood to leave.

"So after all the hype about this guy Cade, does it really come to nothing?"

Kennedy narrowed his eyes in thought before answering.

"The evidence would suggest that's the case, yes."

"So the government has spent a fortune hounding and persecuting a mental health patient because he got lucky with some wild theories about science fiction." Her tone was mocking, and put like that he felt ashamed and his face began to flush. "Save your blushes, it will be Whitehouse it falls on not you."

"You can guarantee that?"

"He has more to lose and he's easily flustered when faced with a barrage from all angles. If it comes to it he'll take a battering in the Commons and come across as incompetent."

Kennedy nodded and half smiled, satisfied. She turned to leave as the door opened. Healy walked in. She ignored him. He ignored her. He had papers for the Major General from the Defence Secretary: nothing important, an insignificant page of information, no more important than he himself.

Kapoor put down the phone for the umpteenth time with a

complete feeling of dejection. No one wanted to speak to him. He was a leper, ostracised by a ringing bell and a call of 'unclean'. Suddenly he realised just how indiscreet his multiple contacts were and how the squeeze had easily been put on them. How long had they been following his movements, tracking his feeble attempts at gathering information? He had been a fool to think it was so easy.

The words of his last call still echoed in his ears: "I can't tell you anything Surjeet, I wish I could but things here are difficult. There are men here, we are being monitored." Raphael Weizmann had been a friend ever since Louis Vost had first instructed him to contact him for information on a case about a set of mysterious lights seen over Israel in the late 90's. Kapoor, keen to keep hold of valuable contacts, had maintained the relationship from a distance with his friend at the Sackler Institute of Astronomy in Tel Aviv, just one of many such confidants who usually were more than happy to share what they knew with a trusted partner keen on seeking the truth without the desire to sensationalise a big story. The lights over Israel had turned out to be gas clouds drifting in our upper atmosphere, a story which at the time Kapoor was dubious of but accepted for he saw no reason for Weizmann to lie about it.

Over the years they had shared many small snippets of information to their mutual benefit, so now to receive a frosty response could mean only that something big was happening.

Who were the men that were monitoring things at the Institute?

Had it been this alone he would have taken it for an isolated incident, a local problem, a security issue which, being Israel, was highly likely. But this was not isolated; it was as though he had been blacklisted.

He couldn't help but wonder why. So they knew he had been digging on his own and using contacts he should have given up years ago when he left MI17. So they knew he was obsessed with the John Cade case. What he couldn't figure out was why it mattered. Who would care that much? What danger was there to anyone else? Cade officially was being discredited - the case closed. There had to be more.

He knew Kennedy on his own didn't have the clout to affect all the global departments he had been calling around this morning, which meant that someone else was cutting him off. There were groups he'd heard whispers about; you can't be an investigator into

UFO's and not be drawn into the conspiracy theories about secret organisations seeking for global dominance and maintaining a lingering relationship with alien life-forms as they manipulated the world stage and dangled the world leaders from strings like puppets. On occasion he thought he had seen glimpses of work that could be attributed to such groups, but he preferred to sit in denial of it, preferring to believe the world was innocent and that only he knew its true secrets, that he was the one with the insider knowledge. He was the only one who truly believed in Cade, the only one who knew he was an alien, the only one who knew the impact it had on the rest of us, and how only he, Surjeet Kapoor, could find the key to an alternative life in the universe.

How long had he fooled himself with this assumption, allowing his ego and pride to deceive him? There were others, he saw that now, more powerful and insightful orchestrating the events playing out. Were there aliens out there ready to attack? John Cade's V'hihyon, or the rebellious mechas, or someone else, some other threat hidden from the world. He had seen the footage of the hidden technology to fire upon and destroy objects in space, much of which had gone viral in recent years. He wondered whether that was being prepped. He wondered whether an attack was imminent. He wondered whether he should just get back to doing his job and that maybe, just maybe he had bitten off more than he could chew. If the rumours about these secret all powerful groups were right, then he had probably already got on their radar, and they had people primed to deal with things that could be considered annoyances, or loose ends.

Yes, he was eager to encounter the alternative vessel for his soul and follow the religion of faith he had bought into with Abadd'on as his prophet - but not that eager.

Part Four

Christmas

Sui cuique mores fingunt fortunam
(one's character fashions his fate)

1

It had been three weeks since the explosion on the International Space Station (ISS) which had killed all six of its crew. NASA, Roscosmos, JAXA, ESA, and CSA all told the same story about the events onboard that led up to the catastrophe which had caused headline news and was destined to put space exploration back by at least a decade.

Roskosmos's Mission Control Centre at Korolyov in Russia handled the main output of the press release regarding the official flight status and what went wrong so far as Mission Control was concerned. Naturally experts from around the world chipped in their opinion for the press, most vocally the American's who tried to bat off the ludicrous accounts of mysterious objects captured by amateur astronomers hours before the explosion. Some even went as far as to suggest that the space station had been destroyed by aliens invading the planet and that a secret Earth missile defense initiative had been triggered by a collective council of world leaders. Various titbits of evidence were produced online within minutes of the event and spread globally within hours. Most, if not all of the supposed incriminating footage and circumstantial evidence was discredited or removed just as swiftly as it appeared, almost as though the countermeasure had been orchestrated and prepared in advance, either that or the conspiracies were just that, and would fall back into the realms of fantasy and urban legend along with Bigfoot, the Loch Ness Monster, and the Roswell incident.

A meteor, it was claimed was to blame for the devastation to ISS, reigniting the fears of an impact to the planet from such a hazard. It was a small one the authorities reassured, but nonetheless fatal to the vessel whose path could not be altered in time, and the crew who could not be evacuated. Excuses were made as to why no radar had picked up the threat, and mumblings about essential maintenance being carried out at the time meant that the station's thrusters were off-line, underlining the incident as an unfortunate and unavoidable accident. NASA showed footage of the projected path of the space rock that had approached unseen in the vastness of space before it collided with ISS with little warning. The expected fallout of space junk, including the bodies of the six astronauts was expected to continue for the next couple of weeks as slowly the debris fell to Earth. The public was being warned not to approach any debris that survived the burn up in the atmosphere as it was vital every piece was collected and collated by the investigators.

It was a news story that was likely to rumble on for some time and would probably feature in the memories of most until at least the Hollywood version eclipsed the reality of the actual event.

Following the ISS disaster Sentinel was reorganising and regrouping its assets globally. Its Board deemed it necessary to rein in some of its fringe interests in a move which had clearly been pre-planned but executed in the favourable light of the misery that befell the aeronautics and space community. The company, which had close links not only with the UK government but also with others around the world, began cementing its ties with authorities, which on outward appearances gave the impression that they were bowing to political influence and control in order to protect a financial interest: however, on closer inspection it could be viewed with an opposite approach as certain parliamentary personnel could be seen as being in the pocket of the company, a company whose private board members had enough personal wealth to pay off the majority of the substantial national debt.

Various installations owned by Sentinel were drawn into a fold of assets to be sold off. All information relating to the various projects owned by the company were to be collected and scrutinised for their financial value in order to be sold off to keep the company afloat.

All this seemed quite predictable and obvious in light of the inspections of its equipment installed at the Roskosmos Mission Control as well as onboard ISS itself. However, were anyone to make further inspection of the selloff that ensued, an inspection that would never take place due to political assurances, one might observe that the purchasing companies were also subsidiary companies of other companies owned by various members of Sentinel's Board.

No matter how suspicious the business activities of Sentinel appeared, the details of which would never see the light of day, this made no difference to the Bansteads: their fate was sealed along with many others who may have been able to shed any authoritive light on matters concerning the fatal descent of ISS.

Although the Mauna Kea Observatory had no clear line of sight of the direct strike on the space station, they were in a position to monitor the fallout and had been well placed to detail any cross referenced data of meteor movements prior to that fatal day.

A senior official from Sentinel arrived on the day the downed space station hit the news and requisitioned all the data from the couple and gave them notice at the facility. Marcus and Julie had vehemently argued their case to no avail. They could apply for the same post or another at an alternative facility but there was no guarantee a position would be granted. A generous severance would be paid to accommodate their relocation and a note of thanks for their years of service was offered. It was all very polite and professional with no hint of wrong doing by the couple and not discounting any future employment with the company, yet despite this they felt betrayed and dismissed without warrant and couldn't help but wonder if there was more than met the eye.

Following enquiries the Bansteads found that it did appear to be a companywide move and that many of their colleagues were in the same boat, but they couldn't help but think that this was more about why Fiona Roberts had been snooping on the facility, and despite the claims that it was a knee jerk reaction to the potential legal damage the company faced with regards to the lack of foresight and procedures in place for identifying stray meteors, the Bansteads couldn't help but wonder how a company employee had made the long trip to Hawaii all prepped to serve them notice and claim their research on the very day the accident took place.

Of course he didn't get everything: the research Julie had taken home to study away from the prying eyes of Fiona Roberts was still there safely tucked away under her bed awaiting boxing up with the rest of their things, including details of that damning communicae sent into space from the observatory by Fiona before she left the island. It was enough of a trump card should they wish to use it against Sentinel, but after much consideration the couple were satisfied that at long last they had an answer to their lifetime's work.

2

The mysterious case of John Cade was now deemed insignificant, at least so far as Dave MaCaan was concerned. The destruction of ISS had eclipsed everything. There was plenty for MaCaan to question, plenty of assumptions he could make; he was never great at maths but even he could put two and two together and come up with a cover-up conspiracy theory that would satisfy the masses. Would he be believed? Possibly. Was he likely to be met with a randomly bizarre accident if he exposed what he knew? Most probably.

He had every incentive to keep his mouth shut.

He missed his conversations with Malachi. He had only managed to listen in on one further session before he was ordered to pack up and prep for another operation. He didn't know whether the two still met for their counselling sessions, he hoped so, he thought Cade needed it.

He missed too his daily dalliance with the blonde on the train, despite her obvious rejection of him in the end. Now he was having to listen in on an aide to the Defence Secretary himself and submit the files directly to Kennedy; it was an off the books op for which Kennedy had him seconded to for his own purposes. He didn't care for the reason why, so long as his transfer over was legit and all he could be pulled up for was following instructions, besides, the regular journey in was colourful and he had already identified a few regulars he could sidle up to - there was no harm done so long as his wife didn't find out.

3

Vost heard about what had happened to Cade from both Kennedy and Kapoor, seemingly they both thought he would like to know, but in truth he wasn't all that interested nor surprised; he didn't want to get drawn back into it, especially following the ISS disaster. There were too many coincidences to account for and it was a minefield he didn't want to step into.

His wife was glad to have him home without distraction, and why complicate life? There was a time when he wondered if we were alone in the universe, and whether there was life after death, but having spent most of his professional career searching for answers to such questions he now felt as though he just needed to live. Could the knowledge of such things, having all the answers to life's mysteries, change anything? Unlikely. There wasn't much chance that it would alter how he lived his life and would ultimately bring him no more peace of mind.

His wife wanted him to start going back to church. She said that could make a difference to his outlook on things. In God there was something to chase after, something to live for now that would also affect his eternal soul. If the whole John Cade investigation over the years had taught him anything, it was that there was still a desire and a hope for an eternal soul buried in all of us. We all wanted to live on in some form, and he couldn't help but wonder whether we could affect that in this life. He didn't know the answer, but maybe his wife was right, maybe church had a simpler and more honest answer than any he had investigated thus far. He believed in it once: that Jesus showed the way, but somehow had lost faith, allowed himself to be distracted by the fantasies of others. Was it as deluded as the religious fanatics of Cade's imagined race? Maybe, but in that maybe Cade was just echoing a truth he himself denied. Maybe we were all in denial.

He dusted off his Sunday best. Why the hell not.

4

It happened a week after ISS went down. John Cade sat in a cell, graffiti written or scratched into the walls slagging off those who had confined them. The bench come bed he sat on was cold and hard, not built for comfort. The door was firmly shut, the shutter closed to peering eyes.

He'd made his one phone call, to the one person he felt he could turn to.

As he sat waiting he felt his ribs, he was pretty sure they were broken, possibly a finger too. One officer had stamped on his hand after knocking him down with his asp to the back of the leg. The rawness around his eyes was still tender but at least the grating crystals that tore at his eyeballs no longer aggravated. The effects of the full can of CS spray that had been expelled into his face had done its job admirably, blinding him and causing his eyes to stream uncontrollably and painfully allowing officers to pummel in as he doubled over senseless. Despite this it still took six of them to restrain him in cuffs.

He didn't know the full extent of his injuries and despite his wounds the FME was conveniently stuck in traffic. He wondered whether that was a line they always used when their own had taken a beating trying to bring in a prisoner. No doubt their officers had all seen the doctor they claimed was delayed, or had taken themselves off to hospital. The FME was probably patching them up first as he sat there wallowing in his own guilt.

He had fought bigger and better and this defeat was humiliating. He put it down to his Earthly body being inferior to that of Abadd'on's, and they were armed and wearing protective clothing. All he had was his wits and his fists and the combat knowledge of a lifetime away.

They would interview him soon, under caution. This wouldn't be like the interviews with Vost and Kapoor, or even Kennedy. This was different. This wasn't to be hidden away from the public eye. This was to be a permanent record against his name, against his character. This would have repercussions. Whatever he said in that interview room would stay with him.

He hoped to have some guidance before they got to him.

He waited, and waited. It seemed an age. Eventually he heard the footsteps in the corridor of the custody suite and the keys turning in the heavy metal lock. Malachi stood in the doorway as it pulled open to reveal the dark looming figure.

Left alone for a moment to confer, Malachi was uncomfortably blunt.

"Is it true, John Cade, did you kill her?"

Cade thought for a moment. Had he? He remembered confronting Gemma about her conversation with Lucy. He remembered it getting heated. He remembered rising up in superiority. No, he had hadn't killed her - Abadd'on had. Abadd'on was the one who didn't want her around complicating things, an emotional attachment he didn't need.

Cade shook his head, a tear tipping over the edge of one eye. John Cade loved her.

"You haven't changed, Abadd'on. I had hoped to save you from yourself. I had hoped you would embrace your new life here and leave John Cade to live it. All this time I was trying to rescue you from yourself. But you are as arrogant and warlike here as you were there. You are a callous butcher amongst men. You were a good captain and commander but a poor human being, Abadd'on."

"I don't understand, do you mean you're not going to help me?"

"Help you, what do you think I have been trying to do? I tried to get you to see the mechas for something more, but your prejudice blinded you."

Cade looked at him blankly, no emotion showed but Malachi saw the embers of fear and realisation burning in his eyes.

"It is a far, far better thing that I do, than I have ever done," whispered Malachi as he turned to leave.

5

Two men, inconspicuous on a crowded high street, blurred in the mix of lunch time shoppers and those trying to escape the confines of a town centre workplace, even if it were for the few minutes' freedom from the desk that held them prisoner for the majority of their waking life. The bench was just one of many clumped together at intervals along the pedestrianised walkway between the parallel parades of shops where once upon a time cars and even buses used to traverse.

One man ate a sandwich bought from the nearby supermarket, a fizzy drink in a bottle accompanied it as it reserved the space beside him for no one in particular, or so he gave the pretense of appearance.

The second man took the space as the bottle was moved

politely with barely a look up to see who wished to sit on the wooden bench. The sun had dried a splattering of whitish grey bird mess on the seat but the dark skinned man paid it no attention as he dropped heavily into the seat and read the front page of the paper he held now in his lap.

"Any loose ends?" asked the first man without turning his head or making eye contact, the words almost lost to the bustling crowd about them who barely noticed their presence.

"No. What will happen to him?"

"He'll be treated like any other mentally insane killer. Why concern yourself over it?"

"We have history, in this life and beyond."

The first man took a bite of his sandwich and gave a gesture of muted understanding.

"Was the threat completely destroyed?"

"Thanks to the information you provided and what Kennedy was able to verify, yes we believe so."

"Could you tell which fleet it was?"

"You mean was it friend or foe, yours or his?" Healy turned his head to look Malachi in the eye. "You're all foe as far as we're concerned."

Malachi saw the menace in the look, took a gulp and pushed himself up from the seat and walked away. He was confident they would call on him again should another V'hihyon appear; there would be others he was sure, something deep within him told him there always had been. For now he understood the fear and distrust of his kind, and despite his betrayal and his failure to help the likes of Cade adapt, he was glad of the path he'd chosen and the opportunity to live his Earthly life.

6

The background noise at first had been intense. He could hear the mature banter of groans from both sides of the house as the various parties sprang to life at a cheap jibe at the PM from the leader of the opposition. He could hear the gavel calling time, trying to restore order. He could hear himself coughing and then choking as he struggled to draw in breath. He could hear the sudden rush of blood to his ears as his face flushed and his shoulder blades seized up, all just before his knees gave way and he gripped at his left arm. He slumped rather than fell, into the lap of the Chancellor. He hadn't been fully stood anyway, merely perched like others in active defense of his leader's reputation, otherwise he'd have toppled dramatically over into the lectern to sprawl before all in the centre partition in full view of government and the national populace as a whole. As it was, his collapse was sure to have been captured by the television cameras dotted about the room and broadcast live on national TV, and no doubt repeated on every news channel and across the World Wide Web. People were obsessed by death, especially one they could watch played out for real on camera. He would wonder later whether he would ever get to see the footage.

The background noise, which had risen to the concerned voices, both calm and anxious, raised and whispered, which echoed around his head as he squinted his eyes shut and tried to block out the pain, soon was drowned out by the one repetitive sound which ticked along in a slow countdown, getting slower the louder it got and the more he focused on it. Even after it stopped he imagined he could still hear it, even after he detached from the physical realm and was sucked through the spiral of the cosmos into uncharted realms. That heartbeat keeping him conscious as he searched for a place to land, knowing beyond hope that he had left his old self behind for good.

Then all went black - and all went silent.

He didn't know for how long, but when he awoke he was a different person, yet the same.

The skies above him were a strange tinge of purply grey. Tall sharp ridged buildings rose up like stalagmites, ornate and expensive in their construction. Platforms hovered between the buildings like outdoor elevators which didn't move. Instinctively he knew these were teleportation platforms between floors and even buildings. There were no vehicles moving, they didn't need them. He could see figures on the various platforms: grey skinned ganglian creatures with an overarching spine that curved into a narrowly jagged, almost square head with teeth and eyes that glittered as though they were made of glass, no, not glass, crystal.

It took him a moment to realise that he too was stood on a platform, a little girl was holding his hand, not that she looked like a girl but instinctively he knew. She garbled something unintelligible and throaty, grating like coal hung as tonsils in her mouth. He replied, "No, we're not there yet." It didn't come out the way he expected it but the words lost nothing in translation. "We'll be there soon, honey."

He lent forward and looked over the barrier of the platform at the sea of crystal that formed the planet's crust out of which the towers were built and from which their whole civilization survived. As he looked down the pain struck him, not the pain that he had as Philip Whitehouse died in the chamber of the House of Commons upon being questioned about the destruction of the ISS and the external threat from space, but a new pain which struck to the core of his mind as two lifetimes of thoughts and personalities merged.

He stumbled back thrashing at his head with the three fingers of one hand, his daughter staring at him with worry crunching the crystals of her forehead as the platform blinked into life and transported them to somewhere else entirely.

THE END

If you enjoyed reading this book then please leave a review on Amazon or visit my webpage at:

www.cpclarke-author.com

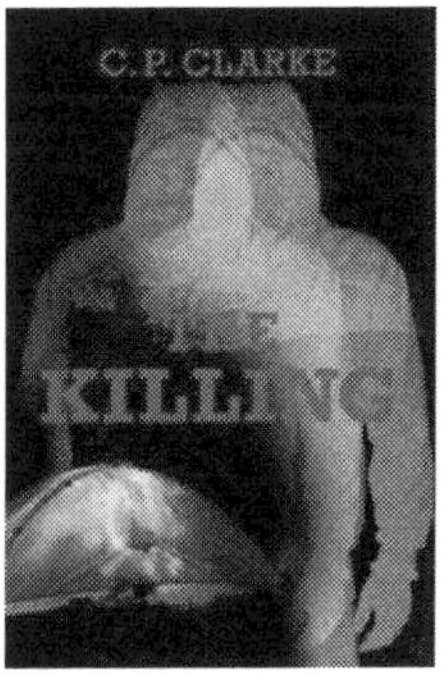
C.P. CLARKE
KILLING

C.P. CLARKE
VICKI
RIVERS

C.P. CLARKE
LIFE IN
SHADOWS

C.P. CLARKE

C.P. CLARKE
POV
A PERSONAL PERSPECTIVE
OF THE BIBLE

C.P. CLARKE
POV
A PERSONAL PERSPECTIVE
OF THE BIBLE

Made in the USA
Charleston, SC
16 September 2016